WITH SIX YOU GET WALLY

A JOHN BEKKER MYSTERY

WITH SIX YOU GET WALLY

AL LAMANDA

FIVE STAR
A part of Gale, Cengage Learning

GALE
CENGAGE Learning·

Farmington Hills, Mich • San Francisco • New York • Waterville, Maine
Meriden, Conn • Mason, Ohio • Chicago

GALE
CENGAGE Learning·

LIBRARY OF CONGRESS CATALOGING-IN-PUBLICATION DATA

Names: Lamanda, Al, author.
Title: With six you get Wally / Al Lamanda.
Description: First edition. | Waterville, Maine : Five Star, a part of Cengage Learning, Inc. [2016] | © 2016 | Series: A John Bekker mystery
Identifiers: LCCN 2016007146| ISBN 9781432832599 (hardcover) | ISBN 143283259X (hardcover)
Subjects: LCSH: Bekker, John. | Private investigators—Fiction. | Compulsive gambling—Fiction. | Inheritance and succession—Fiction. | BISAC: FICTION / Thrillers. | FICTION / Mystery & Detective / General. | GSAFD: Mystery fiction.
Classification: LCC PS3612.A5433 W58 2016 | DDC 813/.6—dc23
LC record available at http://lccn.loc.gov/2016007146

First Edition. First Printing: October 2016
Find us on Facebook– https://www.facebook.com/FiveStarCengage
Visit our website– http://www.gale.cengage.com/fivestar/
Contact Five Star™ Publishing at FiveStar@cengage.com

Printed in the United States of America
1 2 3 4 5 6 7 20 19 18 17 16

WITH SIX YOU GET WALLY

CHAPTER ONE

A few weeks before my grandfather passed away, I visited him in the hospital. I was just a kid and didn't know any better at the time, so when he called me at home before the family left for the hospital and asked me if I could smuggle in a pack of Camel cigarettes, some sipping whiskey and the Marilyn Monroe *Playboy* issue from nineteen fifty-two, I did as he asked.

The last year of his life, my grandfather came to live with us in the family home and occupied the spare bedroom on the first floor. I spent a great deal of time with him alone in his room, so I got to know his haunts and secrets pretty well.

One afternoon after school, early in his sickness, he spoke to me of many things. "Life," he said, "is nothing but one long circle. Everything that's been said will be said again. Everything that's been done will be done again. Every mistake, repeated. Every lesson learned will be learned again. What happens today will have happened yesterday and will happen again tomorrow. Always remember that."

I told him I would, even though I had no idea what he was talking about.

That day I visited him in the hospital was the last time I saw him alive. I had a four-ounce bottle of sipping whiskey hidden in my left pocket, the pack of cigarettes in the right and his prized Marilyn Monroe *Playboy* issue down the back of my pants.

Fifteen minutes prior to the end of visiting hours, my grandfather told the family he wanted some alone time with me, and they obliged him and left us alone. The second they filed into the hall and closed the door, my grandfather jumped out of bed and closed the white curtain to give us privacy.

"You bring what I asked for?" he asked, excitedly.

I produced cigarettes, whiskey and Marilyn.

"Good boy," he said, and rubbed my hair.

He got back into bed and hid his smuggled goods under the covers.

"Remember what I told you," he said. "Life ain't nothing but one big circle of events that goes 'round and 'round."

Two weeks later he was dead. He waited until he knew the time was at hand before he broke out his smuggled goods.

Nurses on duty at the desk rushed to his room when his monitors went blank and they found him smiling in his bed, lit cigarette in one hand, four-ounce whiskey bottle in the other and Marilyn Monroe on his chest.

My grandfather knew how to live and he knew how to die.

My grandfather's words ran through my mind as I sat in the bank and talked to the loan officer about mortgage rates and loans.

Life ain't nothing but one big circle.

Twenty-plus years ago, as I signed my life away when my wife, Carol, and I purchased a home, there was a knot in my chest and a lump in my throat. The loan officer explained I didn't earn enough money to buy the home we actually wanted without a bigger down payment. I worked a second job, as did Carol, and we borrowed the rest from family and then we purchased the home where she was murdered in front of our five-year-old daughter.

All these years later, a loan officer at the bank told me that my forty-percent early-retirement pension wasn't enough to purchase the home I wanted to buy to give Regan a decent place to live in. Not without a steady second income. As I was in forced retirement as a private investigator at the moment, I needed to upgrade my income or settle for less house.

We discussed emptying my savings account and that familiar lump in my throat and knot in my chest took my mind to my grandfather.

"Perhaps a less expensive home would allow you to make the payments without dipping too far into your savings?" the loan officer suggested.

"It would, but this home serves a very important purpose to me," I said. "If I put one hundred thousand down, what does that do to the monthly payments on a twenty-year mortgage?"

The loan officer did some calculating on his computer.

I did some of my own. If I removed one hundred thousand from my savings, I would be left with seventy-five thousand, more than enough emergency money.

"It's doable," the loan officer said. "But there isn't much left over every month in your pension check."

"That would be my problem," I said. "Your concern is that I make the payments every month, and if the bank can arrange to have the funds automatically transferred from my direct deposit account to the mortgage payment account then you don't have any concern at all. Yes?"

The loan officer looked at me. "I can arrange that," he finally said.

"Good."

"When will you put the bid on the house?"

"As soon as I leave the bank with all the paperwork signed."

The loan officer nodded. "I'll get the papers," he said.

Karen Hill, associate vice-president of the Five Star Real Estate Agency, one of the largest agencies in the state, met me for coffee a block from the bank. I was already in a booth by the window, sipping away and reading the bank documents, when she showed up.

Around thirty-five, tall and blond, dressed in a miniskirted power suit, Karen slid into the booth opposite me and gave me her best real-estate-broker-smells-commission smile.

"You got it?" she said.

"Right here."

"Let me see."

I slid the documents across the table. While Karen read them, I ordered a coffee for her and a refill for me.

I sipped.

She read.

I sipped some more.

She read some more.

"Well?" I said when she lowered the documents.

"I can put the bid in today," she said. "If you'd like?"

"Do it," I said. "And call me later with the answer."

The house in question is a four-bedroom, two-bathroom home on the beach about a mile and a half from my trailer. It has a finished basement and attic and is the ideal place for Regan to live in, as the closest home to it is a hundred and fifty yards away.

While my daughter has grown by leaps and bounds in the past two years, she is still very much plagued by witnessing her mother's murder and is far from where she needs to be at this point in her life. A lot of nosy neighbors are exactly what she doesn't need.

When I left the beach trailer hours ago, Regan and Oz, my one and only neighbor on the beach, were seated in chairs and having a late breakfast.

By the time I drove my fourteen-year-old Marquis onto the beach and parked beside the Impala I'd bought Regan a few months ago, Oz was standing beside a pile of junk wearing a confused expression on his face.

I got out of the Marquis, removing the red tie I wore with my gray, pinstriped suit. "What's going on here?" I asked.

"Regan be cleaning," Oz said. He had a rich, baritone voice and often spoke in truncated sentences.

A rusted, dented toaster flew out the open door and landed at Oz's feet.

"Cleaning what?" I asked.

"She said she . . . go ask her yourself," Oz said. "I already been hit once in the noggin with a radio."

"I own a radio?"

Oz looked at the busted portable radio in the pile beside his feet. "Not no more," he said.

I stepped into the trailer, where my daughter, dressed in a tank top and shorts, was on her hands and knees, scrubbing the tiled kitchen floor.

"Regan, what's this about?"

She paused in her scrubbing and looked up at me. "The mold on this floor is growing mold," she said.

"It's not that bad," I said.

"I can make penicillin with what's under my fingernails," she said, and resumed scrubbing.

"How long will you be cleaning?"

"Until this entire place shines or I die of old age."

I nodded. "Okay."

I stepped around Regan, entered my bedroom, and changed into comfortable sweats and jogging shoes. When I returned to the kitchen, she was holding half of a pepper mill.

"What's this?"

"It used to be a pepper grinder."

"What is it now?"

"Broken."

Regan tossed it outside, then lifted the bucket of water and poured it down the sink, and then glared at me.

"I'll be outside," I said.

Oz wore a smirk on his well-worn face when I stepped outside.

"She's cleaning," I said.

I had a nice bonfire going and burgers on the grill by the time an exhausted Regan stepped out of the trailer and flopped into a chair next to Oz.

"End of phase one," she said.

I glanced at Oz, who gave me his smirk again.

"What's phase two?" I asked.

"Redecorate."

"About that," I said.

"We can't keep living like this, Dad."

"I know, but . . ."

"How am I supposed to take care of you in this rust bucket if . . ."

"Regan, listen a minute."

"I thought my bedroom window was frosted glass until I wiped the dirt off of it," Regan said.

From her hiding place under the trailer, Molly suddenly appeared and jumped on Regan's lap.

"There you are," Regan said to the tiny calico cat.

"Would you just listen for a second," I said. "I agree with everything you just said."

Stroking Molly, Regan raised an eyebrow at me. "You do?"

"Yes," I said. "Just not here. I made an offer on that beach house we looked at . . ."

"Dad, that house cost . . ."

"I know what it costs," I said. "And my offer was accepted this afternoon. The real-estate agent called while you were on your cleaning rampage."

"The house we looked at on the beach with the big yard for Molly and the bedroom for Oz?"

"Yup."

"How can we afford that?"

"I moved some money around," I said. "We can afford it."

"What's this bedroom for Oz stuff?" Oz asked.

"You're as much a part of the family as Molly," Regan said. "We can't leave you here all alone on the beach. You're old. Something could happen. That's why we looked at four-bedroom homes."

"I right up there with the cat, huh," Oz said. "And who you calling old, squirt?"

"Just go with it," I told Oz.

"Can we show Oz?" Regan asked.

"I'm meeting the real-estate agent at the house at ten tomorrow morning," I said.

"Can we bring Mark?" Regan said. "I'm sure he'll be staying over a lot."

"We'll pick him up on the way."

"Can we eat them burgers now?" Oz asked. "This old man needs his strength."

CHAPTER TWO

I drove Regan's Impala to pick up Mark, Janet's fifteen-year-old son. He is the closest thing to a brother Regan has, and is like a son to me. Even though my engagement to Janet came to a screeching halt several months ago, Mark remained close to me, to Regan, and even Oz.

Oz sat next to me, Regan in back with Molly on her lap. I looked for Clayton's car when I pulled into the driveway of Janet's suburban home. It wasn't there.

I didn't need to toot the horn as the front door opened and Mark, wearing a blue backpack, came rushing out to the car. From the kitchen window, Janet watched as he got into the back seat next to Regan.

"So what's with the house?" Mark asked.

"It's a place to live in, dummy," Regan said.

I pulled out of the driveway and Janet disappeared from the kitchen window.

"I thought you had a place to live," Mark asked.

"The giant tuna can doesn't cut it anymore," Regan said.

"I like the tuna can," Mark said.

"That's because you don't live in it," Regan said. "What's in the backpack?"

"Stuff."

"Stuff? Stuff ain't no country I ever heard of. Do they speak English in stuff?"

"Ha-ha," Mark said. "You've been spending too much time

14

with Uncle Jack."

"Who wants pizza for lunch?" I said.

"Oh, thank God for Uncle Jack," Mark said.

"Why?" Regan asked.

"Mom is on one of her diet kicks again," Mark said. "I eat nuts for breakfast like I'm some kind of squirrel. How am I supposed to grow eating a bowl of nuts for breakfast?"

"Diet?" I said. "What for?"

"I don't know," Mark said. "The other day I heard her screaming in the bathroom about sagging, and when I asked her sagging what, she told me to mind my own business. Then she went out and bought nuts and fruit and tossed out all the ice cream, and went jogging."

"Sounds serious," Regan said.

"So, what kind of pizza are we getting?" Mark asked.

Karen Hill met us at the front door with the key.

"This is Oz, my neighbor, my daughter, Regan, and my nephew, Mark," I said.

"And Molly," Regan said, as she held the cat in her arms.

"Well, shall we take a look at your new home?" Karen said and opened the door.

The moment we were through it, Molly jumped down from Regan's arms and went exploring on her own. Void of furniture, the place appeared gigantic.

"Wow," Mark said. "Which room is mine?"

While Karen led the gang on a guided tour of the house, I went to the backyard. It was divided into two sections. Half was fenced in; the other half had a path that led to the beach about a hundred yards away.

After a while, Karen joined me as I stood at the fence and looked at the ocean.

"How soon before we can move in?" I asked.

15

"Thirty days."

"Can we do some fixing up?"

"I don't see why not."

"Good."

"So, Jack, are you free for . . . ?" Karen asked.

And the back door burst open and Regan, Mark and Molly came running out.

"This place is great," Mark said.

"We settled on our rooms," Regan said.

I looked at Oz. "Okay?"

Oz nodded. "I get the view of the beach."

"I get the view of the front," Mark said.

"Mine has a view of the beach and a walk-in closet for all the new clothes I'm going to buy," Regan said.

"What did I get?" I said.

"You get a view of the kitchen," Oz said.

I looked at Mark. His backpack was now flat. "What was in the backpack?" I asked.

"Something for Molly," Mark said. "I got it for when she stays over with Regan, but I think she'd like it better here."

We entered the house and in the otherwise barren kitchen, Molly was curled up in a tight ball in the cushy, fleece-lined cat bed on the hardwood floor.

"Well, let's go for pizza then," I said. "Karen, join us?"

"Why not."

"Regan, better grab her before she gets too comfortable in that thing."

Rose's Pizza Palace near the beach served a hell of a pizza. We ordered two, smothered with everything, and we ate in the backyard at a picnic table.

Karen ate her slice with a knife and fork. The rest of us were slobs, spilling grease on just about everything as we gobbled up

16

several slices each.

"When is the closing?" I asked Karen as we walked back to the car.

"Two weeks, then another two weeks for processing."

"Okay."

I drove back to the house so Karen could retrieve her car. She leaned in my open window. "I'll call you later," she said.

Oz and I sipped coffee from our chairs in front of my trailer while Mark and Regan tossed a Frisbee down at the water.

"How you gonna pay for this new castle?" Oz asked.

"A hundred thousand down and a decent mortgage over twenty years."

"Twenty years make you old as me," Oz said. "Twenty years a long time."

"I know, but my pension covers most of the monthly nut, so all I need is some part-time work," I said.

"I thought you promised the kid you'd give it up."

"I didn't say that kind of work."

Oz sipped coffee and gazed down at the ocean. "Walt tell you why the board rejected your reinstatement?"

"They said my age and time away from the job was the deciding factor."

"Sound like a load of crap to me."

"Walt is going to ask for an appeal."

Walt was Captain Walter Grimes, and my one-time partner. We started out in the police academy together, made sergeant at the same time and remained very close friends ever since despite my many stumbling blocks.

"My pension from the post office be pretty good, you know," Oz said.

"Meaning?"

"Meaning I can pay my own way," Oz said. "Help out with

the bills and such. I got nothing else to spend it on since I quit drinking."

"You're as much my family as Regan," I said.

"Don't mean I live for free," Oz said. "I don't pay my share, I stay on the beach."

"We'll work it out," I said.

Oz looked toward town where the beach ended and the municipal parking lot began. A car had entered the beach and was driving toward us on the sand.

"Somebody coming," Oz said, squinting. "Is that Walt?"

"If it is, he went and bought a ninety-five-thousand-dollar Benz," I said.

A few minutes later the Benz arrived and parked next to my Marquis. The door opened and Frank Kagan stepped out and looked at me.

"Bekker, it's been a while," he said.

"Want some coffee?" I said as he approached the trailer.

"Sure. I see you got some new chairs."

While Kagan sat, I went inside for a cup, filled it and carried it out to him.

He sipped, then looked at me.

"I need your help," he said.

Oz looked at me.

Down by the water, Regan and Mark looked at me.

I looked at Kagan.

Frank Kagan was mob boss Eddie Crist's private attorney on civil matters. While he never represented Crist, or any other mobster, in criminal matters as far as I could tell, he knew where many a body was buried. So to speak.

"I'm out of the P.I. business, Frank," I said. "Two months now and counting."

"It's not about investigating," Kagan said. "And it pays really well for practically no work."

"Let's take a walk," I said. "Oz, I'll be right back."

I stood and Kagan followed me as I walked down the beach out of earshot of Regan and Mark.

"I'm a full-time parent to Regan now, Frank," I said. "I can't afford to get involved in anything time-consuming or danger-ous."

"Who said anything about dangerous?"

"If it weren't, it wouldn't 'pay really well,' as you put it."

"You were a cop and that was really dangerous; did it pay really well?"

I looked at Kagan. "Okay, tell me about it."

"A straight-up baby-sitting job," Kagan said.

"You mean bodyguarding job is what you mean."

"Trust me, it's baby-sitting."

"Where, when and how much?"

"That doesn't sound like you," Kagan said. "Since when have you ever been motivated by money?"

"Since I bought a new house for me and Regan, and the mortgage is more than I'd like to think about."

"Then come to my office at three tomorrow and hear me out, and meet the client," Kagan said. "And that mortgage will all but disappear."

"All right."

I walked Kagan back to his car. Regan and Mark were with Oz now, and Regan said, "I remember you, Mr. Kagan. You're a friend of Dad's."

"Yes," Kagan said. "And I remember you, too."

"I'll see you at three, Frank," I said.

After Kagan drove away, Regan said, "What did he want, Dad?"

"I'm not entirely sure," I said. "I'll find out tomorrow at three."

"Come on, Regan, let's take a walk and find some seashells," Mark said.

They took off for the beach and I flopped into my chair next to Oz.

I could feel Oz's stare and I looked at him.

"What?" I said.

"Frank Kagan is the mob lawyer," Oz said.

"Was, and he only handled civil and personal cases."

"For the mob."

"All right, okay, for the mob," I said. "His connection died with Crist."

"You believe that?"

"No."

"But you go see him anyway."

"Apparently he needs a babysitter," I said.

"A . . . to babysit who, the new godfather?"

"If the pay is as good as he says I might need an assistant."

"How good and how much?"

"Never mind how much. Where do you want to take the kids for dinner?"

"Let them decide."

"That's never a good idea."

My cell phone rang. I checked the number and pushed *talk*.

"I'm taking him to dinner with us and then I'll run him home," I said. "No later than nine o'clock."

"I wasn't calling about Mark, Jack," Janet said. "School's out and he's fifteen now. He can spend time with his uncle if he wants."

"Then what?" I said.

"We need to talk," Janet said.

"About?"

"Don't play stupid, Jack."

"Who's playing?"

Janet sighed heavily.

"Okay, what do we need to talk about?" I asked.

"Not on the phone. I'm sick of the phone. I'm on the day shift tomorrow. Can you and Regan stop by for dinner? We can talk privately afterward."

"What time?"

"Seven thirty."

"We'll be there."

I set the phone on the table beside my chair.

"I'm going home and change," Oz said. "You pick the place for dinner or we be eating pizza again."

Oz walked down the beach to his trailer. A shower and a change of clothes sounded pretty good to me and I was about to go into my trailer when my cell phone rang again.

I checked the call. It was Karen Hill.

"Nothing is wrong with the paperwork, I hope?" I said.

"No, everything is fine with that," Karen said. "I was calling about something else, Jack."

"And what would that be?"

"You strike me as a boob when it comes to women, Jack, so I thought I'd make the first move and ask you to dinner."

"I appreciate the offer, but that's not such a good idea right now," I said. "I'm sort of ending a relationship that's not quite over and . . . it's just not a good idea."

"Well, let me know when it's over," Karen said. "Maybe it will be a good idea then?"

"I will. Thanks."

Regan and Mark returned to the trailer and my daughter kissed me on the cheek and sat in Oz's chair.

"Who was that?" she asked.

"Just someone who thinks I'm a boob."

"That could be almost everybody," Regan said. "I'm going in and take a shower and change for dinner."

After Regan went inside, I looked at Mark. "What about you, do you need to change for dinner?"

"What for?" Mark asked. "I eat with my mouth, not my clothes."

"You know something, I agree with you."

CHAPTER THREE

I awoke early the next morning mostly because I'm a terrible sleeper. I got out of bed and listened to my bones crack as I walked to the kitchen to brew a pot of coffee.

Age is just a number, I told myself as my knees snapped, crackled and popped on the way to the bathroom. A number that doesn't reverse, my lower back reminded me as I changed into gray sweats and jogging shoes.

I returned to the kitchen, filled a mug with coffee, and went outside to take my chair and watch the sunrise over the ocean.

I craved a cigarette I couldn't have because I made a promise to Regan that I would quit for good.

Going on thirty days now and the urge to light up with coffee was as powerful as ever. One puff and I'd be back on the nicotine express train. However, as I'd been sober going on nineteen months now, I knew what it took to stay nicotine free.

Willpower.

That and a daughter that has the uncanny ability to pop up the moment a cigarette is lit and scold me like the dominant lion when a cub gets out of hand.

I finished my coffee, stood up and walked down to the beach. I touched my toes and my knees sounded exactly like my knuckles when I cracked them. I stretched for a bit more and then took off jogging along the water.

It took a mile for my body to warm up and all cracking of bones to cease. I ran another two miles and then reversed direc-

23

tion and headed back to the trailer. I was covered in sweat when I stopped alongside the trailer where my little homemade gym is set up. Elevated pushup bars, one hundred-twenty-pound heavy bag, pull-up bar stand, weighted jump ropes, speed bag.

I grabbed the jump rope. Each handle weighed one pound. I jumped for five minutes or so, switching off from forward to backward, and ended with a mad Rocky-like flurry.

I hung the jump rope back on its hook, dropped to the pushup bars, and did as many reps as my arms, shoulders and chest would allow. I rolled over, rested for a few minutes and then repeated the process.

I stood and wiped sweat out of my eyes, grabbed the pull-up bars and cranked out a few sets of wide-grip pull-ups, reversed the grip and ended with chin-ups. I rested a few minutes and did it again.

More sweat wiping and then I slipped on the heavy-bag gloves and pounded the bag non-stop for about thirty minutes. I ended the workout with the speed bag, working it until my shoulders were on fire and my forearms gave out.

Regan was at the tiny kitchen table with Molly on her lap and mug of coffee in her hand. I filled my mug and took a seat.

"You're up," I said.

"Who can sleep with World War Three going on out there?"

"I was thinking of putting a home gym in the basement," I said. "Less noise."

"There is a God, and he is kind," Regan said.

"I have a three o'clock appointment today."

"I know."

"I'll ask Oz to . . ."

"I'll be fine, Dad," Regan said.

"I know, but . . ."

"You can't keep a leash around my waist forever, Dad."

I sipped coffee and nodded.

"Maybe you might want to get together with Oz and start shopping for some new furniture for the house," I said. "We are going to need some, you know."

"I can open my trust fund and . . ."

"The old man isn't quite ready for the poor house just yet," I said. "The last two cases I worked I deposited the money in my checkbook and it's just sitting there. We might as well put it to good use."

"I'll get ahold of Oz and we'll do some homework on my laptop and then I'll work on a budget while you're gone," Regan said.

"Good."

I wore a gray suit minus a tie to Kagan's plushy office located downtown. His receptionist ushered me into his office and asked if we wanted some coffee for our meeting.

Kagan told her yes and she closed the door.

"Have a seat, Jack," Kagan said.

I took a leather chair facing the desk.

"So what's this all about, Frank?" I asked.

"I handle a great deal of civil cases for the general public, wills and inheritance disputes, things like that," Kagan said. "Since Crist died, I've stayed away from any mob-related civil cases and I've been busier than ever."

"How nice," I said. "Is that what you asked me here for, to listen to your new resumé and client list?"

The door opened and the receptionist ushered in two mugs of coffee. She set them on the desk and closed the door behind her.

"I just wanted to let you know our business has nothing to do with the mob or anything criminal," Kagan said. "It's strictly a civil matter and totally legitimate."

I lifted my mug and took a sip. "I'm listening."

"Ever drink Sample iced tea?"

"Not if I can help it. Why?"

"They make thirty-four flavors and it's sold around the world," Kagan said. "Richard Sample, founder and owner of the company, died a billionaire and left his entire estate to his six children. His wife passed away before him. However, the fortune was not divided up equally among the six heirs."

"Unless I'm one of the lucky six, why do I care, Frank?" I asked.

"Would you just listen, Bekker?"

I sipped and waited.

"Five of the heirs, two sons and three daughters, turned out just fine," Kagan said. "Normal, well-adjusted members of the company as officers and family people. The sixth is the rotten apple."

"Ah, and said rotten apple is your client?"

"Not exactly. His father is."

"You said he was dead."

"He is, but his last will and testament isn't."

"Maybe you might want to start making some sense here, Frank," I said.

"Wally Sample is the sixth heir and the family outcast," Kagan said. "However, his father was not without love for this loser and put a clause in his will that when Wally turns forty he is to be given a lump cash settlement of ten million dollars and a full partnership in the company equal to his five siblings."

"Why?"

"Like I said, his father wasn't without love for his . . ."

"I mean, why did he wait until he turns forty?" I said.

"Oh," Kagan said. "Well, Wally has a little bit of a problem."

"How little?"

"He is a degenerate gambler. He bets on anything and everything, and his father knew that and kept him away from the family fortune until the time he felt Wally was responsible enough to handle money."

"Only he's not," I said.

"Far from it. In fact, he's worse than ever."

"And you want me to do what about it?" I asked.

"Here is the deal, Jack," Kagan said. "In thirty days, Wally Sample turns forty, and on his birthday he will inherit ten million dollars and become an equal partner in the company if he can prove to a court-appointed psychiatrist that he hasn't gambled for thirty days prior to the hearing."

"So stick his loser ass in Gamblers Anonymous and let them deal with him," I said.

"He wouldn't last one day before he jumped the wall."

"And now it becomes clear," I said. "You want me to wet-nurse him for thirty days so he can collect his inheritance, so he can turn around and just blow it all in Vegas or whatever."

"That is not my concern or yours," Kagan said. "Richard Sample was one of my first clients when I started out nearly forty years ago in New York. I wrote the will some twenty-five years ago. He had it revised, not by me, to include the clause for his son Wally prior to Wally turning twenty-one. I became aware of this change after Richard died ten years ago. I would like to honor the commitment I made to him and follow through on this as any good attorney would."

"If I take this on, and I say *if*, what's my compensation?" I said.

"Two and a half percent of his inheritance."

I did the math in my head.

"Three percent, plus expense money for the month up front." Kagan looked at me.

"In writing before I leave your office."

Kagan opened a drawer, removed a folded document and slid it to me.

"Fill in the three percent," he said. "Twenty thousand for expenses should cover it. There is more if you need it."

I used his pen to sign my name and fill in three-percent compensation.

Kagan picked up his phone, waited a moment and then said, "Bring Mr. Sample into my office, please."

A few moments later the door opened and the receptionist led Wally Sample into the office.

He stood about five feet six inches tall and was shaped like a pear inside his cheap suit. His hair was long and shaggy and mousy brown. His beard was scraggly. Blue eyes hid behind thick glasses. He looked at me and licked his lips.

"Mr. Sample, this is John Bekker, the man I told you about," Kagan said.

"Everybody says I have a problem," Wally said. "I don't have a problem. I have a system that I'm trying to perfect and when I do I plan to empty Vegas as if the whole town went on Weight Watchers to prove my point to the world."

"That will be enough, Wally," Kagan said.

"The world has a problem, not me," Wally said.

"That will be enough, Wally. Sit," Kagan said.

"The world," Wally said. "Is the problem."

"Sit," Kagan commanded.

Wally sat next to me. He reached into his jacket pocket and produced a stack of scratch tickets three inches thick.

Kagan gave the signed agreement to his receptionist. "Make a copy of this for Mr. Bekker," he said.

She snatched the paper and glared at Kagan. "Next time you babysit him," she said and stormed off.

I looked at Wally. He was scratching a ticket with a quarter.

"Am I on the clock?" I said to Kagan.

"Yes."

I grabbed the stack of scratch tickets from Wally's hand.

"Hey, those are my . . ."

"Not anymore, scratch boy," I said. "Let's go."

"Where?"

"Wherever I say go for the next thirty days."

"Mr. Kagan, this isn't . . ." Wally said.

"Do you want your inheritance?" Kagan asked.

"Yes, of course."

"Then shut up and go with Mr. Bekker."

I stood and yanked Wally to his feet.

"I'll be in touch, Frank," I said and shoved Wally toward the door.

In the hallway, the receptionist all but threw my copy at me.

"Asshole," she said under her breath.

"Is this piece of crap your car?" Wally said as we walked to the Marquis.

I'd parked in the office building lot beside Kagan's Benz.

"It isn't locked," I said. "Get in."

"I've seen homeless people sleeping in better cars at the city dump."

"In," I said. "Now."

Wally opened his door. By the time I went around to the driver's side, Wally had produced another stack of scratch tickets.

I reached over and grabbed the stack of scratchies from his hand.

"Hey, those are my . . ."

I stuck them in my pocket and started the car.

"In thirty-one days you can do what you want," I said. "You can scratch tickets or your rear end to your little heart's content. Until then, you do what I want and only what I want. Are we clear?"

"You need a better car," Wally said. "It's embarrassing for me being seen in a car like this."

"I need you to shut up and behave yourself," I said. "And those snazzy clothes of yours aren't exactly *GQ* material."

I pulled out of the lot and headed for home. Ten minutes into the hour-long drive, Wally started to rock back and forth in his seat.

"Take it easy, Wally," I said.

"Let me have just one," he said.

"If I give you one you'll want more. It's like eating potato chips."

"I promise I won't."

"We both know that's a lie," I said. "Now just relax and try not to think about it."

Wally fell silent and concentrated on his rocking, but ten minutes later he let out a loud yelp, jumped from his seat and hopped into the back, and disappeared on the floor.

"Wally?" I said.

I couldn't see him, but I could hear him moving around on the floor.

"Wally?" I said again, louder.

"What?"

"You're on the floor of the back seat of my car; what do you mean 'what'?" I said.

"It's comfortable back here," Wally said.

I steered to the curb and put the car in *park,* and then opened my door and got out. I yanked open the back door. Wally was on his belly, rubbing scratch tickets with a quarter.

"Oh for . . ." I said, grabbed Wally by his long shank of hair and pulled him out of the car.

"Hey, that hurts," Wally yelped.

"Give them to me," I said. "Right now."

Reluctantly, Wally handed over the stack of scratch tickets.

"All of them," I said.

"That *is* . . ." Wally said.

I stuck my hand into his left jacket pocket, pulled out a stack of scratch tickets and waved it in his face.

"All of them," I said.

"Come on, Mr. . . . ?"

"Bekker."

"Come on Mr. Bekker; leave me a crumb or two."

"I will turn you upside down and shake you like a piggy bank until all your pockets are empty."

"All right," Wally said and started unloading.

By the time he was done I had somewhere between two hundred and fifty and three hundred tickets, not counting the first and second stacks.

"Now get in and be quiet until I tell you to talk," I said.

Wally started for the rear seat.

"Up front," I said. "I'm not your damn chauffeur. And put on the seatbelt."

Sulking, Wally sat in front and we arrived at the beach forty-five minutes later. As I turned onto the sand, Wally looked at me.

"Are we going swimming?"

"No."

I drove to my trailer and parked beside Regan's Impala. She and Oz were out front at the table with Regan's laptop in front of them.

I got out, went around, opened Wally's door and pulled him out by his jacket.

"We're here," I said.

Regan and Oz stared at me.

"Here?" Wally said. "Where is here?"

"Your home for the next thirty days," I said.

"This shithole?" Wally said. "I'm used to better accommodations."

Regan and Oz stared at Wally.

"Never mind shithole," I said. "Plant your ass in that chair over there and don't move until I come back."

I walked past the table and Regan said, "Dad?"

"I'll be right out," I said.

"This gonna be good," I heard Oz tell Regan. "He go to a meeting and come back with a real life Smurf."

"Smurfs are blue, Oz," I heard Regan say.

I went to my bedroom and changed into a lime-colored warm-up suit and jogging shoes, stopped in the kitchen for a mug of coffee, and joined the gang outside.

Oz and Regan were looking at her laptop. Wally was scratching tickets with a dime.

"For crying out . . . Oz, don't you see this?" I said.

"See what?"

"He's . . ." I said and grabbed the tickets from Wally's hand, "scratching scratch tickets."

"So what?" Oz said.

"Yeah, so what?" Wally said.

I pointed to Wally. "You shut up."

"Dad, who is this guy?" Regan asked.

"Yeah, who is this guy?" Oz said.

I sat in my chair and sipped coffee. If ever there was a time to light up a cigarette this was it. Instead I took a deep breath and said, "Okay, remember the visit from Frank Kagan?"

"The mob lawyer," Oz said.

"He's not a . . . would you just listen?" I said.

"I thought I was messed up," Regan said after I concluded my tale of woe on the meeting with Kagan.

"He's not that bad," I said.

"He looking in his shoe," Oz said.

I turned. Wally had his shoes off and was removing scratch tickets from under the removable insoles.

I snatched the tickets and set them in front of Oz.

"You keep them," I said.

I stood and went to my car, opened the door and glove box, and returned with a six-inch-high pile of scratch tickets and dumped them on the table.

"And these, too," I said.

"Can I have some?" Regan asked.

"I don't care what you do with them so long as they disappear from my sight," I said.

Oz gathered the tickets in both hands and stood up. "Come on, girl, let's go down the road and leave these two to discuss their important matters in private."

Regan stood and fell into step beside Oz. "You got a quarter?" she said.

I waited until they were inside Oz's trailer and then I said, "Okay, Wally . . . strip."

"Strip what?"

"Your clothes," I said. "Take them off until you're down to your birthday suit."

"I can't."

"Why not?"

"I don't have any clean clothes."

"Where do you live?"

"Riverdale."

"New York Riverdale?"

"I didn't know there was another."

"Wally, how did you wind up at Kagan's office?"

"I took the train."

I glared at him, but he seemed oblivious.

"Why? I mean why now?"

"I'm well aware of my father's will," Wally said. "I went to see Mr. Kagan because, like he told you, I turn forty in one month."

"Did you know about the part where you must pass a psych exam?"

"No."

"Do you realize what happens if you don't pass?"

"Yes."

"Do you have any money on you?"

Wally stood up, rifled through his pockets and produced thirteen dollars rolled in a crinkled ball covered in lint.

"I had more but I bought . . ."

"Scratch tickets, yeah I know," I said. "Okay, let's go."

"Where?"

"The mall," I said. "I have expense money and you need some clothes."

"Wait a minute," Wally said. "Where am I supposed to sleep for the next month?"

"Let's climb one mountain at a time, Wally," I said.

Wally looked around at the flat beach. "What . . . ?"

"Figure of speech, Wally," I said and walked to my car.

CHAPTER FOUR

On the rare occasion that I buy athletic clothing, it's usually from the sports clothing store at the mall. They carried every brand of every type of athletic wear on the market and could fit just about any body type and size.

Except for Wally Sample.

His pear-shaped body, sunken chest, twig-like legs and bulbous stomach sent the salespeople running for cover behind clothing racks.

I took matters into my own hands and mixed and matched three sets of warm-up suits, six tee shirts, a dozen pairs of athletic briefs, the same amount of socks and two pairs of jogging shoes.

We left the mall with Wally wearing a teal-colored warm-up suit, black jogging shoes and a blue tee shirt, all of which made a six-hundred-dollar dent in Kagan's expense check.

"Can we hit the food court?" Wally said. "I'm kind of hungry."

"If you hurry," I said. "We need to get back and get you settled."

We entered the food court and set the shopping bags on a table.

"Grab two coffees," I said.

"My money is in my pants," Wally said. "In one of those bags."

I gave him a ten-dollar bill and he walked to the Coffee Hut.

As soon as Wally was out of sight, I pulled out my cell phone and called Janet. She was still at work, but answered the call anyway.

"Jack, I'm still on duty," she said.

"I know, I'm sorry," I said. "I don't think I can make it tonight. I have a job and I don't think it would be a good idea at this time."

"What kind of job?" Janet said, coldly.

"Something for a lawyer."

"Something?"

"Let's just leave it at that, okay?"

"How long is this something going to last?"

"A month at least."

After a short pause, Janet said, "Is this about Clayton? I want to . . ."

"No, it's not about . . . look, I have to go," I said. "If I can I'll call you later."

"Jack, wait . . ."

I ended the call and placed the phone in my jacket pocket just as Wally arrived with two containers of coffee.

"Can we get something to eat?" Wally said. "I haven't had . . ."

"When we get home," I said.

"Do you live in that thing?" Wally said. "With the girl and old man?"

"The girl is my daughter and the old man is . . . never mind," I said. "Look, I need some background info here."

"On what?"

"On you."

"Like what?"

"Are you married?"

"I was, but she left me like eight years ago. I'm not sure why."

I thought I knew why, but I kept it to myself.

"Do you work at all?"

"If you mean a job, the answer is no."

"What do you live on?"

"I receive an allowance of sixty thousand a year from my father's company, and the home in Riverdale was my parents' original home. It's paid for and the taxes are paid for out of my father's estate."

"Education? Did you go to college?"

"I went to MIT."

"MIT in Boston?"

Wally nodded.

"That's the hardest technical college in the country to get into."

"I was always good with numbers. The idea was I would graduate and run the logistics department at Sample."

"Would graduate?"

"In my third year I was expelled."

"Why?"

"I was using MIT resources to create a program that would allow me to count cards at a Vegas table," Wally said. "It was beautiful. I was close to completion when they caught me and tossed me out."

"Your father couldn't . . . ?"

"It was my fifth offense," Wally said. "I was caught designing a program to beat the lottery, and another one to . . ."

"I get it."

"I can beat them, you know. The bastards."

"That's not the point," I said. "In your present state of mind you would never pass a psychiatric evaluation. You stand to lose your inheritance unless you can convince them you're addiction free."

"It's a hobby," Wally said. "They would penalize a man for his hobby?"

"Collecting stamps or butterflies is a hobby," I said. "Walking around with three hundred scratch tickets in your pockets and shoes is an addiction. Come on, let's go."

"Can I use the bathroom first? This coffee."

"It's right over there," I said and pointed to the hallway between the pizza joint and Chinese take-out place.

Wally stood and walked across the food court to the hallway. I watched him open the men's-room door and disappear as the door closed.

I took my coffee and Wally's shopping bags with me and left the food court and entered the parking lot. I turned left and walked along the sidewalk to the bathroom windows. One of the windows opened just enough for Wally to squeeze out and fall on his face by my feet.

He looked up at me.

"So, are you ready then?" I said.

CHAPTER FIVE

Oz and Regan were seated at the table in front of the trailer when I parked the Marquis beside the Impala.

Regan dashed from the table to me with a scratch ticket in her hand.

"I won five hundred dollars," she said. "Oz won two-fifty."

"Then you can pay for dinner," I said.

"Technically, I won," Wally said. "See, I purchased the . . ."

"Shut up, Wally, and have a seat," I said. "Regan, you, too."

I stood while Wally and Regan took chairs.

"Regan, have you and Oz found anything you like furniture-wise?"

"We're whittling it down," Regan said.

"Good. Your project for the next thirty days is to furnish the entire house," I said. "You and Oz. That goes for my room, too. Okay?"

"Dad, the money . . ."

"Don't worry about it," I said. "I have the funds in my checkbook."

"I pay for my own stuff," Oz said.

"Fine."

"It's only right."

"I said fine," I said.

"Ain't no free lunch in life," Oz said.

"Next time we go to lunch, you can pay for it," I said. "Now, can we . . . ?"

"That was an allegory," Oz said. "I wasn't talking about a real lunch."

"I know."

"Those tickets were mine," Wally said.

I glared at Wally. "Say one more word and I'll staple your lips together."

"Dad, he has a point," Regan said.

"No, he doesn't," I said. "Now listen to me a minute. I've agreed to help Mr. Sample with . . ."

"Who?" Oz asked.

"Mr. Sample. Wally. Weren't you listening earlier?"

"Earlier you said his name is Wally," Oz said. "Nobody said nothing about Sample."

I glared at Oz.

"Dad, what are you trying to say?" Regan asked.

"I explained to you before that I've agreed to help Wally with his problem so he can collect his inheritance," I said. "The only way this can work is if I don't let him out of my sight and that means he sleeps in the trailer."

"Dad, he's a slob," Regan said. "I mean, look at the guy. Even in new clothes he's a total slob."

"But I'm a deep thinker," Wally said. "Einstein never combed his hair."

"Wally, shut up," I said. "Oz, can Regan use your spare bedroom for a few weeks?"

"Yes, please," Regan snapped. "Oz, I beg of you."

"Will you do the cooking?" Oz said.

"The cooking, cleaning and I'll even mend your socks so long as I don't have to bunk with Mr. Deep Thinker here."

"Deal."

"Good. In the meantime you and Oz can spend your days furnishing the new house," I said. "I figure in two weeks after the closing you and Oz can move in and do some fixer-upping."

"Can I paint my room?" Regan asked.

"It's your room."

"Can we get something to eat now?" Wally asked.

"Why not? My daughter is buying," I said.

I drove the Impala to the steak house near the mall. We feasted on steak and salad and, despite scratch-ticket winnings, I footed the bill using Kagan's expense money and we were back at the trailer by eight thirty.

Wally, silent for most of the dinner, was sweating, mumbling under his breath and rocking on the drive back to the beach.

"Dad, Wally is sort of having a fit," Regan said.

"I know the feeling, Wally," I said. "Believe me, I do. Tomorrow we'll keep busy to take your mind off things."

Seated beside me, Regan turned around and looked at Wally.

"He's drooling on himself, Dad," she said.

"And me," Oz said. "Cut that out, boy, you ain't no English bulldog."

I pulled the Impala onto the beach.

"I gonna hit this boy in the nose with a rolled-up newspaper he don't quit drooling on me," Oz said.

"We'll be home in five minutes, Wally," I said. "A hot shower, a good night's sleep and a fresh start in the morning will help a lot."

"A front-row seat at a blackjack table would help," Wally said. "That's what would help."

"In thirty-one days you can do . . ." I said.

"Dad, somebody is at the trailer," Regan said. "There's a car parked next to yours, and the lights are on."

"I see it," I said. "That's Janet's car."

"This should be good," Oz said. "Wally and the ex."

"Never mind 'this should be . . .'," I said.

"Is somebody sick?" Wally said. "She looks like a nurse."

I parked beside Janet's sedan. Janet was seated at the card table with a mug of coffee.

Except for Wally, we got out of the car and walked to the table.

"I still have a key," Janet said. "I made coffee."

"I need to get my stuff together," Regan said and ducked into the trailer.

"I'll wait and give her a hand," Oz said.

"Jack, what's going on around here?" Janet asked.

"This is Wally Sample," I said, unaware that he was still in the car.

Janet stared at me.

"Wally still be in the car drooling," Oz said.

I turned around. "Oh, for . . . Wally, get out here. Now."

Slowly the car door opened, and Wally crept out and walked to me.

Janet stared at Wally. "What's this?"

"This be Wally," Oz said.

Regan suddenly appeared with a small suitcase in one hand and Molly in the other. "Let's go," she said. "That show about duck calls is on."

"The what?" Oz said.

"Never mind. Do you have popcorn?"

Oz took the suitcase and they walked down the beach to Oz's trailer.

"Jack, what is . . . ?" Janet said.

"Do you have any scratch tickets?" Wally said to Janet.

"Any what? Jack, who is this person?"

"Wally Sample. Wally, this is Janet."

"Why are you dressed like a nurse?" Wally asked.

"Because I am a nurse," Janet said. "Jack, we need to talk."

I looked at Wally. "Go inside and get comfortable," I said. "I'll bring in the shopping bags later."

Wally walked to the door of the trailer and paused.

"What do you mean by comfortable?" he asked.

"Relax," I said.

"Oh, okay."

"And Wally, don't try jumping out the window," I said. "I'll see you and I don't want to have to tie you up. You might drown in your own drool."

Wally nodded and entered the trailer.

"Why would he jump out the window?" Janet asked.

"He . . . I need some coffee first," I said.

I went inside and filled a mug with coffee, and then returned to Janet and took my chair at the table.

"So this is why you broke our date?" Janet said.

"He's my . . . the job I told you about concerns him and his family-owned company."

"What company is that, Jack?"

"Sample Iced Tea."

"Sample Iced Tea," Janet said. "I love Sample Iced Tea. I drink it all the time. The raspberry cream is delicious. What does that drooling goofball have to do with anything?"

"I really can't go into it," I said. "He's a client and that entitles him to privacy."

"I didn't come here to discuss Wally Sample, anyway," Janet said. "I wanted to talk to you about us."

Wally stuck his head out the door. "Where is your computer?"

"I don't own one," I said.

"That laptop?"

"My daughter's and she probably took it with her."

"Can I . . . ?"

"No. Now go inside and relax."

Wally disappeared.

"Jack, are you listening to me?" Janet said.

"Yes."

"Can we walk down to the beach and talk privately?"

"I don't want to leave Wally alone where I can't see or hear him."

"Is he going to turn into a pumpkin at midnight?"

"It's . . . complicated."

Janet sipped her coffee.

I sipped my coffee.

Wally poked his head out the door again.

"Which bedroom is mine?" he said.

"See the bedroom with the pink curtains and bedspread and stuffed animals on it? That one isn't mine," I said.

"Oh, okay," Wally said and disappeared.

"Jack, please," Janet said.

Wally appeared again. "So the other room is yours?"

"Yes," I said.

"Okay," Wally said and disappeared again.

Janet glared at me.

"I told you I'd be tied up for a month," I said.

"This can't wait a month."

"Then say what it is you want to say."

Janet took another sip from her cup.

"Clayton wants to get married again," she said. "He feels we're more mature and better suited to make it work a second time."

I drank some coffee and set the mug down on the table.

"And you said?"

"Nothing yet."

"Why not?"

"I wanted to discuss it with you first."

"Do you want to know how I feel about it?" I said.

"For one thing."

"I don't really know or like Clayton all that much," I said. "He stepped up when you were in the hospital and took care of

Mark, but Mark is his son so that's what he's supposed to do. But I'm not marrying Clayton, so how I feel about him one way or the other really doesn't matter."

"How do you feel about me?"

"How I feel about you hasn't changed. How I feel about myself has."

"I don't . . . what does that mean exactly?"

"I'm not some puppy to be brought home and molded into the kind of dog you want me to be," I said. "I'm a flawed individual who happens to be pretty good at being a cop even if I'm not one anymore. I'm not nine-to-five, dinner-at-six, take-out-the-trash-on-Wednesday-and-Saturday material. I have to live with me first and I can't live a lie. Not anymore."

"I was doing that, wasn't I?" Janet said. "Molding you into the kind of man I wanted you to be and not who you really are."

"If it means anything, the man you want me to be is probably the better man," I said. "Just not the real one."

"I understand, Jack."

"After this job is done I may or may not ever work another," I said. "But if I do or don't, the choice is mine alone. It's no different than if you decide to quit being a nurse."

Janet nodded. "I guess I'll go home now."

"There is something you should know," I said. "I bought that house on the beach we looked at. The closing is in two weeks."

"I see," Janet said. "I guess there is no more to say, then."

"Not tonight, anyway."

Janet stood and I walked her to her car.

"I wasn't that bad, was I?" she said as she got behind the wheel.

"If it wasn't for you I probably wouldn't have gotten or stayed sober," I said. "You were probably the best thing that happened to me in twenty years."

"Thank you for that."

I returned to my chair and watched her drive off the beach.

When she was gone I took my mug inside and found Wally at the kitchen table playing blackjack with himself and scribbling in a notebook.

I sat. "What are you doing?"

"Working on one of my systems," Wally said. "See, there's five decks in a dealer's . . ."

"Go to bed right now," I said.

"I'm not tired," Wally said. "I'm used to late hours."

"Let me rephrase that," I said. "Go to bed right now or I'll break both your arms and legs and you'll sit out the next month in a wheelchair."

Wally looked at me. "Are you serious?"

"Want to find out?"

"No."

"Then go into the bedroom, close the door and try to get some sleep."

"What are you going to do?"

"I'm going to say good night to my daughter and then hit the bed myself," I said.

Wally stood, nodded, walked into Regan's bedroom and closed the door.

I took the deck of cards, stood over the trash bin by the sink and ripped them into pieces. Then I stepped outside and walked around to the side of the trailer and stood in the dark. The moon was bright and high and I could see the lights of town in the distance.

Wally must have figured five minutes to walk to Oz's trailer, five to say goodnight and five to walk back, because by my watch five minutes passed before he came rolling out Regan's bedroom window.

He hit the beach and started running toward town.

46

The thing about running on sand is that it's much more tiring than running on the road or grass, especially if you're in terrible shape like Wally. The half mile to town must have seemed like a marathon to him because after a hundred yards he stopped, placed his hands on his knees and sucked wind.

After a minute or so, he continued on, ran another fifty yards and stopped to rest again. He looked toward town and started running again. He made about a hundred yards before he fell to his knees and gasped for air.

I went to my car and drove to Wally. I parked beside him and opened the passenger door.

"Get in," I said.

"I . . . can't . . . my . . . I need to . . ." Wally sputtered.

"Get in or I'll tie you to the rear bumper and drag you back like a buck deer."

Wally slowly stood, then flopped into the car and closed the door.

I made a U-turn and drove back to the trailer. "Inside. Go," I snapped.

Wally got out and slunk into the trailer. I walked around the side to my makeshift gym and opened the large box where I store kettlebells and extra chains for the heavy bag. I grabbed a four-foot-long chain and a forty-pound kettlebell and carried them inside.

I set them on the table while I went to my bedroom to fetch a pair of handcuffs, then carried ball and chain into Regan's bedroom, where Wally sat on the bed with his head between his legs.

"Oh, man," Wally said.

"Wally?" I said quietly.

Wally looked at the kettlebell. "What the hell is that? You're not going to hit me now, are you?"

"That's a tempting offer, but no," I said. "Give me your right leg."

"What?"

"Your right leg, stick it out."

Wally extended his right leg. I snapped one handcuff around his skinny ankle, then threaded the chain through the handle in the kettlebell and cuffed the second loop through the chain.

"There," I said. "Now anywhere you go that forty-pound kettlebell goes with you. So get some sleep and we'll start on your program in the morning."

"What program?"

"Diet and exercise."

I left the room and closed the door.

"What are you . . . what diet? What exercise?" Wally called after me. "I have food allergies. Hey, wait."

"Good night, Wally," I said, and entered my bedroom and slammed the door.

Chapter Six

I was up before the sun, brewed a pot of coffee, poured it into a carafe, and took it and a mug outside to my chair. I could hear the waves at the shore but not see them as I drank the first cup of the day. The urge to light up a cigarette was strong and I had to choke it back.

Coffee and cigarettes are a lethal combination.

After a second cup of coffee the nicotine urge subsided and my nerves calmed down enough for me to start a workout. I began in darkness and ended ninety minutes later in bright sunlight.

Drenched in sweat, I filled my cup with coffee from the carafe and flopped into my chair. It was around seven thirty in the morning and I doubted Wally ever stirred before ten.

I decided to take advantage of Regan's cleaning jag and make breakfast in the now-spotless kitchen. I warmed up the waffle maker while a pound of bacon cooked, mixed the batter, and made six waffles and whole wheat toast.

Just before everything was ready I went to Regan's bedroom to free Wally, who was still asleep under the covers.

"Let's go Jimmy the Greek, up and at 'em," I said as I shook Wally awake.

He rolled over and opened his eyes. "What time is it?"

"Almost nine. I made breakfast."

"I never eat breakfast."

I used the key to unlock Wally's ankle. "You will today. Get up. Meet me in the kitchen in five minutes."

I returned to the kitchen and set plates at the table. Wally stumbled in looking like he'd spent the night in a cardboard box under a bridge somewhere and flopped into a chair wearing the warm-up suit he'd slept in.

"I can't eat all this," he said. "I'll just have coffee."

"You can eat it and you will," I said. "You'll need the fuel for your workout."

"What workout?"

"Eat."

I allowed Wally one hour to digest before starting his workout. We sipped coffee at the table outside, and Oz and Regan walked over from Oz's trailer.

"We're going to that furniture store on Beaumont and do some window shopping," Regan said.

"I ate waffles," Wally said.

Regan looked at him. "What's wrong with you?" she asked.

"He chained me to the bed," Wally said.

"He . . . never mind. Nothing he does surprises me anymore," Regan said. "Oz, my car or yours?"

"Mine," Oz said. He looked at me. "Any of them waffles left?"

"We'll eat in town," Regan said.

"Can you bring me a newspaper?" Wally said.

"No newspapers," I said.

"A newspaper can't hurt," Regan said.

"Newspapers contain horse racing results and coded numbers bookies use for bets," I said.

"Almost, Wally. Almost," Regan said.

"Be back this afternoon," Oz said.

"We left the door open for Molly," Regan said.

After they left, I stood up and said, "Are you ready?"

"To do what?"

"I don't know, but we're going to try."

Wally managed to do three situps, three and a half push-ups, no pull-ups or chin-ups, and jumped rope five times before he tripped and fell on his face.

"Okay, end of phase one," I said.

"What's phase two?"

"We're going down to the water and take a little jog."

"You're a crazy man, you know that?"

"Maybe so, but I can run more than a hundred feet without puking. Let's go."

"I didn't . . ."

"Move."

We walked down to the water where it was low tide.

"We'll walk a half mile and then take it up to a power walk for another half," I said.

We started walking at a slow pace.

"I'm not exactly clear on this power-walking thing," Wally said.

"You will be."

Twenty minutes later by my watch we arrived at the half-mile mark I'd memorized after a thousand runs along the water.

"Let's kick it up a notch," I said and broke into a quick walk.

"Hey, wait," Wally said.

"Shut up and stay with me."

Looking much like a drunken ostrich, Wally kept pace with me for several hundred feet and then gasped, wheezed and started to fade.

"Stay with me, Wally," I said.

"I . . . can't."

"You can and you will or I'll stick your head in the ocean."

We made it nearly to the mile mark before Wally fell to his knees and puked.

"That wasn't so bad, was it?" I said.

Wally puked on his hands, rolled over and looked up at the sky.

"I'm gonna have a fucking heart attack," he said.

"No, you're not," I said. "Get up and let's head back."

"I can't."

"I'll stick your head in the water and drag you back by the ankles."

Wally rolled over and managed to get to his feet.

We power walked a few hundred yards and slowed to a regular pace to keep Wally from passing out, and made it back in just under an hour.

Wally collapsed into a chair in front of the trailer.

"Don't get too comfortable," I said. "We're not done yet."

"I need a nap."

"You just woke up three hours ago."

"That's when I usually nap, three hours after I get up," Wally said. "It's refreshing."

"Not today," I said and yanked Wally from the chair. I walked him to the side of the trailer and said, "Put on those bag gloves."

Wally picked up the gloves and put them on.

"You're going to hit that bag five hundred times, then we'll work on the speed bag," I said.

Wally stared at the heavy bag.

"Hit it," I snarled.

Wally punched the bag with the force of a three-year-old.

"Harder."

Wally hit the bag hard enough for it to wobble and he winced in pain.

"Just four hundred and ninety-nine to go."

Wally made it to around a hundred before his arms quit on him.

"I just can't do anymore," he sniveled.

"Okay," I said. "That's enough for today."

We returned to our chairs and I poured coffee.

"Tomorrow we'll include the speed bag," I said.

"You're a crazy person," Wally said. "You know that?"

"And you're an addict," I said. "One way to keep your mind occupied and not think about your addiction is to keep your body occupied."

Wally looked at me defiantly. "What are you, an expert?"

"Yes."

Wally raised an eyebrow at me.

"I'm a drunk, Wally," I said. "I crawled inside a bottle and spent ten years there before I got sober. If there is one thing I know about it's craving your addiction. Believe me, keeping your body and mind occupied helps a great deal in the battle."

"What . . . what happened?"

"I was a cop. I got too close to a mobster and his son sent somebody to kill me. He killed my wife instead and my daughter, five at the time, witnessed it," I said.

"Jesus," Wally said. "What happened to the mobster?"

"He died of cancer fourteen months or so ago."

"Your daughter, the room I'm sleeping in, she was the five-year-old?"

I nodded.

"Jesus."

"You said that already," I said. "Go take a hot shower and change, you'll feel better."

"Yeah, okay," Wally said.

He stood and entered the trailer, then poked his head out. "I'm sorry about all that mob stuff and your daughter," he said.

"Sure," I said and Wally disappeared again.

I picked up my cell phone and dialed Walt's private office number. He answered on the third ring.

"Walt," I said.

"Jack."

"I need a favor."

"Of course you do. Asking for a favor is how you say hello."

"Can you . . . ?"

"It's not like I have a police department to run or anything."

"I realize how . . ."

"In fact, I was just thinking I should call you and ask if you needed any favors I could help you with that you will never pay back."

"Are you going to listen or not?" I said.

I could hear Walt's sigh and then he said, "What?"

"Can you do a background check on Wally Sample?" I said. "Son of Robert Sample and one of six heirs to the Sample Iced Tea company."

"I love that stuff," Walt said. "The black cherry cream is delicious on a hot day with some ice."

"The background check, can you do it?"

"Of course I can do it," Walt said. "Can you buy me lunch?"

"Don't you want to know why?"

"I know why," Walt said. "Because you're a pain in the ass."

"Call me when you have it."

Walt hung up and I set the phone aside. I went inside and found Wally at the table wearing the lime-colored warm-up suit, one of the three we bought at the mall. He was scribbling in the notebook with pencil.

"I warned you about . . ." I said.

"No, see, this is logistics," Wally said. "For the company."

I sat beside Wally and looked at the notebook.

"What is that?"

"Basically it's a math problem that would logistically save the company one hundred million in shipping costs over five years," Wally said.

I scanned the page and tried to follow the breakdown analysis of shipping costs to production ratio, but it was like trying to learn Chinese from reading a book without English translations.

"Have you shown this to your family?" I said.

"Once, a couple of years ago," Wally said. "It wasn't perfected then. They threw me out of the office and told me never to come back. I've made some changes since then based upon the prices of sugar and certain flavors and central locations to customers and some other factors like the price of gas and mileage."

"Wally, if you can hang on for twenty-nine more days and pass a psych exam they won't be able to toss you out if you're an equal partner," I said. "Right?"

Wally looked at me.

"I don't know if I can hold out for another twenty-nine days," he said.

"What it comes down to is how badly you want to be a part of the company your father spent his lifetime building," I said.

Wally nodded and closed the notebook.

"Okay if I take a nap?"

"Sure."

Wally stood and walked to the bedroom door, and paused to look at me. "Are you going to chain me in?"

"No."

Wally nodded and entered the bedroom.

I brewed a fresh pot of coffee and took it outside.

Wally was a pathetic figure to be sure. But in a lot of ways so was I.

My thoughts turned to Janet. She deserved better and more than I could give her. If we went through with the wedding, it might be okay for a year or so, but I would always have an itch I couldn't scratch and that would lead to problems, and we both knew that. I'm an old dog and I only know one trick and maybe I could learn another or forget the one that I know, but as someone once said, *to thine own self be true,* and a lie is no way to start a marriage, but a good way to end one.

On the second cup of coffee I spotted Molly walking toward me from Oz's trailer. When she finally arrived she hopped onto my lap and rubbed her head against my stomach. I scratched her ears, and she purred and settled down and curled into a ball.

"You wouldn't happen to have a pack of smokes on you, would you, girl?" I said.

Molly opened one eye and quickly closed it.

"That's what I thought."

Down the beach I spotted Oz's car turning onto the sand.

"Your mistress returns," I said.

Molly rolled over and slept with her belly exposed.

I watched the car as Oz drove beside mine and parked. Excited, Regan came dashing out with a cardboard box in her arms. "We got swatches," she said.

"I have a watch," I said.

"No, Dad, rug samples."

Oz came and joined us at the table.

"Where the degenerate?" Oz asked.

"Taking a nap."

"He just got up, didn't he?"

"He's delicate."

Regan emptied the swatches on the table. They were samples of various colors and patterns of rugs.

"I like the peach for my room," Regan said. "Oz likes the light gray. What do you like for yours?"

Molly, suddenly awake, leapt to the table and used the swatches as a scratching board.

"Hey, stop that," Regan said. "We have to return those."

"Better get used to that," I said. "Rugs and cats don't mix."

Regan grabbed Molly and took a chair.

"I'll go with Oz's pick," I said.

"That just leaves the rest of the house," Regan said.

I nodded. "I need a favor from you two," I said. "I have a meeting with Walt tomorrow and I can't bring Wally. Can you babysit him for a few hours?"

"He run off, I ain't chasing him," Oz said.

"If he runs off he'll probably have a heart attack," I said.

"In that case, we watch him," Oz said.

CHAPTER SEVEN

"When you said lunch, you didn't mention I'd need a second mortgage to pay for it," I said.

Walt sliced into his perfectly prepared sixteen ounce rib-eye steak and smacked his lips. "Police resources aren't cheap," he said and forked a slice into his mouth.

I cut into my steak and said, "Police resources are paid for by tax dollars. So as a taxpayer I'm actually paying for this twice."

Walt shrugged. "Splitting hairs."

"So what am I getting for my money?"

"The file is in my car," Walt said. "You can have it later. The gist of it is Wally Sample has been arrested three times in Vegas at three major casinos for cheating, twice in Atlantic City, twice in Biloxi and twice in Connecticut. His credit cards are maxed out and overdue. He applied for but was rejected by the bank for a second mortgage."

"Ever convicted?"

"No. Charges were always dropped in exchange for his guarantee he would never return to the casino," Walt said.

"His family name might have something to do with that," I said.

"Ya think."

"Anything criminal?"

"Those were criminal."

"Besides those."

Walt ate another slice of steak. "This is so good, and no, no other arrests."

"Okay, thanks."

"What shall we have for dessert?"

"The cupcakes are thirty-five bucks apiece in this joint," I said.

"One cannot put a price on the public's safety," Walt said.

Regan was attempting to teach Wally how to hula hoop on the sand when I returned from lunch with Walt.

Regan had a custom-made hoop that lit up in the dark. Wally had the standard fare. Oz, from a chair, and Molly, from the table, watched as Regan danced and twirled while never losing the spin of the hoop and Wally . . . well, Wally couldn't seem to get the hoop to revolve even once.

"Use your hips like I showed you," Regan said.

I took the chair next to Oz.

"I didn't know she had those until the last visit to see Sister Mary Martin and the two of them put on a show," I said to Oz.

"The nun hula hoops?" Oz said.

"They teach fitness classes at the home," I said. "The nun also teaches kickboxing and judo."

"Damn," Oz said. "The nun like Chuck Norris."

Regan dropped her hoop and turned to Wally. "Look," she said. "Follow what I do without the hoop first."

My cell phone rang and I removed it from my pocket. "Bekker," I said.

"Uncle Jack, it's Mark."

"Hi, Mark, how's it going?"

"Tomorrow is Saturday," Mark said. "Mom said I could go striper fishing with you if that's all right."

I looked at Wally, who was trying his best to follow Regan's hip-swaying movements, but more resembled a giant weeble trying not to fall down.

"That might be just the thing," I said.

"Cool."

"Pick you up around seven."

"I'm spending the night with my dad."

"No problem."

I hung up, looked at Wally and shook my head. "I was thinking tonight might be a good night for a bonfire and barbeque," I said. "And some striper fishing with Mark tomorrow morning."

"Sounds good, Dad," Regan said.

"Oz, I'm going to town and pick up a few things," I said.

"I'll keep an eye on Fred Astaire there," Oz said.

I took the Marquis to town and hit the meat market and supermarket, and returned inside of ninety minutes and found Wally doing math equations in the sand with a stick while Regan and Mark watched with puzzled expressions on their faces.

"What's this?" I asked as I carried bags to the trailer.

"Wally is showing us how logistics could save the post office millions each year by consolidating pick-up and drop-off points in a given area by . . ." Regan said.

"Never mind," I said. "Wally, see that trash can? Gather up dry driftwood off the beach and fill it. Regan, give him a hand."

I took the bags into the kitchen and unpacked the groceries. I seasoned chicken and steak tips, and readied potatoes for the grill, along with ears of corn. Then I made fresh coffee and took a mug outside to my chair.

Regan and Wally were filling the trash can with driftwood from the beach.

"Oz, you want to do the honors?" I said.

Oz picked up the can of lighter fluid beside the grill, squirted some onto the driftwood, struck a match and tossed it in. Immediately the wood burst into flames.

"That's not enough," Regan said to Wally.

While Regan and Wally gathered some more wood, I added fresh coals to the grill, squirted on some fluid and struck a match.

"Give them a half hour to get hot enough and gray," I said.

I took my chair and sipped some coffee, and noticed a man walking alone on the beach. During peak summer months that wouldn't be so unusual to see dozens of people walking the shoreline even close to dark.

This wasn't peak season and the man was wearing a suit.

Nobody wears a suit for a stroll on the beach.

I kept my eye on him as he walked along the water's edge, turned and looked in our direction.

He seemed to focus on us for a few moments and then turned and started walking back to town.

By the time he reached the municipal parking lot it was getting dark and he was a dot on the horizon. I watched the lot. Car lights came on and then vanished as the car turned onto the street.

Regan and Wally dumped stacks of driftwood beside the trash can.

"I think we're good, Dad," Regan said.

Oz checked the grill. "We good here, too."

"I'll get the food," I said.

Around ten o'clock, Regan and Oz called it a night and went to his trailer. I sat with Wally for a bit in front of the dwindling bonfire.

"What started you gambling?" I said to Wally.

"I was always good at math," he said. "Dad always sent us to private boarding schools where I was bored out of my mind all the time, except for math. Numbers just seemed to make sense to me. Even in first grade I could do high-school calculus. When I was twelve I became fascinated with the lottery. Not the money aspect, but the odds of winning. One in a sixteen-million chance of hitting the exact six numbers to win. In my young mind I saw one giant math problem that needed to be solved. That's all gambling is really, math problems. Games of chance with a mathematical-based solution."

"And later?"

"Horse racing, card games, roulette, any and all of it fascinated me to the point all I could think about was finding the right system to beat the odds for the sake of solving what to me is a giant math problem."

"Which got you kicked out of every major casino in the country."

"I tried to explain to them I wasn't cheating to win money, that I was trying to find a logical solution to winning a game based in logistics, but they wouldn't listen."

"How badly in debt are you?" I said.

"About one hundred and fifty thousand on my credit cards," Wally said. "Mostly from online gambling sites."

"I know about that," I said. "What else?"

Wally lowered his eyes.

"Loan sharks?"

"Maybe a few."

"Maybe?" I said. "You do or you don't. Which?"

"Do."

"Who and how much?"

"Tony 'Angel Eyes' Marco, about eighty thousand. Bobby 'The Butcher' Bannister, around a hundred thousand, and May 'Sunshine' Jackson, about a hundred and fifty thousand," Wally said.

"Wally, in twenty-eight days you need to pass an evaluation or it's no inheritance and partnership in the company," I said. "Right now if I let you out of my sight for five minutes you'd be on the phone placing bets or worse."

"I know." Wally looked at me. "I need help."

"I know you need help, and tomorrow you're going to get some," I said. "Right now I want you to go to bed and get some sleep. We're going fishing in the morning. Early."

"Do you need to chain me to the bed?"

"Can I trust you?"

"No. I got the taste in my mouth."

"Go on in," I said. "I'll be in to chain you in a few minutes."

Wally nodded, stood up and entered the trailer.

I drank another mug of coffee, missing the cigarette that usually accompanied it and when the mug was empty I went inside to my bedroom. I grabbed the key for the cuffs, went next door and found Wally in bed, but still awake.

I cuffed his ankle to the kettlebell. "I'm going to say good night to my daughter," I said.

Wally nodded. "I'll see you in the morning."

I went back to my room and opened the closet. Shortly before Regan moved in I purchased a heavy-duty gun safe and had it bolted to the floor. I opened it using the combination. Inside were several different models of handguns, and a pistol-grip, 12-gauge shotgun. My arsenal of handguns included a .357 hammerless Magnum revolver, a Glock .45 and a .44 Smith & Wesson.

I selected the hammerless .357 because I could stick it in a pocket and not have to worry about the hammer getting snagged if I needed it in a hurry. I opened the wheel and added six rounds, closed it and stuck it in my right-front pants pocket.

I tossed on a windbreaker and left the trailer. I didn't run, but walked at a brisk pace to the municipal parking lot. The deli across the street was still open and I ducked inside for a container of coffee.

Then I entered the parking lot, where only a dozen or so cars were parked and went to the rear where the street lamps didn't shine, and sat on the metal rail fence to wait.

About an hour passed before a car turned into the lot and parked close to the exit. A stocky man wearing a suit got out and started walking toward the beach. He never noticed me on the rail.

I waited until he entered the beach, and then I hopped over the rail and raced to him from behind and tackled him at the knees. We went down hard with me on top. He was a big guy, strong, but I shoved his face into the sand and drew the .357 and pressed it against his face.

"Are you armed?" I said.

"Yes," he rasped.

I frisked him and removed a Sig .380 pistol.

I stood up. "Get up slow and face me."

He stood up and looked at me. There was just enough light from the street lamps to see faces.

"Who the fuck are you?" he asked.

"That isn't the question," I said. "The question is who are you and what do you want?"

"That's none of your business."

"This .357 says it is," I said. "Are you Angel Eyes or The Butcher, because you don't look like Sunshine to me?"

"I'm . . . how did you know? Wally tell you he owed money?"

"Yes."

"I'm Jimmy Marco. Tony is my brother. I work for him."

"Wally owes you eighty grand," I said.

"Sounds about right."

"How did you find him?"

"Dumb luck," Jimmy said. "Tony sent me to collect and he was leaving his house in Riverdale. I followed him to the train. I thought he was skipping town so I followed him. I rented a car at the station and tailed his cab to that lawyer's office, and then to you. I followed you all over town and decided I better have a chat with him and find out what's going on."

"Let's go talk to him," I said.

"Where?"

"My trailer."

I lowered the .357 and put it away. I held the Sig in my hand. "I'll give this back to you later," I said.

Jimmy nodded. We started walking.

"You work for that lawyer?" he said.

"I'm doing him a favor."

"Cop or private?"

"I was a cop, now I'm private."

"Wally paying you for protection?"

"No," I said. "Wally needs to dry out."

"He ain't a drunk."

"His addiction is gambling," I said. "He has thirty days to kick his habit or he won't collect his inheritance. I'm helping him."

"I didn't know about any of that."

"Why would you?"

We reached my trailer.

"Have a seat," I said. "I'll get Wally."

Wally was in a dead sleep when I removed the cuffs from his ankle and shook him awake. "Mr. Bekker, is something wrong?"

"Company. Get dressed. Meet me outside."

I joined Jimmy at the table in front of the trailer. Five minutes later, Wally stumbled out and froze when he saw who the company was.

"Honest, Jimmy, I wasn't trying to ditch out on you," Wally said with fear in his eyes.

"Relax, kid, your friend here explained things to me," Jimmy said.

Wally came to the table and sat next to me.

"I'll pay you back, Jimmy," he said. "Every cent plus the vig.

All I need is a month."

"I'll tell Tony that you'll pay one hundred thou in thirty days," Jimmy said. "But Wally, don't make me come look for you."

"It probably will take several days for Wally's inheritance to clear," I said. "Make it forty days."

"Then make it one-ten for the extra trouble," Jimmy said.

"Agreed, right, Wally?" I said.

"Yes, agreed."

I looked at Jimmy. "Can I give you a ride back to your car?"

"Why not?"

"Back inside," I told Wally. "Lock yourself up."

I drove Jimmy back to his car and handed him his Sig before he got out.

"You handle yourself pretty good," he said. "Ever think about collecting, let me know. We could use you."

"I'll keep it in mind," I said.

When I returned to the trailer, Wally was asleep with the cuffs around his ankle.

I locked the front door and decided to call it a night. I set the alarm for five thirty, and then crawled between the sheets and fell asleep almost immediately. It was a comforting thought to know that if my present career went bust there was a Tony Marco in the wings who would hire me.

CHAPTER EIGHT

Mark was dressed and waiting for me in front of Clayton's condo when I arrived at five to seven the next morning.

He came to the car. "Morning, Uncle Jack."

"Wait in the car, Mark," I said. "I want to see your dad for a moment."

"Okay, but we don't want to miss them biting."

I walked to the front door of the condo. It was unlocked. I opened it and stepped inside to the living room. I found Clayton drinking coffee at the kitchen table with a *New York Times* at his elbows.

He looked up at me. "Jack?"

Fear was in his eyes.

"Relax, Clayton," I said. "If I wanted to hurt you, you'd never hear me or see me coming. You'd just wake up in a hospital."

"Then what do you want?"

"You could have waited until we officially broke up before you came sniffing around Janet's nest," I said.

"I love her, Jack. I always have."

"I know. But what you did tells me you still can't be trusted. Maybe Janet thinks you've changed; I don't know. That's up to her to decide. Thing is, you and I know better. If I find out you've cheated on her or hurt her in any way, I'll break both your fucking legs and remove the family jewels with a rusty knife."

Clayton stared at me.

I turned around and walked out.

"Jack, wait! Please!" Clayton called after me.

I ignored him and went out to the car.

I stuck four plastic sleeves in the sand near the water and placed a surf caster into each one. Oz lined up five chairs behind the poles and he, Regan, Mark and Wally sat.

There were two thermos bottles next to Oz's chair. One held coffee, the other was full of hot chocolate.

"I don't know a thing about fishing, but aren't we supposed to have bait?" Wally said.

I held a pitchfork and used it to dig holes in the sand.

"Dad is digging for worms," Regan explained.

I went down a foot before I came across the first few sandworms. "Grab the cooler, Mark."

Mark brought me the empty cooler. As I dug, he loaded worms into it until we had about two dozen.

While I baited Wally's hook, he said, "I didn't know worms had legs."

"These are sandworms," Regan said. "Different from earthworms. They're not as squishy."

Lines were cast, coffee and hot chocolate were consumed, nibbles and bites were had, and finally the first striper was caught.

By Wally.

A nice one just short of a keeper.

But that didn't matter. We weren't keeping any.

After Wally's first catch, the stripers woke up and started hitting the bait at a record pace. Seventeen stripers were reeled in during the next sixty minutes, the largest being Mark's at forty-two inches, the smallest being Oz's at seventeen inches.

Then, as quickly as they bit, the stripers swam out and the

poles went silent.

"How about breakfast in town?" I said.

While Regan took a shower and Oz went to change, I left Mark with Molly and took Wally for a walk along the water.

"Those other two goons you owe money to," I said.

"Bannister and May Jackson."

"Those two," I said. "Are they likely to come looking for you like Jimmy boy?"

"Bobby Bannister might, I don't know," Wally said. "I hadn't thought this whole thing entirely through when I called Mr. Kagan."

"May Jackson?"

"That one is a shark," Wally said. "She's bad news if you're late on the vig. She runs a large loan-sharking business out of Harlem in Manhattan."

"Where can I find Bannister?"

"Fordham in the Bronx," Wally said. "He's half Italian and runs his business out of Little Italy on Arthur Avenue."

"I suppose you're late on payments by now."

Wally nodded. "Like I said, I didn't think things fully through."

"I have an idea, but you need to trust me," I said.

Wally nodded again. "I trust you."

"Good. Let's go have some breakfast. We'll be back in plenty of time for when the stripers bite again around four."

While the gang fished for stripers, I sat at the table in front of my trailer and made a phone call to Hope Springs Eternal, the Catholic home for traumatized children where Regan spent most of her youth.

Around six the stripers quit biting and we returned to the trailer.

"Your mom wants you home by seven thirty," I said to Mark. "Wally, take a ride with us."

On the way back to the beach after dropping Mark off, I said, "I worked something out for a few days, Wally. I need you to cooperate with me so I can get those two monkeys off your back."

"What do you want me to do?" Wally asked.

"Talk," I said.

Wally nodded. "I can do that."

Chapter Nine

Hope Springs Eternal is a large facility right on the county line. It sits on forty acres of woodlands in a countryside setting. The facility is owned by the Catholic Church, and run by Father Thomas, a psychiatrist and medical doctor. His assistant is Sister Mary Martin, and she is also a trained psychiatrist specializing in child care.

While I was drinking away a decade, Regan, through no credit of my own, received all the loving care and treatment she needed as a traumatized child.

Father Thomas met us at the main office building, where Regan ran from the car and embraced the priest in a warm hug.

"Where is Sister Mary Martin?" Regan asked.

"Umpiring a game," Father Thomas said.

"I'll be right back, Dad," Regan said and dashed around the building to the athletic field.

Father Thomas looked at Wally. "And you must be Wally Sample?" he said.

"Yes, Father," Wally said.

"Let's go to my office and talk," Father Thomas said.

Father Thomas served coffee in his office and then took his place behind his highly polished oak desk. "So, Mr. Sample, Mr. Bekker tells me you have a bit of a gambling problem," the priest said.

"It's not about the money, Father," Wally said. "It's about

mathematically beating a system against the odds. It's mostly about solving problems and logistics."

"I understand," Father Thomas said. "Mr. Bekker has asked me to put you up in our guest lodging for a few days while he takes care of something for you."

"He mentioned that on the drive," Wally said. "I don't want to be a burden to anybody."

"The twenty-five thousand dollars you've agreed to donate to our library will go a long way, Mr. Sample," Father Thomas said.

"How long will I be here?"

Father Thomas looked at me.

"Three or four days," I said.

"And you can help me?" Wally said to the priest.

"I'd like to think so."

"Fifty thousand will go further," Wally said.

Father Thomas looked at me. "I'd like to speak to Wally alone for a bit. Okay?"

I stood up. "See you later, Wally."

I found Regan sitting in the stands at the athletic field, where a softball game was in progress. The kids playing were between eight years old and early teens. A nun acted as first-, second- and third-base umpire. Behind the plate, dressed in shorts, tee shirt, mask and chest protector, Sister Mary Martin called balls and strikes.

"Score is five to four with one inning to go," Regan said.

In the bottom of the ninth, the losing team rallied and loaded the bases with two out. A kid of about twelve hit two foul-line drives and then took a called third strike to end the game.

The kid was furious at the call and immediately argued with Sister Mary Martin. The kid's team manager, also a nun, rushed to home plate to argue as well. The kid kicked dirt on Sister

Mary Martin's shoes while she went nose to nose with her fellow nun.

Everybody was having a great time arguing with everybody else, and then suddenly Sister Mary Martin called lunch and the field cleared.

Regan went down to the field and met the nun. They embraced warmly. Sister Mary Martin looked up at me. "Will you join us for lunch?"

The dining room was filled to capacity and abuzz with various conversations. Regan and I sat with Sister Mary Martin and several other nuns.

"Mr. Bekker, I am very glad you brought Regan with you today," Sister Mary Martin said. "There is something I've been meaning to discuss with her, and you, and I was going to ask Father Thomas to drive me to your home next week."

I was slicing into meatloaf and slipped a hunk into my mouth. It was pretty good. I chewed, sipped some water and said, "Glad I could save you the trip. What's on your mind, Sister?"

"I need an assistant," she said. "I'm not as young as I once was and I could use help around here with the physical activities as well as other things. I need someone young and inspiring, and as I consider Regan to be my crown jewel, I would like it to be her."

I looked at Regan. Her face was as white as a ghost.

"I . . . don't think I can," she said.

"Of course you can," Sister Mary Martin said.

"Will I have to speak in public?"

"Not unless you want to. I need help with the games and physical-education classes and in the classrooms with the shy ones. You remember how that was, don't you?"

Regan nodded. Then she looked at me. "Dad?"

"You're an adult now, sweetheart," I said. "I can't make your

73

decisions for you anymore."

"Can you still give advice?"

"That I can do."

"What do you think about it?"

"I think it might be a good opportunity to bring you out of your shell," I said. "You're fine with me and Oz and the family, but around strangers you're still very much in a cocoon. You would be helping Sister Mary Martin and Father Thomas and yourself at the same time. It would be difficult to attend college if you're afraid to mingle in a crowd and even more so in life."

Regan nodded. "Do I get paid?"

"Of course you get paid," Sister Mary Martin said. "And you get to pay taxes, which is something you need to get used to."

"I'll do it."

"We'll start with three days a week, say from ten to five," the nun said. "We'll fill out the paperwork right after lunch."

I shook hands with Wally and Father Thomas in front of the office.

"I understand Regan is joining us," Father Thomas said. "Excellent news."

"I start on Monday," Regan said.

"I'll see you then," Father Thomas said.

"A moment, Father," I said.

The priest walked me to the car. Regan stayed behind with Wally.

"Father, don't let him out of your sight, and for God's sake don't trust him for one minute," I said. "A scratch ticket to him is like booze was to me."

"I'll take good care of him, Jack," Father Thomas said. "Work in the garden, therapy sessions twice a day, exercise time and plenty of chores."

"I'll see you on Monday," I said.

I changed into comfortable sweats and decided to go for a run. Oz and Regan were drinking tea with honey at the table when I went out, sat and strapped on five-pound ankle weights.

"Girl went and got herself a job," Oz said. "She be married before you know it."

I looked at Oz.

"But there be plenty of time for that," he said.

"I need a favor," I said.

Oz looked at me. Regan looked at me. Molly jumped onto the table.

"I'm going to New York on Wally's behalf for a few days," I said. "Oz, can you keep . . . ?"

"She can stay with me or, God forbid, I sleep in your bed," Oz said.

"Dad, I'll be fine on my own for a few days," Regan said.

"I know, but I won't be," I said.

"You're turning into an old hen," Regan said.

"So, humor me until I outgrow it."

"Is it okay if we do some shopping for the house?"

"I'll leave you the checkbook," I said.

I stood up and headed for the water. I jogged at a leisurely pace for about a mile and then kicked it up for the next two. On the return trip I ran in ankle-deep water. The canvas straps and casing for the weights took on water and after a mile or so doubled in weight. By the time I returned to the trailer my legs felt like rubber and my feet felt encased in cement blocks.

Oz and Regan were gone. They left a note.

Gone shopping. Will try not to empty the checkbook. Love, Regan.

I flopped into my chair and removed the soaked ankle weights. Molly came out and jumped on my lap and demanded

I pat her by rubbing her head against my stomach.

"Of course," I said, and stroked her ears.

CHAPTER TEN

The six-fifteen business flight to New York City put me down in Kennedy Airport before eight thirty.

I brought just a small carry-on, so I skirted baggage claim and went straight to the car-rental counter, where I rented a sedan with GPS.

I knew Manhattan fairly well, but the Bronx was more or less a mystery. I punched in the address Wally gave me for Robert "The Butcher" Bannister and let the GPS guide me from Queens to his Bronx neighborhood.

The directions read nineteen miles and forty minutes' driving time. They lied. I was in bumper-to-bumper traffic on I-678 North for fifty minutes, moving at a snail's pace before reaching 278 W, where I sat for another twenty minutes before merging onto I-95 South to the Bronx.

I finally arrived at Arthur Avenue, gateway to Little Italy, and drove around for a while until I found a nearby parking space on the street.

Crossing Arthur Avenue was like passing through a time warp to another generation. Meat markets, delis, coffee shops and bakeries lined the streets. A large church was a major focal point of the close-knit, Italian neighborhood. Side streets were lined with two-story homes of every style and color. Tourists were everywhere, sampling wares and dining in authentic Italian restaurants.

Robert Bannister, according to Wally, was Italian on his

mother's side, English/German on his father's side and ran a large loan-sharking business out of the meat market his mother's family owned going back one hundred or more years.

I found Bannister drinking espresso in a bakery a block away from his meat market. He was a large man about my age with a thick gut from too much rich food, black hair slicked back across his skull and thick, black eyebrows. I saw none of the English/German in him; he was all his mother's son. His suit was expensive, although he wore no tie.

Bannister sat alone with his coffee and the horse-racing section of the *Daily News.*

At the next table, three men, also wearing suits, sat with cups of espresso and watched me like a hawk as I approached Bannister.

"Mr. Robert Bannister?" I said when I was a few feet from the table.

Immediately the three men were on their feet and approaching me. Bannister looked up from the racing section.

I looked at the three men. "Relax," I said. "I'm unarmed. I just need a few minutes of Mr. Bannister's time."

"Who are you?" Bannister asked.

"My name is Bekker," I said. "My wallet is in my inside jacket pocket."

Bannister nodded. One of the three men came to me, reached into my suit jacket for my wallet and gave it to Bannister. He flipped it open and read my private investigator's license.

"Private cop," he said.

"I was a real cop until I retired."

"What do you want?"

"Talk to you about Wally Sample."

"Wally, huh? He owes me a hundred large."

"I know. Can I sit? That coffee smells wonderful."

Bannister nodded and as I sat, one of the three bodyguards

went to the counter.

"So, what about Wally?" Bannister said.

The man returned with a cup of espresso and set it before me.

"Thank you," I said. "The coffee on the plane was undrinkable."

He nodded and returned to the other two, and they took their seats.

"In about forty days Wally Sample will inherit a large sum of money from his father's estate," I said. I sipped espresso. It was excellent. "If you can wait that long, he will pay you in full what he owes plus interest."

"Is this on the level?"

"Yes."

"Forty days?"

"The will takes effect in another twenty-seven, but the papers need time to process and all that," I said. "I rounded it off to forty days."

"Two hundred thousand in cash and we're square," Bannister said. "Otherwise my three friends there pay him a visit. Understood?"

"Yes."

Bannister nodded. "I don't think I've ever met a real PI before."

"Like I said, I was a cop once. I retired and now I do this."

"Are you hungry?"

"A bit. I missed breakfast to catch my flight."

"You like Italian?"

"Who doesn't?"

"Take a walk with me," Bannister said. "We'll have some lunch."

Bannister stood. I stood. His three men stood. Bannister walked to the bakery door, opened it and we walked out to the street.

The three men fell into step behind us.

"Know why Wally borrowed the money?" Bannister asked.

"No."

"Some system for beating the odds at blackjack and the gaming tables," Bannister said. "He called it research for logistics. I don't really care what people borrow the money for so long as their payments are on time, but Wally is really out there."

Bannister turned down a side street and the shops all but disappeared, replaced by private homes.

"I've seen his work, so to speak," I said. "He really does know his stuff when it comes to math and logistics."

"In my business the only math we care about is on time payments and the vig," Bannister said.

We stopped in front of a two-story, red-brick home with a two-car garage and flower garden out front.

"This is my ma's house," Bannister said. "I was born in this neighborhood and I'll probably die here. My ma is seventy-nine years old and healthy as an ox. She has lunch ready for me and the boys. You're welcome to join us."

Sara Bannister was born Sara Marie Boscarino to Sicilian parents who came over in 1911 and settled in the neighborhood. She fell in love with Robert Bannister Sr. when she was just seventeen and married him three years later against the advice and wishes of her parents and the pastor at the church, who advised her not to marry outside the race.

While her husband could never become a member of the mob, a right reserved for pure Sicilian blood lines, Robert Sr. was given a nice loan-sharking territory inside the Bronx.

Robert Jr. inherited the business after his father passed away twenty years earlier, when he was struck by a car one night walking home from the meat market owned by his mother's family. At the time, Robert Jr. worked there as a butcher.

I learned all this during conversation over lunch with Robert and Sara. Spry, thin, a workhorse of a woman, Sara served a three-course lunch of pasta with meatballs, Italian steak and salad.

Over coffee, Robert said, "I can live anywhere I want, but I live on the first floor of my mother's house. Do you know why?"

"No."

"I love my mother," Robert said. "Tell Wally to come see me after he inherits his money."

"I'll make sure of it."

"My guys will walk you back," Robert said. "I always take a nap after lunch."

The drive back to Manhattan, a ninety-minute trek, was made even more uncomfortable by a bloated stomach that felt as if I'd consumed lead for lunch.

I had a reservation at the Sheridan on 53rd and Seventh Avenue. I parked the car in an underground lot around the corner, carried my overnight bag with me to the lobby, checked in, went to my room on the twentieth floor and collapsed in a heap on the bed.

I awoke four hours later feeling sluggish and old, but the knot in my gut from the rich lunch was gone.

I unpacked my bag, changed into sweats and black running shoes and rode the elevator down to the basement gym. As gyms go, it wasn't much, but they had a Stairmaster and jump ropes and that was all I needed to work up a sweat.

I started on level one to warm up and finished an hour later on level twelve. After that I did push-ups, sit-ups and jumped rope for fifteen minutes.

When I felt human again I returned to my room for a hot shower and changed into jeans, a teal-colored pullover shirt and walking shoes. It was well past rush hour when I left the hotel and headed south on foot, but New York City never took a timeout and the streets were clogged with pedestrian traffic.

Times Square was lit up like a Christmas tree when I arrived at the crossroads of the world, 42nd Street and Broadway. I stopped in the Disney Store and picked up sweatshirts for Oz and Regan. I darted in and out of gift shops until I found a jewelry store on 47th Street and purchased a pair of gold and pearl earrings. Satisfied with my haul, I walked north on Broadway to my hotel and dropped off the bags in my room.

I headed back out around eight to the burger joint across the street. I stopped for a newspaper on the corner and sat at the counter, read, and ate a burger with fries and coffee.

I was back in my room by nine thirty and called the desk for a seven A.M. wakeup. I flicked cable channels and found an old John Wayne western to lull me to sleep.

A full stomach and the Duke was a lethal combination.

I hit the hotel gym at seven thirty for ninety minutes, then took a shower and changed into my suit and went for breakfast at the coffee shop across the street. It took several attempts to flag a cab until one pulled over. By law, a driver has to take you where you want to go once you're inside the cab, but this guy didn't want to go deep into Harlem.

I bribed him with the promise of doubling the tip and gave him the address Wally gave me for May Jackson. She operated her loan-sharking business out of a Baptist church on 155th Street and 8th Avenue in Harlem.

The driver knew how to get us there fast. He headed west to the Henry Hudson Parkway, drove us north to 158th Street, where we got off and backtracked three blocks to the massive Baptist church.

I paid the fare, got out and stood on the sidewalk for a minute to look around. Many of the old apartment buildings had been refurbished, along with a few brownstones. The church looked pre-1900, but was in excellent condition. A few shops and stores lined the end of the block. The neighborhood was no longer entirely black. Along with the improvements to the area came the yuppies that bought buildings and made the improvements.

Even so, and as the cliché says, I stood out like a sore thumb.

I walked to the church. The front doors were open. As I climbed the steps a huge black man in a blue suit came out and blocked my path.

"Help you with something?" he said.

"I'm here to see May Jackson."

"Cops usually come around the first of the month."

"I'm not a cop."

"What's your business here?"

"I love Jesus."

The man glared at me for a moment, then his entire face lit up and he smiled.

"But does Jesus love you?" he asked.

"A little runt named Wally Sample owes Miss Jackson one hundred and fifty thousand dollars," I said. "He wants to pay her back in full. I represent him."

"Come in and let me wand and frisk you," he said.

I stepped into the vestibule of the church where he ran a metal detection wand over my body, and then frisked under my arms and the small of my back.

"Name?"

"John Bekker."

"Wait here," he said.

He entered a narrow hallway and took a flight of stairs. I glanced into the church for a quick look around and then he was behind me. "Follow me," he said.

"A beautiful church," I said.

"It is," he said.

He led me to the stairs and I followed him up to a loft-style office.

May Jackson was behind a large desk next to an open window. She was whippet thin with snow-white hair and wore glasses. I couldn't guess her age, but I put her around seventy-plus.

Her soft, brown eyes were bright behind the glasses. "Come closer, Mr. Bekker," she said. "I won't bite."

I walked to the desk.

"You're no pretty boy," May said. "But handsome like a young Robert Mitchum back in the day. By the looks of your nose I'd say you've spent some time inside a boxing ring. Have a seat. Coffee?"

"Sure."

"Gregory, bring us two coffees, please."

The big man nodded and went downstairs.

"My great-grandson," May said. "Have a seat."

There were two leather chairs facing the desk and I took one.

"Now, what's all this here about Wally Sample?" May asked.

"Very shortly, inside of forty days, Wally will inherit a fortune from his father's estate," I said. "He will repay his entire loan plus interest as soon as the paperwork clears. He authorized me to tell you that."

"All plus interest?"

"That's the deal."

"I've been putting paper on the street for sixty years and this is a first," May said.

"Sixty years," I said. "I pegged you for around seventy."

"I'm eighty-seven, Mr. Bekker."

Gregory returned with two cups of coffee. "Anything else?" he asked.

"No, thank you," May said.

Gregory returned to the vestibule.

I sampled the coffee. "Very nice."

"Thank you," May said. "You were once a cop, weren't you?"

"I'm retired," I said. "I work privately now."

"He hire you?"

"His lawyer did. I'm helping him stay clean until his inheritance is finalized."

"That's good," May said. "I would not have enjoyed sending my people to collect from him. He's such a squirrely little boy."

I nodded. I didn't see a one of them on the way in, but my guess was a dozen pairs of eyes watched me enter the church from various checkpoints on the street.

"May I ask you something?" I said.

She nodded.

"Why this church?"

"I own the building," May said. "A dozen or more years ago, the church was condemned by the city. I purchased the property and spent one million dollars to refurbish it, and now it has an active parish and pastor. The pastor is another of my grandsons, by the way. I have eleven, and four great-grandsons. I could operate anywhere I wish, but I like to be close to God."

I could see the twinkle in her eyes and a tiny grin on her lips.

"And it doesn't bother you to operate an illegal business out of a church?"

"You strike me as the sort of cop who would bend the rules to the breaking point to catch and put a murderer behind bars," May said.

"He who is without sin," I said.

May chuckled.

"If I were forty years younger I would starch your hair and curl your toes, Mr. Bekker," she said.

"If you were forty years younger I think I'd let you."

Gregory was suddenly behind me. "Time for your walk, Grandma."

"So it is," May said. "Mr. Bekker, are you in a rush?"

"My flight doesn't leave until seven."

"Come walk with me."

May slowly stood up from behind the desk and produced a telescopic cane that, with a flick of her thin wrist, extended to standard length.

"My right hip ain't what she used to be," she said. "Doctor said I should walk a mile a day rain or shine."

She walked to me and extended her right arm. I took it and with Gregory behind us, we descended the stairs to the street.

"What a beautiful day," May said. "One complete loop around Eighth Avenue is about a mile."

Our pace was slow. We stopped at every corner for May to take a quick breather. Along the way she did most of the talking.

"I must have put a million dollars in loans on this block alone," she said. "And not all of it black. During the last five or six years, twenty or more white, yuppie couples have moved into apartments and brownstone buildings. I've lent money to half of them when the banks wouldn't give them a mortgage because of the address."

"At twenty percent," I said.

"True, but at least they got the loan where a bank rejected them," May said. "Some of them even attend Sunday service out of respect."

A yuppie couple on bikes rode past us and the man nodded hello to May.

"Mind if I ask you how you entered into the business?"

"My daddy started it around nineteen hundred to help poor blacks coming up from the South to escape the KKK," she said. "He was born in New York during the Civil War. He died in sixty-two at the age of ninety-nine. I took over for him some sixty years ago when he went to prison on a fifteen-year stretch for racketeering. Truth is, he got tired of paying off the cops and they set him up with the feds out of revenge."

We paused at the corner for May to catch her breath.

"I've had nine children, five husbands, eleven grandchildren and four great-grandchildren and nothing tires me out like this simple mile-walk," she said.

"Is it bothering you, your hip?" I said.

"Only always."

We'd come full circle and stopped in front of the church.

"We part ways, Mr. Bekker," May said. "I'll expect payment in full as you outlined in forty days. Please remind Wally that I would really dislike it if I had to send somebody to visit him."

"I will, and don't worry," I said.

"I've enjoyed your company," May said.

"Same here," I said.

She turned and, followed by Gregory, she entered the church.

Oz and Regan had a bonfire going in the trash can when I drove the Marquis onto the beach to my trailer.

Regan greeted me at the car with a hug and kiss. Oz greeted me with a hot dog off the grill when I reached the table.

"I bring gifts," I said. "On the back seat."

Regan retrieved the bags from the car and brought them to the table. Oz got Mickey, Regan got Minnie, and I got a hot dog.

"What's in the small box?" Regan asked.

"A congratulations on your new job," I said.

"More like my only job. Can I open it?"

"It's yours."

Regan ripped off the gift wrap and flipped open the box. "Dad, you shouldn't spend . . ."

"Try them on," I said.

Regan placed one pearl earring into each ear and looked at me. "Well?"

"Ready for work," I said.

"Want another hot dog?" Oz said.

"Sure, and then I'm ready for bed."

CHAPTER ELEVEN

"I could have driven myself," Regan said as I turned off the road and passed through the gates to Hope Springs Eternal.

"I know, but I need to see Wally," I said. "It seemed silly to take two cars."

"Do I look okay?" Regan wore black slacks with matching shoes, a white, button-down blouse and her new earrings.

"You've asked me three times this morning," I said. "And each time I said you look beautiful."

"I'm not going for beautiful," Regan said. "I'm going for professional."

"Oh. In that case you look professionally beautiful and ready for work."

"You should have been in politics."

"No; I've never been good at taking bribes."

I parked in front of the office where we got out and took the stairs. We found Father Thomas in his office. Regan greeted him with a kiss on the cheek and a warm hug.

"Sister Mary Martin is waiting for you in her office," the priest said.

Regan nodded and left.

"Can you sit for a moment? There is something I'd like to discuss with you," Father Thomas said.

I took a seat.

"I've been having sessions with Wally," the priest said. "I feel that I can help him. I was wondering if you wouldn't mind if he stayed here for a bit more."

"I don't mind. What does he say?"

"He's in favor of staying a while longer. We've had two sessions a day and in between he works in the yard and kitchen. I think he wants to get well, but doesn't know how."

"Sure. I really can't do much for him besides baby-sit him anyway," I said. "I would like to talk with him before I leave, though."

"Certainly. He's probably having breakfast with the staff."

We left the office and walked down a long hallway to another hallway that led to the cafeteria. Regan was at the table for nuns and teachers. Wally sat with the rest of the staff workers. The other twenty-five tables were occupied by children between five and eighteen years of age.

Father Thomas tapped Wally on the shoulder and said, "Would you mind if we joined you at your table?"

"Not at all, Father."

"Scoot over and we'll be right back."

Father Thomas and I went to the serving line. I loaded up on French toast with bacon and coffee. Father Thomas had an omelet with toast. We returned to the table and sat beside Wally.

"How are you, Mr. Bekker?" Wally asked.

"I'm fine, and don't you think it's time you called me Jack or John?"

"Okay. Jack."

"Father Thomas tells me you want to stay here for a while?"

"Is that okay?"

"It's fine. He can help you much more than I can."

Wally nodded.

"About that other thing?" he asked.

"I went to New York and spoke with your creditors," I said. "They've all agreed to wait until you receive your inheritance."

"That's good. I was worried. Thank you, Mr. . . . I mean Jack."

"You're welcome, Wally."

I finished breakfast, shook hands with Wally and Father Thomas, and then went to say hello to Sister Mary Martin and good-bye to Regan.

"She gets off at five sharp," the nun told me.

"I'll be here," I said.

The nun stood up. "Okay, Regan, let's go to work."

I worked off the heavy breakfast with a six-mile run along the ocean wearing ankle weights. After a change of tee shirts, I did another hour in the home gym beside the trailer, then took a shower and changed into a light-blue warm-up suit.

I brewed a pot of coffee, poured it into a carafe, and took it and a mug outside to the table.

I was happily sipping and unhappily missing the usual cigarette that accompanied my coffee when I spotted Oz walking toward me from his trailer.

I sat up and took notice when I saw Oz was walking quickly, something he never normally does, and when he was close enough I could see the *bad news* expression on his face.

"What?" I said when he arrived.

"You need to turn on the TV," he said.

"Why?"

"Something interesting you want to see."

"On network or cable?"

"That's right, you don't have cable," Oz said. "Best come over with me."

I filled my mug and followed Oz three hundred feet to his trailer. We entered the small living room, where the television was tuned to a cable-news network.

"They show stuff on a loop," Oz said. Oz had a dish on his

91

roof and picked up over two hundred channels, but all he ever watched was the news and ball games.

We sat and waited for whatever it was he wanted me to see. I didn't ask because he wouldn't have told me and ruined the anticipation.

Then there it was.

A blond woman in a too-tight minidress gave the report.

"Early this morning, just minutes after seven A.M., Wallace Sample, sixth child of Sample Iced Tea–founder Robert Sample, was killed in a massive gas explosion that destroyed his Riverdale home and that neighbors described as sounding like a bomb going off.

"Firefighters are investigating a gas leak in the basement that might be responsible for the blast that killed the thirty-nine-year-old heir to the company fortune. The youngest of six children, a loner estranged from his family, Wallace Sample was set to inherit millions and a seat in the company on his fortieth birthday, just weeks from now.

"We'll have more on this story as details develop.

"And now this."

Oz hit the mute button and looked at me.

"Where's your phone?" I said.

Oz handed me his cell phone and I punched in Walt's number.

"Walt, where are you?"

"At the moment I'm in my car on the way to see you."

"About Wally?"

"You heard?"

"Just now."

"He wasn't in . . . ?"

"No."

"I'll be there in twenty minutes."

I hung up and gave Oz the phone. "Walt's on the way over."

Oz and I walked back to my trailer. I used my own cell phone to call Hope Springs Eternal. A cheerful-sounding woman picked up and I asked for Father Thomas.

"Mr. Bekker?" the priest said when he came on the line.

"Father, do me a favor and keep Wally and Regan away from the news until I get there later."

"Is something wrong?"

I told him what I knew up to this point and he said he would keep both away from television and radio.

I'd barely set the phone down when it rang. I checked the incoming number and answered the call.

"Jack," Janet said. "I just saw on the news, the little guy you're . . ."

"If you mean Wally, he's fine," I said.

"But the news said . . ."

"I know, but they're wrong," I said.

"So who . . . ?"

"I don't know. Walt's on his way over. Maybe he has some news."

"Well, I'm glad the funny little guy is okay," Janet said.

"Thanks. I'll talk to you soon."

"Wait, Jack . . ."

"Can't. I see Walt coming. Talk to you later."

I set the phone down and watched Walt's sedan approach the trailer.

"I'll get another mug," Oz said and went inside for a moment.

Walt parked and got out. Oz returned with another mug.

"Is it clean?" Walt asked.

"What you asking me for, it's his," Oz said.

"It's clean," I said. "Or Regan would have thrown it away."

"Why would she . . . ?" Walt said.

"Never mind that now," I said.

Oz filled the mug and gave it to Walt. He sat and sipped, then said, "I called NYPD after I heard the news. They know about

93

as much as you saw on the news right now. So, who died in the explosion?"

"It wasn't Wally," I said.

"Where is he?"

"He's staying at Hope Springs Eternal," I said. "Father Thomas is giving him therapy sessions for his problem."

"I think we should ask him who had access to his home," Walt said.

"That's exactly what I'm going to do," I said. "Want to ride along?"

Walt looked at the Marquis. "So long as we take my car, and I drive."

"Okay, so he's alive, but somebody isn't," Walt said. "Who else was in that house?"

"That's what we're going to find out, isn't it?"

"I forgot to ask," Walt said. "Where's the kid?"

"Actually, Regan is now working as assistant to Sister Mary Martin," I said. "Today is her first day on the job."

"No kidding. That's great."

"It is," I agreed.

"Should I ask about the rest of your screwed-up life?"

"Clayton has asked Janet to remarry him, and she's considering it, and I bought that house we looked at a few weeks ago," I said.

"Well, you screwed that relationship up good," Walt said.

"I didn't ask Janet to run into Clayton's arms when I was in Hawaii," I said.

"Anybody can screw up, Jack," Walt said. "And everybody deserves a second chance. Look at how many second chances you got."

"I know that, Walt. Janet was looking for a way out because she realized I'm not the man she wants and needs me to be,

94

and I gave it to her because I'm not going to pretend I'm somebody I'm not and live a marriage based upon lies."

Walt cocked an eye toward me. "Holy shit. Been talking to that priest shrink, haven't you?"

"Father Thomas, and yes, I have, but mostly as a sounding board for what I already know."

"So, now what?"

"Has your appeal to the board for my reinstatement come through?"

"Not yet."

"Then I don't know. Turn here."

Walt turned down the long street to Hope Springs Eternal.

"My house?" Wally said. "My father built that house. It's all I have left."

"You have insurance, right?" I said.

"Yes, but . . ."

"Then rebuild," I said. "Right now NYPD thinks you died in the explosion. Who was in the house?"

"Has to be Paul Watson," Wally said.

We were in the empty cafeteria, Walt, Wally, and Father Thomas. We had cups of coffee from the vat left over from lunch and some Danish.

"Who is Paul Watson?" Walt asked.

"I went to private high school with him," Wally said. "Well, until I got thrown out. We kept in touch, and I asked him to water my plants and keep an eye on the house while I'm away. He's been doing it for years. God, Paul is dead. I can't believe it."

"You asked him to house-sit your plants before you went to see Kagan?" I said.

Wally nodded. "He's done it like a dozen times. He has his own key and the code to the alarm."

I glanced at Walt and I could read his face.

"Did anybody else know Paul was staying at your place?" I said.

"I didn't tell anybody if that's what you mean," Wally said. "My neighbors might snoop, but that's unlikely. The nearest house is three hundred feet away and I have tall fir trees on both sides for privacy."

"Tell me about the gas. Is it for the stove, heat, what?" I said.

"Stove and hot water," Wally said. "Heat is electric."

"Ever have any problems with leaks before?"

"No, never."

"The entry source for the gas is in the basement?" I said.

Wally nodded. "Comes in through a pipe from underground. Bronx Union Gas is the provider. How could something like this happen?"

"That's what NYPD, the fire department and, I'm sure, investigators from the power company are trying to find out," Walt said.

"What about Paul?" Wally said. "Nobody knows he's dead?"

"He have any family?" Walt asked.

"His parents died a few years ago in a car accident," Wally said. "He has an older sister in Vermont. That's all I know about."

"We'll take it from here," Walt said.

"Can he stay with you a while longer?" I said to Father Thomas.

"Yes, as long as necessary."

"Wally, make sure you don't talk about this to anybody but us," I said.

"What are you going to do?" Wally said.

"Give my daughter a ride home," I said.

★ ★ ★ ★ ★

I peeked through the window in the door to the classroom where Regan was assisting kids around seven or eight with coloring books. It immediately took me back some twenty months to when I visited Regan and I was sober for the first time in years, and she was coloring in a book.

She was an expert at it. Father Thomas explained that coloring inside the lines appealed to her sense of order and discipline.

One girl of eight or so was having difficulty keeping her crayon inside the lines. Regan squeezed beside her on the desk chair, took her tiny hand and guided her through the process. When the girl finally got the idea of things, she smiled at Regan and then kissed her on the cheek.

I turned away from the window and walked down the hallway to Father Thomas's office.

"Is she ready to go?" Walt asked.

"Not yet," I said.

"What's the matter?" Walt said. "You sound all choked up."

"Nothing," I said. "Where's Wally?"

"He insisted on helping in the kitchen," Father Thomas said. "It takes about ninety minutes to prepare the evening meal."

"I know you don't have any real security around here except for gates and a watchman, but make sure Wally doesn't leave his room tonight," I said.

"I understand," the priest said.

The office door opened and Sister Mary Martin and Regan walked in wearing bright smiles.

"Excellent first day, Regan," the nun said.

"I had so much fun," Regan said. She noticed Walt standing behind me and said, "Hi, Uncle Walt. What are you doing here?"

"Your old man was lonely for my company," Walt said.

"And he is also lonely for a pizza," I said.

CHAPTER TWELVE

The weather gods decided not to cooperate and we ate two pizzas with garlic rolls in Oz's trailer so we could catch news updates on Wally's home explosion. Oz muted the sound while we gorged on sausage and extra-cheese slices and dripping, warm garlic rolls.

On the drive to the trailer we told Regan what had taken place and she had a hundred questions we couldn't answer.

A new update came on and Oz turned up the volume. A buxom brunette in a sleeveless minidress—did they ever wear anything else?—gave the report.

"Police arson investigators and the arson squad from the fire department, as well as an investigator from the power company, are still conducting tests on the home of Wallace Sample that was destroyed in a fiery explosion early this morning while he slept.

"While authorities are not ruling out suicide or foul play, the investigation is leaning toward the accidental, so say sources on the inside.

"Wallace Sample, youngest son of Robert Sample, founder of Sample Iced Tea, was set to take his place as a company officer on his fortieth birthday, just three weeks from today.

"The Sample family has yet to provide a statement to the media. And now this."

Oz hit the mute button.

"Suicide, Dad?" Regan said. "Wouldn't they think there's an

easier way to kill yourself than blowing yourself up while asleep?"

"One would think," I said.

"They never rule anything out until the evidence dictates it so," Walt said.

We ate some more slices until both pies were gone and just a few garlic rolls remained.

"Okay if I take off?" Regan said. "Molly needs food and fresh water."

"Sure."

Regan opened the door and stepped out. "Rain's stopped."

"I won't be long," I said.

"You think they'll discover that wasn't Wally in the house?" Oz said.

"That depends if they can scrape together enough of . . ." Walt said.

"Paul Watson," I said.

"Right, Paul Watson," Walt said. "If they can find enough of him left to DNA test. My guess is no."

"You'll tell them, though, right?" Oz said.

"We have to," Walt said. "And right now. Can we conference using cell phones?"

"I don't know how," I said. "I'll bet Regan knows. Let's find out."

Regan was on the tiny sofa with Molly on her lap when we entered my trailer.

"Do you know how to conference call using cell phones?" I said.

"Sure," Regan said.

"Can you set it up for us?"

"Give me the phones and number."

Walt took a seat at the table while I waited on a pot of coffee to brew. I poured cups for us just as Regan finished setting up the call. I sat, and Walt and I took our phones.

Walt identified himself to the desk sergeant at the Riverdale Police Department in the Bronx.

"How may I help you, Captain Grimes?" the sergeant said.

"It's imperative that I speak with your captain immediately."

"He's in a meeting with the detectives at the . . ."

"It concerns information about Wally Sample," Walt said.

"Please hold."

Thirty seconds of music and then a gruff voice snarled at us. "This is Captain Ed Jackman. Who am I speaking to?"

"Captain Walter Grimes, and with me on conference is private investigator John Bekker," Walt said.

"What's this information about Sample?" Jackman barked.

I had the feeling Jackman was used to barking and having his barks jumped to.

"He's alive and well and in my custody," I said.

"What do you mean alive and in *your* custody?" Jackman said.

It took me about ten minutes to run the gamut and when I had finished, Jackman said, "You'll bring Sample to me immediately for verification."

"I don't think so, Captain," I said.

"What?" Jackman barked.

"He's safe where he is and he's getting the help he needs," I said. "Why don't you fly here tomorrow and see for yourself. I'll spring for the ticket."

"He isn't wanted for anything and doesn't have to return to New York if he doesn't want to," Walt said. "Catch a seven A.M. flight and you'll be home for lunch."

"You'll pick me up at the airport?" Jackman asked.

"Of course," Walt said.

"Your ticket will be at the counter for Jet Blue," I said.

"All right, but if he wants to return with me I expect you to cooperate," Jackman said and hung up.

"Swell fellow," Walt said.

"He sounds like an asshole," Regan said from the sofa.

"You don't make captain by being an asshole," Walt said.

I cleared my throat. Walt looked at me. "You shut up," he said.

"See you in the morning," I said.

"We'll take my car," Walt said.

After Walt left, I called Kagan at his home and filled him in on the latest.

"I was waiting for you to call," he said. "So what's all this about him being dead at home?"

"A friend was house-sitting Wally's plants."

"Sorry to hear that," Kagan said.

"I might need some extra expense money."

"No problem."

I hung up, called the airlines and reserved a first-class, round-trip ticket for Jackman to be picked up at the counter. Then I went and filled my coffee mug.

"Want to look at swatches?" Regan asked. "We need to pick out colors."

"Oh, why not," I said and sat beside a sleeping Molly.

CHAPTER THIRTEEN

The first observation Walt made of Captain Ed Jackman as he walked toward the waiting area outside the gate was, "He looks like frigging Lou Grant from the old Mary what's-her-name show."

And he did. Medium height, balding, stocky, Jackman was Lou Grant in a police captain's uniform.

"Goddamn airlines made me check my weapon with the pilot," was the first thing Jackman said when he met us at the gate. The second thing he said was, "Can I get some coffee for the ride?"

I picked up three containers on the way out. Jackman didn't offer to pay for his. When we reached Walt's car, Jackman opened the front passenger door and got in even though I'm a head taller and could have used the extra leg room on the hour-long drive.

As soon as Walt drove us out of the airport and onto the highway, Jackman said, "Okay, you there in the back, explain this to me. What's your connection in all this?"

"I told you last night; Wally is my client," I said.

"Yeah, yeah, you said that, but PI's in New York don't get chauffeured around by police captains," Jackman said.

"I was a cop for sixteen years and Walt and I were partners for most of them," I said.

"Job got to you, that's why you took an early out?" Jackman asked.

"I didn't take an early out," I said. "And I think that's about as up close and personal as I'm going to get with you on the subject."

Jackman looked at Walt. "Touchy."

"Try being his partner," Walt said.

The rest of the ride was without conversation. We met Father Thomas at the main office and he took us to the library where Wally was waxing the floor. A few dozen resident children were reading books at tables.

"Clear the room," Jackman said.

"I beg your . . ." Father Thomas said.

"Everybody out but Sample," Jackman said.

The priest cleared the library of the children. Jackman waved Wally over to a table.

"Wallace Sample?" Jackman said.

"Yes."

"Have identification?"

Wally nodded, dug his wallet out of a back pocket and gave it to Jackman.

"Okay, sit down so we can talk," Jackman said. He looked at me. "You, out. Captain Grimes, you can stay."

"How nice," Walt said.

I looked at Jackman.

"Do you have mud in your ears?" Jackman said.

I looked at Walt.

"Jackman, I think you better not . . ." Walt said.

"I won't tell you again, Bekker," Jackman said. "This is official police business and you may be a hotshot PI around here, but you're no longer a cop."

I grabbed Jackman by his uniform jacket and lifted him off the ground so that we were eye to eye and held him there.

"Jack, put him . . ." Walt said.

"You may look like Lou Grant, but he was warm and cud-

103

dly," I said. "You, on the other hand, are exactly what my daughter said you were."

"Jack, for God's sake, put him . . ." Walt said.

"And I'll tell you something else," I said. "In New York you may be a police captain, but here you're a nothing. Even Walt is outside his jurisdiction on this one, so if you want my co-operation on this, start acting like a professional and I might let you stay in the room."

I released Jackman and he fell a foot to the floor.

"What's going on?" Wally said.

"This is Captain Jackman from New York," I said. "He needs to verify that you didn't die in the explosion."

Jackman rubbed his neck.

"So, who is this Paul Watson who was killed in your house?" he said.

"Like I told you last night, a friend of Wally's who was house-sitting his plants," I said.

"I have . . . had more than two dozen plants in the house," Wally said. "Plants give off oxygen, you know. Paul is . . . was an old friend and he'd done it for me before."

"Can you provide his address for verification?" Jackman said.

"Sure."

"Does anyone in your family circle know you're still alive?" Jackman said.

"I haven't told anyone," Wally said.

"Then they will be delighted when I return you to New York for the unveiling," Jackman said.

"You misunderstand the purpose of bringing you here," I said. "We wanted you to know Wally was alive and the man killed was his friend, but he isn't going anywhere with you. In fact, the media isn't to know about this until after Wally's fortieth birthday three weeks from now. Once that happens you can march him down Broadway in the Thanksgiving parade, but not until his birthday."

"I'm not following you, Bekker. Why?"

"Because we're not sure the explosion was an accident," Walt said. "Somebody might not want Wally to live to see his birthday."

"Why?" Jackman said.

"Like I told you on the phone, Wally is a total screw-up," I said. "A walking IOU to loan sharks and casinos. He's in this place to dry out and get some help from Father Thomas, who happens to be an excellent psychiatrist. And because it's unlikely but possible that somebody in Wally's family doesn't want him to become the sixth controlling member of Sample Iced Tea."

Jackman looked at me.

"I know," Walt said. "He doesn't look that smart, does he?"

"So maybe you can request the arson squad and gas company to reverse direction and look for signs of murder instead of accident?" I said. "Quietly, of course."

"I could do that," Jackman said.

"And then in a few days, the three of us can pay a visit to Sample headquarters and tell the family in confidence that Wally is alive and well, but the information is in media blackout," I said. "And we'll see what happens after that."

Jackman looked at me and nodded. "If it was attempted murder maybe they'll try again?" he said.

"And you in conjunction with the White Plains PD can ride the arrest of the decade to promotion to colonel," I said.

"Maybe even a seat at One Police Plaza," Walt said.

"You think one of my family tried to kill me?" Wally said.

"That's the first thing I thought, Wally," I said.

"Sample Iced Tea is headquartered in White Plains?" Jackman said.

"Yes."

"Captain Willard in White Plains is a good man," Jackman

said. "He'll cooperate fully with my . . . with our investigation."

"How nice," Walt said.

"What about me?" Wally said.

"You're safe here right now," I said. "I see no reason to change that at the moment."

Wally nodded.

I placed my hand on his shoulder. "You wouldn't be the first heir a family member tried to kill off, Wally. Don't take it to heart, okay?"

Wally nodded again. "I knew they hated me, but I didn't think they would go so far as to kill me," he said.

"Money and power makes people do strange things," I said.

"Father Thomas needs me in the kitchen by now," Wally said. "Can I go?"

"Sure."

After Wally left, I looked at Jackman. "Want a steak and some brainstorming?" I said.

"You won't choke me again?"

"Don't let that worry you, Captain," Walt said. "Jack's bark is worse than his bite."

"Woof, woof," I said.

As we entered the beach after a trip to the meat market, Jackman said, "What's this, a beach party?"

"My office is on the beach," I said.

"What are you, the Rockford Files?" Jackman asked.

"More like Rockhead Files," Walt said. "But he barbeques a mean steak."

"That's my daughter, Regan, and our neighbor Oz at the table," I said as Walt parked next to the Marquis.

"Just so I know, what is it your daughter called me?" Jackman said.

★ ★ ★ ★ ★

After lunch, Regan and Oz took off to visit furniture stores. I brewed a pot of coffee and we took chairs at the table.

"Nice kid, your daughter," Jackman said. "Your neighbor, too. No missus?"

"She passed away."

"I'm sorry."

"It was a lot of years ago."

"That doesn't make it any easier. Is that why you retired from the job?"

"More or less."

"I should apologize for my actions earlier," Jackman said. "I need to shout a lot back home to get things done."

"No need," Walt said.

"What are you, Captain Grimes, six two or three?"

"About that."

"Do you know how hard it is to move up the ranks and make captain when you're five foot seven?" Jackman said. "The only way for me to get noticed was through tenacity and toughness. We'll never see a male president less than six feet tall again in our lifetime. FDR would never be elected in a wheelchair today. Sometimes it's difficult to step outside the role I've developed for myself and turn off that fellow your daughter so delicately described me as."

"Captain, I'm the last person to throw stones," I said. "Now, let's talk strategy. I'm not a big believer in coincidence. Wally is the black sheep of the Sample family. He's been an outcast most of his adult life. He has a bad gambling problem and owes money all over town. A few weeks before he's set to inherit ten million and a seat as an equal partner in Sample Iced Tea, his house blows up with what everyone believes is him in it. I don't buy the gas explosion was an accident. I believe it was a murder attempt."

Jackman looked at Walt.

"I agree," Walt said.

"Suspects?" Jackman said.

"His five siblings immediately jump to mind," I said. "Who else benefits by not having Wally around? It certainly isn't the loan sharks and casinos Wally owes money to. I've spoken to them and they've agreed to wait for Wally to inherit his money to be paid off. If they kill him, they get nothing."

"It wouldn't be the first time a family member killed another family member for money," Jackman said.

"How do you want to proceed on this, Captain?" Walt said. "The crime took place in your town, but Wally is here and Sample Iced Tea is in White Plains. It will take some coordinating to connect all the dots."

"Let me do that," Jackman said. "I'll meet with the arson investigators and if they haven't already covered the murder angle, I'll instruct them to do so, but privately. No media, limited personnel. I'll check the backgrounds of the five siblings and see where they stand. You never know. I'll meet with Captain Willard in White Plains and set up a partnership with him, as we will be working in his town. Give me one week before we pay Sample Iced Tea a visit with the news Wally Sample is alive."

"You didn't make captain because you're a prick," I said. "You made captain because you're good."

"Easy for you to say, you're six-four," Jackman said.

Walt glanced at his watch. "About time to make the airport."

Jackman stood and looked at me. "Would you prefer the front seat for the leg room?" he said.

Sometimes honey really does catch more flies.

After we dropped Jackman off at the airport, Walt swung around back into traffic to take me home. "Now that you got Captain

Lou Grant to do the legwork on this, what are you going to do?" he said.

"Keep Wally alive long enough to collect his inheritance."

CHAPTER FOURTEEN

Walt dropped me off at the library in town, where I spent several hours doing research on a computer and at a table with some textbooks. Apparently, homes and apartments were blowing up from gas leaks all over the place. Natural gas, propane and hydrogen are highly volatile and will explode at the drop of a hat, or more likely at the drop of an ignition source.

A home in Colorado developed a slow leak in the delivery hose in the basement when the family was away on vacation. They returned after two weeks, and when the father punched in his alarm code to deactivate it, it blew the house—along with him—to kingdom come.

If enough gas is present when an ignition source is added to it, you get a giant kaboom. A lit match or cigarette will do nicely, but so will a small electrical charge from a large appliance such as a furnace or refrigerator, or even a light switch.

I read and made some notes on scrap paper until a librarian told me she was locking up and I had to leave.

The library was a half mile from the beach, so I walked home. It was a pleasant enough evening and when I reached the sand I could see the bonfire in front of my trailer.

Oz was grilling hamburgers and corn on the cob when I arrived at the table. Regan had her laptop open and said, "Check out the sets we looked at for the living room."

"You want one or two burgers and how many corns?" Oz said from the grill.

"Three and three. I'm starved."

"Want some coffee, Dad?" Regan said. "We just made it a few minutes ago figuring you'd be home soon."

"Sure."

"Check out the photos. I'll be right back."

I turned the laptop toward me and looked at the living-room sets: sofa, two easy chairs, end tables, lamps and glass-top coffee table. The design was modern. The color was tan with black trim. The price tag was eleven thousand dollars.

Regan returned and set a mug down in front of me. "That one is Oz's pick," she said. She touched the screen and another set appeared. "This one is mine."

A sofa, loveseat, easy chair, two floor lamps and one coffee table in a style I would call contemporary. Price tag, ten thousand six hundred.

"So you need to pick a set and we'll put it to a vote and go with the winner," Regan said.

"I can live with whatever you two decide," I said.

"You need to have a say in this, Dad."

"You're talking to the man that furnished this trailer," I said.

"Man have a point," Oz said. "Burgers and corn is done."

"Can you get internet on this thing?" I said and touched the laptop.

"If you steal it from Oz."

"Can I borrow this?"

"Of course, Dad."

Oz carried a platter loaded down with burgers and corn to the table.

"What you need to look up?" Oz said.

"Research."

"On what?"

"How to blow up a house and make it look like an accident."

Regan looked at Oz.

"He's your friend," she said.
"Yeah, but he your father," Oz said.
"Don't remind me," Regan said.

Turns out there are all kinds of ways to blow up a house using natural gas and propane. The trick is to do it on purpose and make it look accidental. Most arson squad professionals can tell an accident from a deliberate explosion from a block away.

Around ten o'clock I knocked off, said good night to Oz and took the laptop back to my trailer where I found Regan asleep on the sofa with Molly curled up in a ball on her stomach.

I covered them with a blanket and headed off to bed. I was close to drifting off when I rolled over, clicked on the lamp, and grabbed my notebook and pen.

Talk to Jane about an arsonist, I wrote and went back to sleep.

CHAPTER FIFTEEN

Regan kissed me on the nose and walked to her Impala. "I should be home by six thirty," she said.

"Do you have your cell phone and some money?" I said and sipped coffee from a mug.

"Yes and yes."

"Emergency numbers?"

"Dad!"

"I just want you to be prepared," I said.

"I'll be fine," Regan reassured me. "Trust me, okay?"

I nodded and sipped from my mug.

Regan got into her car, started the engine and drove away. I waited until she was off the beach and then picked up my cell phone and punched in a number.

"Sheriff's Department," a gruff, male voice said.

"John Bekker calling for Sheriff Morgan," I said.

"Let me see if she's taking calls. Hold for a minute."

I listened to Michael Bolton for ninety seconds or so until Jane came on the line.

"Bekker, I was just wondering what you've been up to," Jane said.

"Ever think of changing the music on hold?" I said.

"Why, what is it?"

"Michael Bolton."

"What? Hold on."

"No, don't," I said, and a moment later Michael Bolton

returned. He serenaded me for thirty seconds or so until Jane returned.

"Assholes at the phone company," she said.

"Sure," I said. "So, I see you won reelection."

"Four more years of this crap," Jane said. "Anyway, what's up?"

"Free for lunch?"

"You buying?"

"Yes."

"I have a meeting with some idiot or another from the county at eleven thirty," Jane said. "Say, one o'clock at my office?"

"Any place special?"

"No, just expensive."

"I'll make sure I wear socks with my good shoes," I said.

There was time for a workout and a run. Six miles along the beach and an hour or so alongside the trailer. I ended with a flurry on the speed bag and flopped into my chair to towel and cool off before taking a shower.

I spotted Oz walking toward me, so I went inside and returned with two mugs of coffee. He arrived, took a mug and a chair.

"They still talking about Wally on the news," he said.

"What are they saying?"

"Spokesperson for the family say they are deeply saddened by the loss of they brother in such a terrible accident," Oz said. "They say he will be deeply missed and it be a terrible loss for all the family."

"They haven't seen the guy in years, and the last time they did, they threw him out of the office," I said. "Anything from the PD or fire department?"

"Just they examining the evidence," Oz said.

I sipped coffee and nodded. "Do me a favor, Oz. When you two get settled on the living room, pick out a nice flat-screen

TV and get us cable."

"DVD or blu-ray?"

"Sure. What's a blue ray?"

"A DVD, only blue."

"What about the kitchen?"

"That's Regan's department," Oz said. "I in charge of the basement. I figure you might want an office down there."

"And a gym."

"You want a shooting range and coffee bar, too?"

I glanced at my watch on the table. "I gotta go. I'll be back around three or so and you can show me your progress."

"My progress for this afternoon include a nap," Oz said.

If you took Marilyn Monroe in her prime and stuffed her into a sheriff's uniform the end result would be Jane Morgan.

I arrived at the municipal building where the county sheriff's office is located, parked, and got out and stood beside the Marquis. Normally this would be a good time to light up a smoke. Instead I sipped coffee from a travel mug.

By my watch Jane appeared fifteen minutes later. She came bouncing down the steps, spotted me and smiled.

"Meeting ran late," she said.

"Where do you want to go?"

"Charlie's Steak House. Know it?"

"Nope."

"Let's take my cruiser," Jane said. "I just had my nails done."

They were bright red and shiny and somehow different. I failed to make the connection between them and my Marquis, but I let it go.

We took her cruiser.

Twelve minutes later we were seated at a window table in the steak house reading menus. Seated opposite Jane I noticed a hint of eyeliner and gloss on her lips. Her red nails looked hard as rock.

"What?" Jane said when she caught me studying her nails.

"Your nails."

Jane showed me all ten fingers. "It's a new thing," she said. "It's a gel that dries like cement. Can't chip or break 'em."

I nodded. A waiter came by and took our orders.

"Seeing as how there is no such thing as a free lunch, I'm assuming there is some favor at the end of this rib-eye extravaganza," Jane said.

"Ever hear of Wally Sample?"

"Is it animal, mineral or vegetable?"

"Sample Iced Tea."

"That story all over the news?"

"Wally Sample."

"What about it? Him?"

"He's alive and well," I said. "Except for being a degenerate gambler in hock up to his ears, he's fine."

"And you know this how?"

Our steaks arrived. I filled Jane in as we ate, and by coffee and dessert she was up to speed.

"So the media doesn't know the little pervert is alive?" Jane said as she forked into her strawberry-chocolate cheesecake.

"Not yet. Not for a while."

"And I fit into this little deception how?"

"Find me an arsonist," I said. "Somebody really good."

"In or out of the prison?" As county sheriff, Jane had jurisdiction over the state prison.

"Doesn't matter, just so long as they're good."

"Give me a day and I'll get back to you."

Dessert consumed, I paid the check and rode back with Jane.

"I don't mean to pry but . . ." Jane said.

"Janet is considering remarrying Clayton," I said.

116

"Are you okay with that?"

"Yes."

"But it floats like a butterfly and stings like a bee, don't it?"

"I thought it would, but then I realized the relationship wasn't based on truth and it didn't hurt like I thought it would," I said.

"When did you become a deep thinker?"

"If I was a deep thinker I would have realized right away that I wasn't right for Janet."

"That's such bullshit I could puke," Jane said. "What is it with fucking women, anyway? They fall in love with a guy, but he's not the guy they really want so they set out to mold him into the perfect creature of their dreams. The one guy who won't leave hair in the sink and puts the toilet seat down."

"I didn't say . . ."

"You didn't have to," Jane said as she pulled alongside the Marquis.

"Call me on my cell phone when you have somebody," I said.

Jane nodded. "Sorry if I sounded a bit rude over that."

"You didn't," I said and opened the car door.

"Whoever I come up with might want some money for talking to you."

"No problem."

"I'll call you tomorrow."

I was at the table with Molly on my lap when Regan arrived in her Impala. She greeted me with a kiss on the forehead and as soon as she sat next to me, Molly jumped from my lap to hers.

"Deserter," I said.

Regan scratched Molly's ears and she started to purr loudly.

"How did it go today?" I said.

"I met a six-year-old girl named Keri who lost her parents in a car accident a year ago," Regan said. "She was in a car seat in back and wasn't even hurt. She's like . . . she won't talk or play and just sits and stares into space all day. Sister Mary Martin asked me to sit with her during arts and crafts and we colored in a book and it was like watching myself years ago. She didn't talk, but she did give me a smile and I thought I would cry right there in the classroom."

Molly rolled into a ball, purred and closed her eyes.

"Is that what it was like for you . . . watching me?" Regan said.

"More or less," I said. "Mostly just painful."

"I can help her, Dad. I know I can."

"I believe you," I said. "Speaking of help, did you see Wally at all?"

"At lunch and working in the garden," Regan said. "He said to say hello."

"It's close to six," I said. "Want to grab some dinner in town?"

"Can I take a quick shower?"

"Sure."

"Oz?"

"I'll call him."

Regan stood and Molly jumped back to me. As she passed my chair, Regan hugged my neck and kissed me on the cheek.

"What's that for?"

"Being a good dad."

While Regan took a shower, I called Walt on his cell phone. "Any word from Jackman yet?"

"He said a week, Jack, and you agreed."

"I know, but that doesn't mean he can't keep in touch with updates."

"Like you ever did."

"Not the reason I called, anyway," I said.

"Really?"

"How heavy a workload does Venus have at the moment?"

"Somewhere between swamped and overload. Why?"

"Maybe she could do some research for us?"

"Us?"

"It's our case, isn't it?"

"What research?"

"Known arsonists in New York State. No, make it the tri-state area," I said.

Walt was silent for a moment. Then he said, "I'll get her on it in the morning. Anything else?"

"Jane is doing me a favor, but I'll fill you in on it tomorrow."

"Somehow I think I can wait," Walt said. "Now if you're all done borrowing favors on credit, I'm going home to a home-cooked meal."

"Elizabeth cook it?"

"I didn't say it was a good home-cooked meal," Walt said and hung up.

CHAPTER SIXTEEN

Waiting is a large part of police work. Days and sometimes weeks go by on a stakeout and you're bored to tears. Waiting for reports from forensics and toxicology to produce a usable piece of evidence. A cop is always waiting for something and the hardest part of the waiting game is to stay focused on what you're waiting for.

When you lose focus is when a case gets away from you and the bad guys win.

Every cop is different in how they deal with the boredom and maintain focus. Some review reports and evidence over and over again, searching for something they missed, some tiny detail that can blow the lid off the case. I knew a team of detectives who would trade off cases with another team to get fresh eyes and perspectives. I knew others who, when stalled on a case, would pound the pavement, hoping someone, somewhere would say or do something that would crack the egg.

Walt was one of those guys.

TV cops kill an average of one bad guy a week, but in real life most cops never draw their weapon in the line of duty.

I had my own system for fighting boredom.

I would clear my mind and go for a run. Sometimes for two hours or more. I'd reset my brain and, after a time, runner's high would take over and my thoughts would free-fall, and sometimes something would click and I'd see some small thing I'd missed.

I ran six miles before breakfast and when I returned to the trailer Regan was out front and talking on the phone. She was still in her pajamas. "Okay, I'll be there right away," she said.

I sat beside her and when she hung up, she looked at me.

"Problem?" I said.

"Sort of," Regan said. "Keri refuses to leave her room. Sister Mary Martin said she won't leave her room unless I'm there to take her to class."

"Well, you better get going then," I said.

Regan nodded, got up and went inside to change. I had a mug of coffee and then went around to the heavy bag and beat on it for fifteen minutes before switching to the speed bag.

Reagan appeared, kissed me on the cheek and asked me to tell Oz she wouldn't be shopping with him today.

After she left, I cranked out several sets of pull-ups, chin-ups and push-ups before returning to the heavy bag again for thirty minutes of nonstop pounding. Drenched in sweat, I went inside for a shave and a shower, and reemerged in a white warm-up suit to find Oz in his customary chair.

"Regan stopped by to say she had to go to work and help a little girl," he said.

"I know."

"She growing up."

"I know."

"And you don't like that."

"I don't want to see her years get ahead of her maturity level," I said.

"She going to leave you one day," Oz said.

"One day."

"I remember when mine left, it was hard to face that empty-nest thing."

"My nest won't be empty," I said. "I still have you."

"You know what you need?" Oz asked.

My cell phone rang.

"Hold that thought," I said, and answered the call.

"Venus threw a fit to be tied, but she started working on it this morning," Walt said. "She said she'd have a list by late this afternoon."

"See if you can find out what her favorite perfume is," I said.

"That constitutes a bribe," Walt said.

"So what?"

"So, I'm not paying for it, that's so what."

"Call me when she has the list complete."

"Yeah, yeah, want I should vacuum your new house, too?"

I hung up and looked at Oz. "Want to take a trip to town for some lunch?"

"You look like an ice-cream man in that getup," Oz said.

"This warm-up suit is Italian silk," I said.

"Then you look like an Italian ice-cream man."

"So, you're passing up a free lunch?"

"Hell, no. I'll just have to wear sunglasses."

Jane called a few minutes after I dropped Oz off at his trailer after lunch.

"Joey Pep," she said. "Want to meet him?"

"I can't wait."

"Meet me at the office. We'll take a drive over and see him. He wants five hundred dollars."

"Doesn't everybody?"

Joey Pep was Joseph Pepitone, professional arsonist with a rap sheet three feet long. His last stretch of eleven years broke his back and he now lived a quiet life in retirement occupying the basement apartment in his daughter's home.

He was sixty-seven years old and collected eight hundred and fifty-one dollars a month from Social Security.

The daughter's house was about a block away from the county line on a quiet, tree-lined street.

"I only agreed to talk to you because I have a soft spot for the sheriff here," Joey said. "She busted me on my last rap that sent me up eleven. Insurance job. Man who hired me broke under pressure and fed me to her. Being frisked by her was a highlight of my career."

We were in Joey's basement apartment at the kitchen table. The four-room apartment was neat and well furnished if not luxurious.

"All told I spent twenty-eight years in one prison or another spread out over five states," Joey said.

On the counter behind us a coffee machine dripped coffee into a pot. "I think it's ready," Joey said and got up to pour three cups.

He sat back down and rolled a cigarette using paper and tobacco from a pouch. "I got into the habit of rolling my own in prison because it's cheaper. Want one?"

I was dying for one, but I politely refused.

"Sheriff?" Joey said.

"I haven't had a rolled cigarette in thirty years," Jane said.

"Take this one," Joey said and passed it to her.

He immediately rolled another and then lit his and Jane's off a wood match. They inhaled and sighed with deep satisfaction.

"So, Joey, I need some information on arson," I said.

"Did she tell you my price for trade secrets?"

I dug out my wallet from the jacket pocket of the warm-up suit, counted out five one-hundred-dollar bills and set them on the table.

"My daughter's birthday is next week," Joey said. "I want to get her something nice. That's why I'm charging for information."

"Sure," I said. Beside me Jane blew smoke out her nose like a

123

blond-haired dragon.

"So, Joey, is it possible to blow up a house on purpose and make it look like an accident?" I asked.

"Lemme tell you something," Joey said. "I must have pulled a hundred jobs in my career and never once got caught from evidence. It was always some client lost his nerve afterward, tried to cut himself a deal and fed me up, the fucking scumbags, all of them. Nothing worse than a scumbag who loses his . . ."

"About the house?" I said.

"I once burned down an entire friggin' forest without leaving a shred of evidence behind," Joey said. "Some paper company in a land dispute. Know how I did it?"

Jane happily blew a smoke ring.

"How?"

"Wood matches," Joey said. "The foot-long wood matches they sell for starting a fire in a fireplace. I tied a hundred in a bundle with a rubber band and pulled the center match out about four inches and set the bundle down on some nice dry pine needles. I sprinkled some lighter fluid on the extended match and lit it. That gave me a minute or so to drive away before the lit match reached the other ninety-nine. When it did, bye-bye forest."

"That's nice to . . ." I said.

"When those dry pine needles go, the whole fucking forest goes along with it," Joey said.

"About the . . . ?"

"Once a pine tree goes up, the sap explodes and spreads the fire to the next tree," Joey said. "It's like dominoes with friggin' fireballs, and just try to find evidence of those matches after the fire rages for a week."

"Interesting," I said.

"How's the coffee?" Joey asked.

"Fine," I said.

"Let me touch it up for you." Joey grabbed the pot and added coffee to the three cups.

"This cigarette is wonderful," Jane said. "Can I get another?"

"For you, doll, I'd roll a carton," Joey said.

As Joey rolled another cigarette for Jane, I said, "Can we talk about the house now?"

"What house?"

"Any house. Does it matter?"

"Matters a lot," Joey said. He passed the new cigarette to Jane. "Here ya go, doll."

"Thank you," Jane said.

"Nice nails, by the way," Joey said as he lit Jane's cigarette.

"It's a new thing," Jane said. "It's gel that gets baked on so they don't chip."

"I knew this safe cracker once who would get his nails painted with clear coat so they wouldn't chip during a job," Joey said. "I think he may have been a fruit if you know what I mean."

"Back to the house," I said.

"Old house, new house, what?" Joey said. "Be specific."

"Around fifty years . . ."

"Because gas systems vary from older to new and if it's a house in the country it probably has a big-ass propane tank on the side," Joey said.

"City house in Riverdale, New York."

"Around fifty years old?"

"Or older."

"Okay, see," Joey said. He stood and went to a kitchen counter, and returned with a legal pad and pencil. "Here's the street." Joey drew two straight lines.

"And the gas pipeline under the street." Joey drew a pipeline between the two street lines.

"Gas enters a house by a direct line into the basement." Joey drew a house and a line to the house from the pipeline.

"Into the basement and then up to the kitchen to the gas stove." Joey drew a straight line up and then drew a small box representing a kitchen range.

"If they use gas for hot water then you got off-shoot gas lines in the basement to a heating tank," Joey said.

"Okay," I said. "So how would you blow up this house and make it look like it was an accident?"

"How big is the house?"

"Three stories."

"I'd cause a slow leak in the basement," Joey said. "The basement door will keep the gas contained and fill it before anyone on the upper floors becomes aware of it. If you do the math per square foot and all that shit you'd know how long that would take. Then I'd put an ignition device on a timer to go off when the gas leak reached maximum and when it goes off it takes the entire fucking house with it like a giant firebomb. Good luck finding evidence in that pile of rubble."

Joey sniffled.

Jane patted his hand. "Are you okay?"

Joey sniffled again. "Memories," he said.

"What kind of ignition device?" I said.

"Gas is highly volatile," Joey said. "Any spark can send it to kingdom come. Even a cell phone can spark it off, but you want to be sure. That's why gas companies always warn people if they smell gas not to use the phone or even flick a light switch. I'd take the ignition device from an expensive self-starter barbecue grill and rig up a timing device based on math calculation so that when it goes off and creates a spark there's no maybe about it."

I sat back in my chair, picked up my cup and took a sip. "And the explosion is big enough to level the house?"

"Destroy everything and everybody in it," Joey said. "With

enough gas I can make water burn. And good luck weeding through what's left looking for evidence. Gas explosions in houses and apartments happen all the time and most are because some idiot didn't notice a pilot light went out or the tank on the grill stored in the basement for the winter leaks. Arson squads hate gas explosions."

Joey sniffled again and wiped his eyes.

"Thank you, Joey," I said.

"Did I ever tell you about the time I blew up a bank for some robbers in New Mexico who . . ." Joey said.

"Next time," I said.

Behind the wheel of her cruiser, Jane all but burst out laughing.

"What now?" she asked when she settled down.

"Let's go talk to Wally," I said.

"Oh, why the hell not?" Jane said.

CHAPTER SEVENTEEN

When Father Thomas escorted Wally into his office, Jane took one look at Wally and said, "This just keeps getting better and better."

"I have a session to attend to," the priest said.

"No problem, Father," I said. "We won't be long."

The priest nodded and left us alone with Wally.

Wally looked at Jane. "Who are you?"

"This is Sheriff Jane Morgan," I said. "She's assisting me with a few things."

"What things?"

"I generally try to keep Bekker from making a fool of himself and from getting his ass shot off," Jane said. "Things like that."

"Sit down, Wally," I said.

We each occupied one of three chairs facing the desk. Jane and I spun ours around to face Wally.

"I want to ask you about . . ." I said.

"You have very pretty nails," Wally said to Jane.

"Thank you," Jane said.

"Wally, I need you to . . ."

"Is that the new gel thing I heard about?" Wally asked.

"Yes, it is."

"Wally, would you . . . heard where?" I said.

"I watch a lot of late-night TV," Wally said. "The infomercials on . . ."

"Never mind," I said. "Back to your house. We need some

information."

"Sure. Like what?"

"Do you know when the house was built?"

"Around nineteen sixty, I think."

"Gas stove?"

Wally nodded.

"What was the setup in the basement?"

"I don't . . . what do you mean, setup?"

"The gas line to the house in the basement," I said. "Do you know where it was located?"

"Against the wall facing the street. It was copper, I think. It went up the wall and then disappeared into a hole in the ceiling."

"So the hot water was electric."

Wally nodded.

"How often did you check the basement?"

"Never. Except when there was a problem or the guy would stop by for regular maintenance. If I had a problem I'd call the power company and I'd go down to the basement with the guy and check things out. Basements give me the creeps, ya know. It's like going underground into a cave or something."

"Did the . . . ?"

"It's always dark and damp down there," Wally said. "And smells like cement."

"Wally, I need you to focus here," I said.

"Sure," Wally said as he looked at Jane's nails.

"Wally!" I said, loudly. "Focus. Look at me."

Wally looked at me.

"Did a man from the gas company come to the house before you went to see Kagan?" I said.

"I'm not . . . yeah, actually, a man from the power company did stop by for a routine check of the gas lines," Wally said.

"How soon before you went to see Kagan?"

129

"I think it was one or two days."

I glanced at Jane.

"Did you go with him to the basement?"

"No. I told you; I don't like basements. Besides, it was just a routine maintenance call," Wally said.

"How often do you get a routine service call?"

"Once, maybe twice a year."

"Okay, good. You did fine, Wally," I said.

"Can I go back to work now?"

"Sure."

After Wally left the office, Jane and I sat for a moment.

"Somebody wanted Wally out of the way before his inheritance kicked in," Jane said.

"Ten million is a drop in the bucket to Sample Iced Tea," I said. "They do two billion a year in sales. It has to be the sixth seat of ownership that Wally would inherit and not the money they wanted to avoid paying."

"How many siblings did you say?" Jane asked.

"Five. Two brothers, three sisters."

"And none of them close to the little screw-up?"

"Wally said they haven't spoken in years."

"That's a pretty good motive for murder, isn't it? Keep a one-sixth controlling interest of a two-billion-dollar-a-year corporation out of the hands of a degenerate gambler," Jane said.

"I want to find Regan before we go," I said.

We entered the large gardens behind the main office building, where dozens of kids sat at picnic tables with visitors or played on the swing sets. Regan sat with Keri at a table. They were coloring in books.

We stayed back and watched.

Keri showed her book to Regan and my daughter smiled at

the little girl.

Jane took my hand and gave it a gentle squeeze as Keri hugged Regan and kissed her on the cheek.

"Let's go," I whispered.

We were silent on the drive back for a while until Jane said, "She's grown up a lot, hasn't she?"

"A great deal," I said.

"If you're worried you're losing her . . ."

"I'm not." I looked out the window.

Jane said, "Mine are all gone now. I'm glad I had them early, but with my husband living with his bimbo girlfriend the nest is way too big and way too empty."

"Any chance he'll come back?"

"I don't want him back, the lying, cheating, good-for-nothing bastard."

"Divorce?"

"Wouldn't you?"

My cell phone rang. I checked the number, hit *talk* and said, "What do you got?"

"A stomach ache from last night's dinner," Walt said.

"Take two Tums and fill me in," I said.

"I ate a roll of them for breakfast," Walt said. "How about I swing by your city dump around seven?"

"I could make some barbeque chicken," I said.

"And I could eat some," Walt said and clicked off.

"You might as well swing by, too," I said. "Save me having to repeat Walt's report."

"Sure."

Jane drove us to her office, where I switched over to the Marquis and she followed me home. I made a pit stop at the meat market for chicken and the Food Mart for some odds and ends. When I arrived at the trailer, Jane, Oz and Regan were at the table outside.

I carried bags from car to trailer. "Oz, get the coals warmed up," I said. "Walt should be by in an hour."

"I have a recipe for chicken," Jane said. "Regan, give me a hand."

They took the bags from me and entered the trailer.

"What am I supposed to do?" I asked.

"What all men are supposed to do; stay out of our hair and come when you're called," Jane said.

CHAPTER EIGHTEEN

"I'm stuffed," Walt announced as he tossed his paper plate into the bonfire burning in the trash bin.

"I'll get the pot of coffee," Regan said. She went inside the trailer for a moment and returned with the pot and cream and sugar.

Oz stood up and stretched. "Me and Regan going over to my place and look at sofa patterns while you grown-ups talk."

"What?" Walt said. "Sofa patterns?"

"Tell you later," I said as Regan and Oz walked down the beach.

Jane filled our mugs with coffee, took her seat and pulled out a crumpled soft pack of cigarettes.

"Do you boys want to draw straws for who goes first?" she said as she lit the cigarette with a paper match.

Walt dipped into his inside jacket pocket for an envelope and passed it to me. The outside floodlight was bright enough to read by. I removed the document from the envelope and gave it a quick scan.

"Eleven names in three states," I said.

"Professional arsonists with long rap sheets," Walt said. "All for hire. Another two dozen in prisons in the tri-state area but I didn't include them."

"Any connections to the Sample family?" I said.

"None on the surface," Walt said. "I'll ask Jackman to take a closer look when we talk to him."

"Jane hooked me up with a retired arsonist this afternoon and we had a nice chat," I said. "He explained how easy it is to blow up an entire house from a slow gas leak and an ignition source on a timer to spark the explosion. It's really simple to make it appear an accident, actually."

"Okay, I buy that for now," Walt said. "So how does he gain access to Wally's home to set things in motion?"

"A few days before Wally contacted Kagan, a technician from the power company paid him a visit for a 'routine maintenance check' of the gas lines in the basement," I said.

Walt looked at me and I could see the gears churning in his mind.

"I admit it's plausible," he said.

"Plausible?" Jane said. "It's a downright smack in the face."

"Maybe, but we need to be sure."

"I agree," I said. "Let's give Jackman a conference call in the morning."

"All three of us?" Walt said.

"Do you want to be the one to tell Jane she's not invited?" I said.

Walt looked at Jane.

She blew smoke out through her nose.

"No, no I don't," Walt said. "Besides, where you got Wally stashed is county."

"What time for the call?" I asked.

"Say ten," Walt said.

"Want a car to babysit the facility where Wally is staying?" Jane asked.

"No one except us knows he's alive at this point," I said.

"I'll have a car do a drive-by anyway," Jane said.

I nodded.

Walt stood up and stretched his back. "I'm taking my very full and happy stomach home," he said.

Jane tossed her spent cigarette into the bonfire and lit another. We watched Walt's sedan fade away into the distance.

"Say nothing happens until the little asshole collects his inheritance; what then?" Jane said.

"I was hired to get him to his fortieth birthday without gambling," I said. "After that he's NYPD's problem."

"I'd hate to see whoever blew up his house make good on a second attempt," Jane said.

"The odds are against that once the story breaks," I said. "It would be like having a spotlight and magnifying glass on you while you tried to commit murder."

"Still, I'd hate to see something happen to him."

"You've got that empty nest thing pretty bad, don't you?"

"Shut up," Jane said. "I do not. Maybe a little. I'm still in the adapting phase of being alone. It's an adjustment, you know."

"I do know," I said.

Jane reached out and took my hand. "I know you know," she said.

"Nice nails," I said.

"Oh, shut up."

"I see my daughter coming," I said. "Want to help pick out sofa patterns?"

"I'd rather have a toothache," Jane said.

"I don't disagree."

She stood up. "Talk to you at ten."

Regan arrived just as Jane was entering her cruiser. "Night, Regan," Jane said. "Your father's a blockhead."

Regan took the chair Jane had vacated. "I know," she said. "But that doesn't make him a bad person."

We watched Jane drive away and Regan took my hand in her tiny one.

"Dad," she said. "We need to have a talk about women."

CHAPTER NINETEEN

"This is Captain Jackman speaking. Who else is on the line?" Jackman said on Walt's office speaker phone.

Walt rolled his eyes. "Captain Grimes and John Bekker," he said. "And County Sheriff Jane Morgan, who is acting as assistant to Bekker."

"That would be me, Captain," Jane said.

"I'm not sure I understand your involvement in this, Sheriff," Jackman said.

"The clinic where Sample is staying is in my county," Jane said. "Technically that's my responsibility."

"Agreed," Jackman said.

"So, how have you made out?" Walt asked.

"I met with Captain Willard and he is on board with a company executive meeting," Jackman said. "As well as a blackout on Sample still being alive. The arson squad and fire department are still actively searching the wreckage for clues and evidence, but I think it would require a small miracle to uncover anything useful."

"What about the Sample family?" Walt said.

"I have a file on each of the five members," Jackman said. "I'll fax it to you after this conference call."

"Anything useful on them?" Walt said.

"If by useful you mean incriminating it would be easier to dig up dirt on Maria Von Trapp," Jackman said.

I looked at Walt.

Walt said, "Jack dug up a nice tidbit of information that should interest you, Captain."

"Two days prior to Wally contacting his attorney and coming to see me, he had a visit from the gas company for a supposed routine inspection of the basement," I said. "I think a phone call to the gas company should verify if that visit was legitimate."

Jackman was silent for a moment.

"Captain?" Walt said.

"I'll make that call personally," Jackman said.

"Let me give you my fax number," Walt said.

"We'll talk again after I talk to the gas company," Jackman said. "Then we'll plan our visit to Sample headquarters."

Jackman clicked off.

Walt said, "Jane, you still there?"

"Let me take a guess and say that Captain Jackman comes up to Bekker's shoulders," Jane said. "On his tippy-toes. Maybe."

"Almost," Walt said.

"Jane, I'm paying Wally another visit this afternoon; want to tag along?"

"Depends."

"I'll buy."

"Then I'll be proud to assist you in any way that I can."

"Pick you up in about an hour."

Walt hit disconnect and looked at me.

"Can I borrow your sketch artist?" I said.

"In that case, I could use a free lunch, too," Walt said.

"Can we at least wait for Jackman's fax?" I said.

We took Walt's car to the home of retired FBI sketch artist and profiler Jason Byrd, who freelanced his talents to police and sheriff departments statewide. He was around sixty, a slender man with thin hair and mousy features.

"How are you, Jay?" Walt said as Byrd got into the back seat.

"This is my former partner, John Bekker."

"I've heard the name," Byrd said. "You know Paul Lawrence in Washington?"

"Old friends," I said.

"We have to pick up Sheriff Jane Morgan, and then I thought we'd get some lunch first before interviewing the witness," Walt said.

"Who buys?" Byrd said.

Walt nodded to me. "Him."

"In that case lunch will be fine."

Byrd was a chili connoisseur and had been planning a visit to the new chili palace restaurant that opened a few months back not far from Jane's office. They have a build-your-own buffet line where you can make a bowl of chili with your own ingredients and as hot or mild as you'd like.

Walt and I settled for mild with salad and lemon-flavored water. Byrd went with flame-thrower status. Jane settled for somewhere in between.

The mild was enough to melt the fillings in my teeth, so I don't know how Byrd ate the five-alarmer as if it were ice cream, but he seemed totally immune to the red-hot capsicum he gobbled down.

On the drive to Hope Springs Eternal, Byrd filled us in on his secret. While active in the FBI, he spent many years in Mexico, Latin America and South America, and over time built up a resistance to capsicum by consuming so much of it.

"They put it on everything down there," Byrd said. "Even breakfast cereal."

Father Thomas brought Wally to the complex library where we met him. He was dressed in work overalls, and I noticed he'd lost a bit of weight around the middle from two weeks of hard work and a proper diet.

"This is FBI Agent Jay Byrd and he's a sketch artist," Walt said. "He's going to draw a sketch of the man from the power company who visited your home. Okay, Wally?"

"Jay Byrd?" Wally said.

"Please, no jokes about the name," Byrd said. "I've heard them all before."

"Jokes about what?" Wally said. "I was just wondering if you were related to Larry."

"No. Now here is how this works," Byrd said.

Jane touched my shoulder and said, "I'll be right back."

"I'll go with you," I said.

We left the library and wandered around the halls until we found the medical office where, lucky for us, a nurse was on duty.

"You wouldn't happen to have any of the pink stuff in a bottle for heartburn we can buy, would you?" I asked.

"I do, but you don't have to buy it," she said.

Jane and I took the bottle to the gardens, sat at a picnic table and passed the bottle back and forth.

"Good God, my stomach," Jane said.

I swigged. Jane swigged. Walt showed. "Gimme some of that," he said.

I passed him the bottle. "How are they doing?"

"I don't know how he ate that five-alarm stuff," Walt said. "I had the mild and I'm dying here."

"I meant the sketch."

"They're somewhere between chin and nose." Walt took a gulp from the bottle and passed it to Jane.

"Dad?"

I turned around. Regan, holding Keri's hand, walked to our table.

Jane took a gulp and passed me the bottle.

"Dad, this is Keri," Regan said. "Keri, this is my father. You can call him John or Jack. And this is Uncle Walt and Jane."

Keri's eyes took us all in.

"Hi, sweetheart," I said and offered the little girl my hand. She looked at it.

"It's okay," Regan said.

Keri extended her tiny hand and took hold of one finger, and we shook.

"What's with the pink stuff?" Regan said.

"Chili for lunch," I said.

"I'll pick up some extra milk on the way home," Regan said. "I brought Molly today. She's hiding around here somewhere. Come on, Keri, let's go find her."

I nodded, gulped from the bottle and passed it to Walt. Regan and Keri wandered away in search of Molly.

We finished the bottle and walked over to the cafeteria, and got three glasses of milk and sat at a table. Thirty minutes later, as we were on second glasses of milk, Byrd and Wally entered the cafeteria and joined us.

Byrd had his sketch pad open and set it on the table.

"That's him," Wally said. "That's the man who came to my house."

On the drive back, I studied Byrd's sketch. The suspect had a thin, narrow face with sharp features and thin eyebrows. A soft scar ran about an inch long on the left cheek. His hair was receding and cut short. The ears were close to the skull. His lips were thin and tight.

I read the side notes.

Approximately six feet tall.

Weight around one-seventy to two hundred pounds.

No accent of any kind. Voice soft and slightly high-pitched.

"I'll make some copies at home and fax one to the FBI

databank for a profile match," Byrd said. "You can do the same locally."

My cell phone rang. It was Wally.

"Mr. Bekker, I mean Jack . . . I just thought of something," he said.

"What's that, Wally?"

"Jane's nails."

I was in back with Jane on my left. "Jane's nails?" I said. "What about them?"

Jane held up her fingers to show me.

"What about Jane's nails?"

"Tell him thirty-five dollars for a session," Jane said.

"See, after you left I got to thinking and I remembered something," Wally said.

"Tell him I have a coupon if he wants a clear coat," Jane said.

"What the fuck is going on back there?" Walt said.

"I'm trying to find out," I said. "Go ahead, Wally."

"The guy, the man who came to my house," Wally said. "I remembered something after you left. After he finished work in the basement he wrote a work order or something and gave me a copy. I saw his fingernails. They were manicured. It struck me odd that a guy who works with his hands all day would have a manicure. Don't you think that's odd?"

"Yes, Wally, I do," I said. "That's very good. If you remember anything else, you call me right away."

"I will. Bye."

I placed my phone in my pocket and said, "Wally remembered that the man in the sketch had manicured nails. It struck him as odd that a man who works with his hands all day would have a manicure."

"Looks like our man from the gas company is a pro," Byrd said.

"With nice fingernails," I said.

141

Jane looked at her fingernails and blew on them.

After we dropped Jane and Byrd off, Walt got Jackman on speaker phone when we returned to his office.

"A sketch?" Jackman said. "Excellent work. I'll run it through channels for a photo match."

"We're doing the same with the FBI databank," Walt said. "The artist is retired FBI."

"What about the power company?" I said.

"They're checking schedules of calls for the day or days in question," Jackman said. "As soon as I know I'll call you."

"Okay, Captain, I'm faxing you the sketch right now," Walt said.

He ran the sketch through the fax machine beside his computer. Once it went through, he sat behind his desk, opened a drawer and rummaged around.

"What are you looking for?" I said.

"Tums."

I reached into a pocket and flipped him my roll. "Take mine. I got it from the nurse," I said.

"Thanks."

"Speaking of faxes, I'll take a copy of the Sample family files home with me."

"Happy reading," Walt said as he chewed a Tums.

CHAPTER TWENTY

I sat in my chair with a mug of coffee and said a silent prayer that somebody somewhere would create the perfectly safe cigarette made from actual tobacco. I knew my prayer fell on deaf ears, so I quit thinking about the cigarette I couldn't have and opened the file Walt gave me on the Sample family.

Robert Junior, age forty-nine, was the CEO of Sample Iced Tea. He was married with three children, one son and two girls. The son, also a Robert, was twenty-three and recently graduated from college. He worked in the marketing department as an assistant. Both daughters were still in college as a freshman and senior. Robert received a salary of fifteen million a year, plus a yearly bonus taken in cash or stock, had stock options, a healthy retirement plan if and when he ever retired, and use of the company-owned jet.

He was well educated, a Harvard Business School graduate, and gave extensively to charity through the corporation. He and his family lived in a nice big house a mile from the corporate headquarters in White Plains. There wasn't as much as a parking ticket on his record.

I flipped the page.

Steven Sample, Vice President of Operations, was forty-seven years old. Also married, father of two, lived in White Plains. Salary of twelve million a year with a benefits package like Robert's. Had a speeding ticket while driving to a convention in Georgia five years ago, but pretty much everybody who drives in Georgia gets at least one speeding ticket.

Susan Sample, at forty-five, was Vice President of Product Control. Salary of twelve million plus the same benefits package as her brothers. A widow with three teenage children, her husband died of cancer three years earlier and she regularly donated ten percent of her income to a charity founded in his name.

Amy Sample, at forty-three, was Vice President of Marketing and Advertising. Salary of twelve million a year, plus the other goodies. Never married. Lived alone with two cats in a condo in Tarrytown, New York.

Barbara Sample, at forty-one, was Vice President of Finance. She drew twelve mil plus benefits like the other VP family members. She was divorced with no children and owned a home in Rye, New York. Like her brother Robert, she was a Harvard Business School graduate.

Except for one speeding ticket and one divorce, they were the Brady Bunch of the corporate world.

It was getting dark. I went inside for fresh coffee and clicked on the outside floodlight. Regan had stopped by Oz's trailer after work to internet shop and would be a while yet, so I claimed my throne and looked at photos. Five photographs from various events were included in the file.

Robert Sample was a decent enough looking man with one distinguishing characteristic. His thick crop of hair was entirely silver, like the actor Richard Gere. I couldn't tell his height from the photo, but he was slender in build. The photo appeared to be taken at a black-tic affair, as he wore a tuxedo with bow tie.

Steven Sample, wearing an expensive, pinstriped suit with a red tie, looked the part of a business executive. Dark hair speckled with gray, sharp features, eyeglasses that obviously weren't a chain-store, two-for-one special.

Susan Sample wore a power suit in her photograph. Blond, her hair was up away from her face and her sharp, angled features stood out. A lapel pin with her charity's name on it was prominently displayed.

Amy Sample, though forty-three, looked fifty-three in her off-the-rack print dress. I wouldn't label her a spinster, but if she had ambitions of marriage they weren't on display. For all I knew, behind closed doors she had a stable of young men lined up, but given her lack of style, I doubted it.

Barbara Sample was the complete opposite of Amy. Her long, auburn hair flowed over the low-cut, black dress she wore for her photograph. Her eyes were piercing green with a hint of speckles in them that spoke of her intelligence. She was smiling, but the overall tone of her appearance was one of being in on a private joke with everyone else in the dark.

I set the file aside and sipped my coffee. So what did I have? Nothing.

For all I knew, the manicured arsonist could have been sent from one of the loan sharks or many casinos Wally frequented.

But I doubted it.

Cops are simple people. If we think the butler did it, most of the time we'll be proven right. There is no magic to solving a crime. You plod along and follow clues and the evidence, and hope lady luck brings you a break. Such as Wally remembering the visit from the gas company and that the man had manicured nails.

And many times it comes down to asking the right questions. A witness may not know what he or she actually saw or heard if the questions posed to them don't stir the memory or make a connection.

"Dad?" Regan said. "Are you okay?"

I looked at her as she took the chair on my left.

"Just thinking," I said.

"Well, the living room and bedroom furniture is all set," Regan said. "Delivery is in thirty days. I figured we needed to wait until after the closing date."

"What about the kitchen, bathroom and family room?"

"That's next."

"I'll take care of the basement."

Regan nodded.

"So, what's troubling you?" I said.

"I'm that obvious, huh."

"To me."

"It's Keri. I don't know what to do about her."

"In what way?"

"She won't respond to anyone else but me," Regan said. "She wants me there seven days a week and Father Thomas said that isn't good for her. He said she needs to grow and come out of her shell, and by clinging to me I'm providing her a crutch."

"I think Father Thomas knows what he's doing," I said.

"I'm supposed to be off tomorrow, but I know she won't leave her room if I'm not there," Regan said. "When I leave she cries and cries. I don't know what to do, Dad."

"Trust Father Thomas," I said. "Know who Robert Frost was?"

"A poet," Regan said. "Sister Mary Martin read us most of his poems in class."

"Know what he said about life?"

Regan shook her head.

"He said, 'Life . . . it goes on.' I think that applies here."

Regan mulled that over for a moment. "That may be true, but it doesn't make it any easier."

"I didn't say it would, and I know about how hard it can be."

"I guess you do," Regan said.

"Tell you what," I said. "I'm playing the waiting game right now, so why don't we spend tomorrow checking out kitchens

146

and den furniture?"

"Okay," Regan said. "Feel like a home-cooked meal?"

"Who doesn't?"

"Uncle Walt."

I was toying with the idea of arm-wrestling Oz for the last pork chop on the platter when my cell phone rang. I checked the number and scooped up the phone.

"Just got a fax at home," Walt said. "Got a match on Mr. Gas Man. I'd fax it to you if you had one."

"Want me to drive over and . . . ?"

"No. It can wait until morning. I'm just giving you a heads-up," Walt said.

"Why do you have a fax machine at home?"

"Because it came with the all-in-one printer, Mr. Stone Age."

"Dad?" Regan said.

I looked at her.

"Tell Uncle Walt to fax it to my email in-box."

"Can you . . . he do that?"

"Of course."

"Walt, fax it to Regan's laptop," I said.

"Can I do that?"

"How do I know? Hold on."

I gave the phone to Regan and she talked him through the procedure.

She hung up and said, "We have to go to Oz's so I can hook up my laptop."

Fifteen minutes later I watched as Regan clicked on Walt's email and then opened the attachment. There was one photo-graph and five pages of text.

"Want me to print it?" Regan said.

"Yes, and then delete it."

Regan connected her laptop to Oz's printer and ran off the

pages. After they printed she deleted Walt's email.

Oz stayed home while Regan and I returned to my trailer. She washed dishes while I sat outside under the floodlight with a mug of coffee and Walt's report.

Adam Roper. That was the name on the arrest report photo taken by a police department in Connecticut.

Age forty-one.

Profession: Arsonist for hire.

His photograph was almost a perfect match of the sketch drawn by Byrd.

Roper had a long and storied history dating back to his first encounter with arson, when he was just eight and set the family cat on fire. By the time he was eleven, little Adam had a school bus, the school cafeteria, several abandoned cars and a street news stand to his credit.

The school counselor remanded him to a state psychiatrist for therapy. During the session the psychiatrist had to step out of his office for a minute, and when he returned young Adam had set fire to his trash can under the desk.

Adam was sent to a state-run school for troubled children where another psychiatrist wrote a report that stated, "Adam has an antisocial attitude and reacts to things that aggravate him by setting them on fire."

Late one night, Adam snuck out of the boys' dormitory, broke into the psychiatrist's office and burned it to the ground. Expelled after that incident, Adam was sent home, where his parents promptly sent him to social services for relocation.

The report had three missing years. It picked up when Roper was fifteen and discovered that people would pay, and pay handsomely, for his particular love of fire. By the time he was thirty-five, Roper was the most sought-after arsonist in the business according to the FBI's Most Wanted list.

His last arrest came eighteen months ago when the factory

owner lost his nerve after the fact and spilled his guts to the police. The charges were dropped against Roper when the prosecutor failed to make his case. Police suspected the factory owner was leaned on by organized crime members to drop the charges because Roper's talents were so very useful to them.

It was rumored that Roper currently commanded six figures for burning down whatever a client wanted burned down, because his fires could never be proven as arson by investigators and insurance companies.

"Dad, I'm going to bed now," Regan said from the open door of the trailer.

"Okay, hon," I said. "I won't be long."

"Hey, Dad? The note on the refrigerator says the closing on the house is day after tomorrow. Can I go with you?"

"I never thought you weren't."

"Night, Dad."

I set the file on the table and picked up Roper's photograph again. Question. How does a well-connected professional arsonist wind up in the home of Wally Sample?

Answer. Somebody paid him very well for the privilege.

CHAPTER TWENTY-ONE

Wally and Sister Mary Martin were engaged in a marathon game of tic-tac-toe at a picnic table in the garden at Hope Springs Eternal when Jane and I arrived.

"Damn you, Wally," the nun said in frustration. "No one wins sixty-seven consecutive games."

"That's not the point, Sister," Wally said. "I'm simply applying the basis of mathematics over chance in . . ."

"Never mind your gobbledygook and start another game," she snarled.

"What's . . . ?"

"Play," the nun demanded.

"Sister?" I said.

She turned and looked at me. "What?"

"I need to speak with Wally for a moment."

Sister Mary Martin stood up and said, "Keep the no-good little son of a bitch and his stupid mathematics," and marched away.

"Wow," Jane said.

"How are you, Wally?" I said.

"She has a temper," Wally said.

"She's an Irish Catholic nun; of course she has a temper," I said.

"What are you guys doing here?" Wally said.

Jane and I sat opposite him at the table. "The police have a match on the sketch," I said. "I need you to look at the

150

photograph."

"Sure."

Jane set the file with the photograph on the table facing Wally and flipped it open.

Wally needed all of two seconds. "That's him, that's the guy who came to the house."

"You're sure?" Jane said.

"Absolutely."

"That man is a professional arsonist," I said. "And most likely a hitman if need be and the price is right."

Wally looked at us. "The loan sharks?" he said.

"It wasn't the loan sharks," I said. "Or any casinos you owe money to. They can't collect from you if you're dead."

"Then who?" Wally asked.

"That's what I hope to find out," I said.

"I don't understand any of this."

"It's not that difficult, Wally," Jane said. "Not really. It comes down to who benefits the most if you're gone."

"I don't . . . wait . . . what are you saying?" Wally said. "That my family tried to kill me? Is that what you're saying?"

"I'm sorry, Wally, but yes," Jane said.

"What about you, Mr. Bekker; do you think my own brothers and sisters tried to have me killed?"

"Wally, try to understand how a police detective looks at things," I said. "It's not about judgment or theory, and things like a hunch are nonsense. We look at facts and evidence and follow that trail to a conclusion. The loan sharks don't benefit if you're dead because you owe them money, and they certainly aren't going to spend the small fortune it costs to hire someone like Roper and pay for the privilege of not collecting from you. Your family benefits if you're out of the way because you stand to gain a one-sixth controlling interest in a two-billion-dollar-a-year company."

Wally looked away for a moment. When he turned back to us, he said, "So, what now? What happens to me now?"

"For the moment no one except us knows that you're alive," I said. "You'll be safe here for the time being, but it will have to become known that you didn't die in the explosion and then it won't be safe anymore. Your survival will be big news and you'll be hounded by the media as a celebrity. But for now you just sit tight and concentrate on kicking your habit with Father Thomas. Okay?"

Wally nodded. "Will I still have to take that test?"

"The psychiatric exam and I'm afraid so," I said. "There's still two more weeks and Father Thomas tells me you're doing very well."

"Do you remember when I said it's not about the money?" Wally said. "It's always been about finding solutions. Gambling is just a way to finding solutions."

"That may be true, Wally, but the court won't see it that way," I said. "You need to prove to them that you've licked the gambling habit in order to collect your inheritance, so for the moment just concentrate on that and nothing else."

"What about my family?" Wally asked. "When will you tell them I'm alive?"

"Soon."

Wally nodded.

"And Wally, no more tic-tac-toe with Sister Mary Martin," I said.

"Okay," Wally said. "She's a sore loser, anyway."

Behind the wheel of her cruiser, Jane said, "I'm getting old and soft, Bekker. I almost feel sorry for the little twerp."

"I know what you mean, but if he can make it through this, there is quite a pot of gold waiting for him on the other side."

"I guess."

My cell phone rang and I scooped it out of my pocket. It was Walt.

"Go ahead, Walt," I said.

"Confirmation from Jackman," Walt said. "The power company had no service people on the block where Wally's home was located for a week prior to it going kaboom."

"No surprise there."

"Yeah, but it's official," Walt said. "Jackman wants to know when you want to pay the Sample family a visit. I do believe the good captain is chomping at the bit to make a name for himself."

"See if he'll go for two days," I said. "I have the closing on the house tomorrow."

"I'll tell him, and good luck with that," Walt said.

"If everything goes okay, I spring for a celebration dinner," I said.

"Sounds good," Walt said. "I'll get back to you after I talk to Jackman."

I stuck the phone back into my pocket. Jane looked at me.

"What?"

Jane shook her head.

"Feel like some lunch?"

"Sure."

"What's bothering you?" I said.

Biting into a bacon burger, Jane looked at me.

"Come on, what is it?" I said.

Jane took a sip of her soft drink and cleared her throat. "Talking to Walt about your new house, it reminded me of the meeting I had a few days ago with my lawyer," she said. "Did you know we live in a no-fault state? Know what that means?"

"Yes."

"It means that cheating son of a bitch I'm married to gets half of everything no matter what, short of murder."

"I know that."

"Including the house I put the down payment on and made ninety percent of the mortgage payments on," Jane said. "And half the bank accounts, and he gets to stay on my health benefits for ten years."

"That's why you decided to run for reelection?" I said.

"I couldn't afford not to," Jane said. "I'm literally paying for my husband's affair with his twenty-five-year-old bimbo."

"He wants the divorce?"

Jane nodded. "Last we spoke at the lawyer's office he said he was head over heels in love with Miss Patty-cake. Hell, even if I didn't run again and retired I'd still be responsible for half plus benefits. I'd have to buy a private policy or go back to work. It just made sense to keep on the job."

I nodded. "Want some comfort food for dessert?"

"Comfort food? If you start feeling sorry for me I'll kick your ass up and down the beach like a beach ball."

"Is that a yes or a no?"

"God, you're so stupid."

"I'll take that as a yes."

I sipped from my mug and studied the photograph of Adam Roper from my usual spot at the table in front of my trailer.

Adam Roper.

Any one of Wally's five siblings could have hired him.

Or only one.

Each had the means many times over to pay Roper for his services. Each had a good enough reason to want Wally out of the way. A one-sixth controlling interest in a two-billion-a-year corporation is a very good reason.

I read the file again and then picked up my cell phone and called Walt. "Did you read the file on Roper?"

"Front to back."

"No last known place of residence," I said.

"I asked Jackman about that," Walt said. "He said the man lived like a ghost using an assumed name. Probably works only on a referral from a known client or associate."

"I figured," I said. "So how does one or more of the Sample crowd have access to a professional arsonist known only inside a very small circle? They make iced tea, for God's sake."

"Yeah, but in thirty flavors."

"Talk to you later."

I hung up and went for a refill on the coffee, sat and thought for a while. I glanced at my watch and punched in the number for Paul Lawrence in Washington, D.C.

A chipper female voice told me I had reached the headquarters of the FBI in Washington, D.C., and asked if I knew my party's extension. I gave her Paul's extension number and was put on hold, and listened to Kenny G for about five minutes before he picked up.

"John Bekker, how the hell are you?" Lawrence said.

"Somewhere between hanging out and hanging in," I said.

"Before you ask for the obvious favor you called for, fill me in on things."

I took a few minutes to bring Paul up to speed on the past few months. He reserved comment until I was through.

"Sorry about Janet," he said.

"Me, too."

"So, what do you need this time?"

"Something simple."

"That will be the day."

"See if you can find the last known address on an Adam Roper," I said. "He's a professional arsonist with a long track record."

"PD couldn't locate him?"

"Nope."

"Got his DOB?"

I read it off to him.

"I'll see what I can do," Lawrence said. "Give me a day or so."

"Sure."

"My best to Regan."

"Will do."

I set the phone aside and looked down the beach as Regan's Impala made its way toward me. She parked next to my Marquis, got out and sat beside me.

"Dad, I need a favor," she said.

"Okay."

"Sister Mary Martin would like to do an outing at the beach for Keri and some of the other little kids at the home."

"By the beach, you mean here?"

"Yes. Of course here. She and I will supervise, but it would be a big help if you could sort of be here."

"Sure," I said. "Did you know Jane was a lifeguard before she became sheriff?"

"No, I didn't. Do you think she'd . . . ?"

"Let's find out."

I called the sheriff's department and asked for Jane. I was put on hold and listened to the best of Barry Manilow for two songs before she picked up.

"Why is it city councilmen think they can park any damn place they please inside the county and not have to pay their parking tickets?" Jane said.

"Is this a multiple choice or true or false question?"

"That's just what I need, Bekker doing stand-up comedy."

"I need a favor, or rather Regan does," I said.

"Ask."

"She and Sister Mary Martin want to throw a little beach party for some of the younger kids and I know you were a lifeguard once; feel like helping out?"

"When?"

"Hold on." I looked at Regan. "Sunday okay?"

She nodded.

"Sunday," I told Jane.

"That gives me time to buy a suit," Jane said. "I haven't worn one in years."

"Around noon should do it," I said.

"I like my steak rare."

"Who said anything about . . ." I said just as Jane hung up.

"Well?" Regan said.

"She'll do it," I said. "For a free lunch."

Regan beamed at me and stood up. "I'll tell them tomorrow. Thanks, Dad."

After Regan went inside, I picked up the photo of Adam Roper.

"What would you do for prime rib?" I said to the photograph.

CHAPTER TWENTY-TWO

Regan and I met the real-estate lawyer and Karen Hill in the conference room of her agency offices.

I wore a tan suit minus a tie. Regan wore her only business suit, a pinstriped jacket and skirt combo that she picked out to wear on job interviews but had yet to wear until today. With three-inch heels she stood all of five foot five inches tall.

The amount of paperwork was staggering.

My signature was needed on a dozen different documents and twice on some of them. I had the check for one hundred thousand prepared and certified by the bank and gave it to the lawyer.

In exchange he gave me the mortgage papers.

On the way to the car, Regan removed her jacket and said, "Let's pick up Oz and take a drive to our new home."

We made a quick pit stop for Regan to change into jeans and a sweatshirt, and to pick up Oz, then headed over.

"Can we start taking deliveries now?" Regan asked as we walked around the empty rooms.

"I don't see why not," I said. "The place is ours. Oz, get a locksmith out here to change the front- and back-door locks. I want them keyed alike. Okay?"

"I call that locksmith next to Pat's Donut Shop," Oz said.

"And call the Triple A Alarm Company," I said. "I want full coverage with a keypad next to the inside front door."

"What about the cat? She won't set things off?" Oz said.

"Only if she's locked out and breaks in."

"After everything is delivered we need to have a house-warming party," Regan said.

"I'll leave all that to you," I said.

Oz and Regan grinned at each other.

"Within reason," I said.

I spent the afternoon working out and when I returned from a long run along the beach there was a message from Paul Lawrence on my cell phone.

I toweled off and made a quick pot of coffee. Armed with a mug, I took my chair and called him back. An operator at the FBI building put me on hold and Kenny G blasted in my ear for ten minutes before Lawrence picked up the call.

"Jack, got something for you," he said.

"Should I write this down?"

"I'll fax it to you if you want."

"Fax it to Walt."

"Got a pen?"

"I do."

"Adam Roper's last known address is in Wachung, New Jersey," Lawrence said. "I can have the local office run a check on it if you want."

"Pick him up if you can," I said. "Wally will ID him in a lineup."

"I'll call you back," Lawrence said.

I hung up and called Hope Springs Eternal, and got Father Thomas on the phone.

"I need to see Wally," I said. "Is it too late for a visit?"

"We lock the gates at eight, but I can make arrangements," Father Thomas said.

"I'll be there by six thirty."

Wally was having dinner at Father Thomas's table when I grabbed a coffee off the serving line and squeezed in beside the priest.

"A friend of mine with the FBI is running down Adam Roper," I said. "I need to know right now if you'll testify in court that he came to your home posing as a power-company employee."

Wally looked at Father Thomas. The priest nodded. "The man murdered your friend, Wallace. And who knows how many other people. He needs to be punished and you're the only one who can identify him."

Wally nodded.

"Good," I said. "We'll get you through this, Wally, and when it's over you'll take your rightful place in Sample Iced Tea."

"I've been working on this plan for logistics based upon their last year's financial reports," Wally said. "A simple relocation of warehouses to a central distribution point can save millions of dollars a year in shipping costs."

"That's great, Wally, but I need you to understand what I'm about to tell you," I said. "If the FBI picks up Roper he more than likely will want to cut a deal for himself, and that means he will have to give up who hired him to kill you. A federal prosecutor will want to make that deal."

Wally stared at me.

"Remember our earlier conversation?" I said.

Wally nodded.

"If it turns out that one or more of your siblings hired Roper, you'd be testifying against them in a sense," I said. "That means prison time for them and a lot of it. Are you prepared to deal with knowing you sent your own brothers or sisters to prison for murder? Possibly for life."

"I know what you're saying, Mr. Bekker, but I don't think I can do that," Wally said. "What if I just took my inheritance money and declined my one-sixth share in the company?"

"You can decline your share, but it won't change what happens in court," I said. "Roper will eventually get picked up and cut a deal, and you'd be subpoenaed to testify anyway."

"What if I just ran away?"

"It won't change anything," I said. "Roper will get picked up and charged with arson and murder, and whoever hired him will be charged as an accessory and convicted right along with him."

"But at least I won't be part of it," Wally said.

"Wallace, look at me," Father Thomas said.

Wally turned in his chair to face the priest.

"You have been running away all your life," the priest said. "If you don't face up to this now you will keep running until the day you die. And if whoever murdered your friend gets away with it because you ran, you will carry that guilt with you here on earth and later on when you must answer for it."

Wally lowered his head and sighed.

"Wally?" I said.

He looked up at me.

"Time to step up to the plate," I said.

Wally nodded. "Okay."

"Good," I said. "Good."

"He has a brilliant mind when it comes to mathematics," Father Thomas said.

We were in the back gardens walking along the well-lit stone path to the guest parking lot.

"How is he doing otherwise?"

"We're getting there," Father Thomas said. "If I had six months I feel I could really do him some good."

"All we have is another two weeks," I said. "Do you think he could pass a psychiatric evaluation prior to his hearing?"

"Today, no. In two weeks he might stand a very good chance."

We reached my car.

"Thank you for everything, Father," I said.

We shook hands and I opened the car door.

"Mr. Bekker?" the priest said.

I looked at him.

"We're all very proud of Regan," he said. "And we're all looking forward to our beach outing."

"Me, too," I said. "See you on Sunday."

Around ten o'clock that night, Paul Lawrence called with the news that Roper's last known address was a vacant lot on a street of burned-out buildings.

I couldn't say I was all that surprised.

CHAPTER TWENTY-THREE

Walt and I took a direct flight into White Plains, New York, where we were met at the gate by Jackman and Captain Willard. Both men wore their dress uniforms, a bit much I thought as Walt wore a simple gray suit and I chose a lightweight pinstripe.

Jackman made the intros. "This is Captain Willard of the White Plains PD," he said. "Captain Walter Grimes and retired detective John Bekker."

"Ed has told me a lot about you, Mr. Bekker," Willard said.

"Our meeting isn't until ten," Jackman said. "We have time for breakfast if you'd like and to plan our strategy."

Willard drove us from the airport to a diner two blocks from the Sample Iced Tea headquarters building. Over breakfast I told them about Adam Roper's last known address in New Jersey.

"Obviously a front," Jackman said.

"Probably, but someone knows how to reach him," I said.

"For the moment let's back-burner Roper," Willard said. "Sample Iced Tea is a major corporation headquartered in my town. The five, as we call them, are some of the most respected corporate officers in the country. This will have to be handled delicately, to say the least. Who speaks for us? By that I mean who breaks the news to them that their brother is alive?"

"Wally is Bekker's client," Walt said. "It's his show as far as I'm concerned."

"I'm okay with that," Jackman said.

"I'll go along with that as well," Willard said.

Willard was around Jackman's age, but the similarities ended there. Willard was at least six foot one and had a full head of dark hair speckled with gray. Somehow I just knew he would run for mayor when he retired from the force.

"If you can do the intros, I'll take it from there," I said to Willard.

"One word of caution," Willard said. "I have to live and operate in this town, so no bullshit."

"Wouldn't dream of it," I said.

Walt rolled his eyes.

"It's almost ten," Jackman said.

The Sample Iced Tea headquarters building was a six-story, nearly all glass, modern building that fit right in with the ultramodern, ultra-clean city of White Plains.

The beautiful lobby was guarded by two uniformed guards at a long desk that faced a bank of three elevators. A well-put-together man of my height and weight, dressed in tan pants and white polo shirt, stood talking to the guards. He had dark eyes and a crew cut, and I put him at around forty-five years old.

He turned to us and smiled at Willard as we entered the lobby. "Captain Willard, right on time," he said.

"Captain Jackman from New York, Captain Grimes and John Bekker, this is Mike Fuddy, director of security for Sample Iced Tea," Willard said.

Fuddy shook hands with Walt, Jackman and then me. His handshake was a bit too firm and his right biceps flexed just a bit too hard when he squeezed my hand.

"I'll ride you up to the sixth floor," Fuddy said.

We followed him to the third elevator. Before the door closed, Fuddy removed a key ring from his pocket and used it to unlock the elevator so it would rise to the sixth floor.

"Six is reserved for the Sample family," Fuddy said.

During the few seconds it took for the elevator to rise to the sixth floor, Fuddy stared at me with a frozen smile on his face. I could see him practicing it in front of a mirror. His eyes had a little something in them I didn't like, but there wasn't time to study them as the elevator door snapped open.

We stepped out onto a plush, white, wall-to-wall carpet, a waiting area with sofas and chairs, and a receptionist behind a counter-type oak desk.

"Susan isn't here yet, Mr. Fuddy," the receptionist said. "She's still fighting that bad cold. She said she would be here in thirty minutes."

"Well, we can kill some time with a tour or a visit to the sixth-floor cafeteria," Fuddy said.

We chose the cafeteria.

It was off to the right and down a long hallway. As cafeterias go, this one was impressive. Spanish-tiled walls and floors, five redwood tables with six matching chairs at each. A kitchen with a serving counter and two chefs on duty. Every flavor of Sample Iced Tea was on display behind the counter.

Fuddy led us to a table with a window view. A chef came out from the kitchen and approached the table.

"This is Tony, our head chef," Fuddy said. "Just ask and he'll deliver."

Walt, Jackman and I asked for coffee. Willard requested strong tea with honey.

"I'll have bottled water," Fuddy said.

Tony returned to the kitchen and brought out a tray with four cups logoed with Sample Iced Tea, and one bottled water.

"Thank you, Tony," Fuddy said.

Tony nodded and went back to the kitchen.

I sampled the coffee. It was amazingly good.

"Mr. Fuddy, you have the look of an ex-cop," Walt said.

"Twelve years on the job," Fuddy said, looking at me.

"What happened?" Walt said.

"I got tired of being poor and decided to enter the corporate world."

"I can understand that," Walt said. "How long have you been with Sample?"

"Almost six years now," Fuddy said. He looked at me. "What about you, Bekker?"

"What about me?"

"How long were you a cop?"

"Fourteen years."

"No pension?" Fuddy said.

"Small one for disability."

Fuddy grinned at me. "You don't look disabled."

"Neither do you," I said.

"Yeah, well, I spend a lot of time working out."

"Me, too."

Fuddy grinned. "We should work out together sometime."

"Love to," I said.

Walt looked at me.

The receptionist entered the cafeteria and walked to our table. "Susan just arrived," she said. "The meeting will be in the conference room in five minutes."

After the receptionist left, I looked at Fuddy and said, "So what does a security chief do around here?"

"You'd be surprised," Fuddy said. "Last year alone there was sixty million in theft globally."

"Sixty million in losses?" I said. "Sounds like you're not very good at your job."

The grin on Fuddy's face froze and then slowly his lips drew back into a tight, angry line. "Shall we go?" he said.

★ ★ ★ ★ ★

The conference room was as elegant as the rest of the sixth floor. The table appeared to be made of oak, as were the padded chairs. The five members of the Sample family occupied one end of the table that held a total of sixteen chairs.

Robert Sample sat at the head of the table. A brass nameplate with each Sample executive's name indicated who sat where.

"Bob, you know Captain Willard," Fuddy said. "This is Captain Jackman from New York, Police Captain Walter Grimes and John Bekker, a private investigator."

"We've been briefed," Robert said. "Please, everyone, sit down."

Except for Fuddy, we took chairs. He stood against the wall to Robert's left. I had the feeling that was his usual place.

Except for Susan Sample, everyone looked pretty much as they did in the photos. Susan had a red nose and watery eyes from her cold and she wore a lightweight trench coat over casual pants. She probably planned to return home immediately after the meeting.

"Now then, Captain Willard, what news have you concerning our brother's death?" Robert said.

"I'll allow Mr. Bekker to answer that," Willard said.

"Before you answer any questions, what exactly is your involvement in this, Mr. Bekker?" Robert asked.

"I'll answer that in my statement," I said. "But before I begin, what I have to say is of a private and personal nature."

"Obviously," Robert said.

"He means he doesn't want Mike in the room, Bob," Barbara said.

"Mike is one of our most trusted employees and head of our security department," Robert said.

"The key word here is 'employee,' " I said. "Trusted or not, what I have to say is for family only."

167

Robert looked at Fuddy and nodded. I didn't look at Fuddy as he left the room, but I could feel his glare.

"I have to tell you, Captain Willard, that I find this procedure very strange and unsettling," Robert said.

"If you think that was strange and unsettling, try this," I said. "Your brother is very much alive."

There were about five seconds of silence.

Then.

"What are you talking about?" Robert asked.

"Who's alive? Wally?" Steven said.

"Are you talking about our brother Wallace?" Susan asked, and sniffled.

"How could he be alive after a gas explosion like that?" Amy said.

"If Wally is alive, then who the hell is dead?" Barbara asked.

"A man by the name of Paul Watson died in the explosion," I said.

"Who is . . . how do you know this?" Robert said. "Captain Willard, who is this private investigator and . . . ?"

"If you will shut the hell up for a moment I will explain," I said.

Under his breath, Walt said, "Smooth, Jack. Real smooth."

"Your father's attorney from a long time ago, Frank Kagan, contacted me two weeks ago," I said.

"I remember him," Robert said. "He handled Dad's last will and testament."

"Then you know about Wally's fortieth-birthday clause?"

"We all do," Barbara said. "What is your point?"

"Wally went to see Kagan about his inheritance two weeks ago," I said. "As you may or may not know, it hinges upon Wally passing a psychiatric exam for his gambling problem. Kagan hired me to help your brother get ready for that exam."

"So the little asshole really is alive?" Barbara asked.

"Barbara, please," Robert said.

"Well, what would you call him?" Barbara said.

"Yes, he really is alive and under my protection for the next two weeks until his hearing," I said. "At that time I will turn him over to Kagan for his court appearance."

"So, wait, who died in the accident?" Susan asked.

"Paul Watson, a friend of Wally's who stayed over to watch his plants," I said.

"Leave it to the asshole to not notice a pilot light was out," Barbara said.

"Why has this been kept from us and the media?" Robert said.

"I didn't tell anyone except for a select few," I said.

"Why?" Susan said.

"Because I don't think the explosion was an accident," I said.

A few seconds of silence passed as my meaning was ingested.

"Wait . . . are you saying someone deliberately set that explosion to murder Wally?" Robert said.

"Yes," I said. "And I've kept this a secret to protect Wally from that someone trying to kill him again."

Robert looked at Willard. "What do you say, Captain?"

"I agree completely," Willard said. "There would be no need to attempt to murder Wally again if it was believed he was dead."

"Even though there is no evidence to suggest that what happened was anything other than an accident," Steven said. "Gas-leak explosions happen all the time. The fire department told us they would . . ."

"The fire department, police and arson squad probably won't find much in the rubble," I said. "The size of the explosion took care of that."

"Then how can you make . . . ?" Robert said.

"There was a witness," I said.

The room fell silent again until Barbara said, "Who?"

"I won't give details at this time," I said. "My first concern is Wally's safety and I don't want to give them the opportunity to try again."

"Mr. Bekker, it is no secret that we don't want Wally to join us in controlling the company," Robert said. "Our plan was to meet in court with our attorneys to try to block the will from being instituted. Our offer was going to be that he keep the ten million, and in exchange for him giving up his one-sixth interest, we would provide him with a tax-free income of one million dollars a year for life. Please tell him this and ask him if he would accept those terms as offered in good faith by his family."

"I'll tell him," I said. "But have you ever considered that Wally might have a great deal to offer you as a company?"

"No, we haven't," Barbara said. "Wally is just short of Rain Man with a gambling problem and we can't have that little dick as a controlling officer."

"We're a family-owned company, Mr. Bekker. We have an image to uphold and Wally just doesn't fit in with that image. His gambling would make every paper and cable-news show in the country," Robert said. "There is no telling what he would do given access to such resources. We have an obligation to protect those resources and our family reputation. He is our brother and we care for him, and that is why we made so generous an offer."

"Like I said, I will tell him, but not one word of this can leak out or Wally's life will be in danger again," I said. "And think of your reputation if it became known that you threw your brother to the wolves when he needed your help."

"We understand," Robert said.

"And not just the media," I said. "Understand that any one person you tell automatically becomes two and then four and so on."

"I don't think you need worry about that," Robert said.

"That's it, then," I said. "I'll be in touch right before Wally's court appearance."

"Hold on, Mr. Bekker," Robert said. "Aren't you going to tell us how our brother is doing? We are his family, after all. We have the right to know."

"I don't think so," I said. "Except for her," I pointed to Barbara, "you're all full of shit in my book."

Barbara smiled at me. It was a very smug smile, to say the least.

"I'll see you all in court in two weeks," I said.

I led the parade to the elevators where Fuddy stood waiting. Glaring at me, he opened the door with his key and we entered the car. We rode down in silence and as we exited the car to the lobby, Fuddy held the door open.

"We'll see each other again, Bekker," he said.

"Looking forward to it," I said.

Fuddy released his hand and the elevator door slowly closed in my face.

Driving us to the airport, Willard said, "You didn't make any friends back there, Bekker."

"Jack has a way of not making friends rather quickly," Walt said.

"I didn't come here to make friends," I said.

"So, what now?" Jackman said.

"Hope that the PD and arson squad find some evidence the explosion wasn't an accident," I said. "And hope my friends at the FBI can find Adam Roper and lead us to whoever hired him to kill Wally."

"And if they don't?" Willard said.

"That's something I need to discuss with Wally and Kagan," I said.

171

"Straight up, Bekker," Willard said. "Do you believe one or more of the Sample family tried to have Wally Sample killed?"

"I do," I said.

"Without any hard evidence or proof."

"Do you think a pro arsonist just fell out of thin air and picked Wally's home to blow up at random?" I said.

"I have to agree with Bekker," Jackman said.

"I didn't say I don't agree," Willard said. "I said we don't have any real evidence."

"All the more reason for the arson squad to find some and for us to find Roper," I said.

"All before his court date?" Willard said.

"Or after," I said. "Either way an innocent man has been murdered. That Wally was the target doesn't really matter, does it?"

"I suppose not," Willard said.

"This deal, do you think he'll go for it?" Jackman said.

"The inheritance money and a million a year to give up his seat at the table?" I said. "I don't know."

Willard drove into the airport and parked in front of the departure terminal. "You'll let me know what Wally says about the offer?" he said to me.

"I'll conference call all of us after I speak with him," I said.

After Willard dropped us off, we entered the terminal building. Jackman's flight to New York was at another airline and we shook hands before heading in different directions.

"Interesting morning," Jackman said. "Do you think they'll leak the news?"

"No," I said. "Not at this time. It would be bad for their precious corporate image."

Jackman nodded. "I'll check on the progress of the arson squad when I get back. We'll talk on the conference call."

We went our separate ways. Our flight wasn't for an hour. I

grabbed two coffees and Walt and I took seats at our gate.

"You went out of your way to get under Fuddy's skin," Walt said.

"I didn't like his handshake," I said.

"I know you too long and too well, Jack," Walt said. "This is no longer about Wally and his court date. Roper threw down the gauntlet and you picked it up. Why?"

"I have a new house to pay for," I said.

Walt sipped some coffee and then said, "You always were a pain in the ass when it came to the underdog, Jack. That's what this is really about, isn't it?"

"Now Walt, as a career cop who knows that crime goes unsolved eighty percent of the time, don't you think we're always the underdogs?"

Walt sighed.

"They're calling our flight," I said.

CHAPTER TWENTY-FOUR

"What do you think, Dad?" Regan asked when I walked through the front door of our new home and looked at the furniture.

Oz was connecting wires to a new flat-screen television that he'd mounted to the wall opposite the new sofa. "Following these instructions be like trying to do Chinese arithmetic," he said.

"Sit. Try it out," Regan said.

I took a seat on the sofa. It was plush and comfortable. I looked at the glass-top coffee table and my daughter read my mind.

"Don't even think about putting your feet up," she said. "The sofa is electric and reclines by remote or by that button on the side."

"Or sit in my Lazy-boy," Oz said, gripping a handful of wires.

"Want some competent help?" I asked him.

"Sure. Who you know is competent?" Oz said.

"Check out the kitchen," Regan said.

I stood and followed her through the connecting door into the kitchen. The butcher-block table with four chairs nestled near the glass doors to the backyard. A matching chef's island separated the appliances section from the table.

"All very nice," I said. "You guys have done a great job. What about the bedrooms and den?"

"Friday delivery," Regan said. "I can't wait to cook you dinner in this kitchen."

I slid open the kitchen doors and stepped into the backyard. Molly was playing with an insect of some kind in the grass.

"We need a new grill and a lawn mower," I said.

"On my list of things to talk to you about," Regan said.

"Okay. What time will you be done here?"

"As soon as Oz is done wiring the TV."

"That long, huh," I said. "I have to see Wally. I'll pick you guys up later and we'll go out to dinner."

"Sure."

I made it to Hope Springs Eternal right after their evening meal and met with Wally in Father Thomas's office. Wally listened as I told him about his family's counter-offer to their father's will.

"No," he said.

"That's it, just 'no'?"

"No is all I have to say about it."

"Are you sure about this?" Father Thomas said. "A ten-million-dollar inheritance plus one million a year for life is quite the compensation in exchange for a place in the company."

"Maybe so, but I have a rightful interest in the family business and I know I can help," Wally said. "I can't contribute if I've given up my seat for an allowance. I've been on an allowance all my life. It's time I earned my way, don't you think?"

"Okay, I'll tell them," I said. "It might get ugly in court, just so you know. The other thing is the competency hearing. You have to get past that for any of this to matter."

"I'll pass it," Wally said.

I looked at Father Thomas.

"We've made some important breakthroughs," he said. "If Wally were a boy in school today they would feed him drugs for a condition that in my opinion he doesn't have. By the time of the hearing Wally will have refrained from gambling for thirty days and thereby would meet the requirements of the will. Correct?"

"As I understand it," I said.

"You said the Sample family will have their attorneys present in court to protest the will and make that offer to Wally?"

"That's their plan."

"What if I prepared a statement for the court and agreed to testify on Wally's behalf?" Father Thomas said. "I am a psychiatrist and I will also be a priest under oath. It would be difficult for them to call me a liar, wouldn't it?"

"It would at that," I said.

"You would do that for me, Father?" Wally said.

"I would, Wally," the priest said. "You have a great mind and a good deal of value, and it would be a shame if that were lost because of prior indiscretions."

"I'll call Frank Kagan and let him know," I said. "He'll be representing Wally in court."

"A common cause makes for strange partnerships," Father Thomas said.

"It certainly does, Father," I said. "I'll call you as soon as I speak with Kagan. I'm sure he's going to want to meet with you before the hearing."

I sat in my car in the visitors' parking lot and made two calls on my cell phone. The first was to Frank Kagan. He was working late and I caught him in his office.

"Problem?" he said when he answered the phone.

I told him about Father Thomas's offer to testify in court on Wally's behalf.

"Son of a bitch," Kagan said. "Why didn't I think of that? Who is going to argue with a priest who is also a psychiatrist, under oath? Genius, Bekker."

"Can you meet with Father Thomas?" I said.

"I insist on it," Kagan said. "Give me his number and I'll call him in the morning."

I hung up and sat for a moment, and waited for the nicotine craving to pass. When the urge for a cigarette finally subsided, I punched in the number for Paul Lawrence. After I'd been put on hold twice and listened to three songs by Abba, he came on the line.

"Jack, nothing new on Roper at the moment," he said.

"I know, but that's not why I'm calling. I need another favor."

"Of course you do," Lawrence said. "My guys sure do love those giant donuts from Pat's. Haven't had any for a while."

"Will two dozen satisfy their donut lust?"

"Two will do, three would be better."

"Overnight delivery okay?"

"Done. What do you need?"

"Any information on an ex-cop named Mike or Michael Fuddy," I said. "Works for Sample Iced Tea as head of security the last six years or so."

"And he's done what to warrant this look-see?"

"I didn't like his handshake."

"Oh, well, as long as it's something important."

"And fast, Paul," I said. "We're running out of time here."

"I'll call you late tomorrow," Lawrence said. "And Jack, I'm partial to the Boston creams and lemon Danish."

"Got it," I said and hung up.

I was about to start the engine when I spotted Sister Mary Martin walking along the sidewalk to my car. She waved and I opened the passenger door for her. She got in beside me. "I'm glad I caught you," she said. "I wanted to talk to you about Sunday."

"Sure."

"Eight children in all. Five girls, three boys, all between six and ten years old. Father Thomas and I and Regan will supervise, but I'm afraid we're not much for swimming. I'm a bit concerned that if any of the children should want to go into the water . . ."

"I'm a pretty good swimmer, and I've asked my friend Sheriff Morgan to attend. She used to be a lifeguard," I said.

"Well, I feel much better; thank you," the nun said.

"You're welcome."

"Good night, Mr. Bekker."

"Before you go, may I ask you a question?"

"Regan has come a very long way since she left us a year ago. She still is not up to par emotionally, but working at a job is giving her more of a sense of self-worth," Sister Mary Martin said. "She's gone from coloring books and silence to driving a car and decorating your new home. Buying the house was an excellent move, by the way. A strong sense of a real home and family is exactly what she needs to continue her progress. She'll have the confidence to finally pursue college and a career and something that is missing in her life."

"What's that?"

"Boys, Mr. Bekker. Boys."

"Oh, I wish you hadn't said that last part."

"If you build that glass dome around her thick enough you're not keeping the world out, you're trapping her inside."

I nodded. "Yeah."

"See you on Sunday."

"Good night, Sister."

"By the way," she said. "I'm really glad to see you not smoking. I wish Father Thomas would quit. Maybe you could speak with him about it on Sunday."

"I'll mention it," I said.

After Sister Mary Martin left, I started the car and sat for a moment wishing a pack of cigarettes would just drop out of the

178

sky and land in my lap.
   One didn't, so I drove home.

CHAPTER TWENTY-FIVE

Armed with a mug of coffee brewed in the new machine on the kitchen counter of the new house, I took a chair at the new patio table and waited for my very old cell phone to ring.

Inside, Regan and Oz supervised the bedroom-furniture delivery. I got up to slide the glass door closed, and Molly dashed out just before I closed it and ran to the grass.

I sat and watched her chase a few bugs. Near the fence a red-breasted bird landed and pecked at the grass. Molly went into full stealth mode.

My phone rang. I checked the number. "Captain Jackman," I said.

"Just thought I'd pass this along," he said. "The arson boys found the remains of what looked like some sort of timing device in rubble they believe came from the basement. The lab is analyzing it for identification."

"No need to mention to them they should be looking for some sort of ignition source the timing device was connected to, right? Maybe something like an electric starter from a barbeque grill that would spark an explosion? They're professionals. They know what they're doing. Right?"

"Right," Jackman said. "What was that again?"

After hanging up with Jackman, I went inside for a moment to refill my mug. Regan caught me in the kitchen.

"Wait until you see your room," she said.

"They done yet?"

"Almost. Delivery included assembly."

"Okay. I'll be outside with Molly."

When I returned to my chair, Molly was stalking a tiny wild bird of some sort that dared venture into her territory. She went low in the grass and all but disappeared.

My phone rang again and I scooped it up. "Get the box?" I said.

"All three dozen," Lawrence said. "My guys are very happy. Me, too."

"So what do you got?"

"Nothing on Roper yet. The man's a ghost."

"What about Fuddy?"

"Now, here is where things get interesting," Lawrence said. "Michael Medford Fuddy. Age forty-four. Born in Hartford, Connecticut. Joined the Army at eighteen. Discharged at twenty-one. While stationed at Dix he took the Connecticut State Police exam and finished in the top five percent. That plus his military service got him called after only two years of waiting. He spent twelve years on the job before resigning under prejudicial circumstances."

"Like what?"

"Like more than twenty complaints of brutality in the line of duty. Involved in five shootings, he killed three," Lawrence said. "Those were cleared by IA. It's the beating up of suspects on those so-called resisting arrest that forced him off the job."

"What did he do before hooking up with Sample Iced Tea?"

"Spent a few years as a bouncer for nightclubs in Connecticut and Manhattan," Lawrence said. "Some rumors he did some strong-arm stuff for local mobsters, but it's unsubstantiated. He was arrested for assault on a man who supposedly took his parking space at a club he worked at, but charges were later dropped. So, besides his handshake, what else don't you like about this character?"

"It doesn't fit that a family-owned, squeaky-clean company like Sample would hire this jerk," I said.

"No, it doesn't."

"Fuddy and Roper are both from Connecticut," I said.

"You noticed."

"Find a connection?"

"Not yet."

"Keep at it."

"Not to worry. I'm finding this very interesting, not to mention tasty."

"Go easy on the Boston creams."

"It's the lemon Danish that will do you in."

"Talk to you later."

I hung up and sat with my coffee for a while, watching Molly chase birds she couldn't catch.

A bad cop and a professional arsonist from the same state. The cop winds up working for Sample Iced Tea and the arsonist just happens to inspect Wally Sample's house days before it blows up in a gas explosion . . . one month before Wally's inheritance kicks in.

Coincidence?

The door slid open and Regan popped her head out. "Hey, Dad, come take a look."

I followed her to my room to check out the queen-sized bed with matching end tables, lamps, and mirrored dresser and dressing chair that awaited my inspection. Oz's room, a bit larger than mine, housed a similar set of furniture.

Regan's bedroom theme was a bit more modern with a feminine flair to it. I suspected her need for a queen-sized bed was to allow Molly maximum sleeping room.

"You guys did a great job," I said and kissed Regan's nose.

"Last thing is drapes for the windows and some new appliances for the kitchen, and we're ready to move in," she said.

We returned to the kitchen and after I filled my mug with coffee we went out to the patio table. Molly was chasing a butterfly.

"What about the trailer, Dad?" Regan asked.

"It's ours to keep," I said. "I can use it as an office and a place for us to hang out on beach days. I don't think our new location would allow bonfires."

"I'm thinking I should keep mine, too," Oz said. "Nobody in their right mind would buy it anyway."

"What about a grill and lawnmower?" I asked.

"That's our project for tomorrow," Regan said.

"Phones and cable?"

"First of the week."

"That leaves the basement to me," I said. "I'll take care of that next week."

"Dad, something we've been meaning to ask you."

"We?"

"We sort of talked it over and . . . we were thinking of getting Molly some company," Regan said.

"By *we* you mean you and Oz, and by *company* you mean another cat?" I said. "I don't think Molly is the sharing type. A second cat would . . ."

"A dog," Regan said. "A little pug she can run around and play with in the yard."

"A pug?"

I looked at Oz.

"They tiny little dogs," he said. "It be good for the cat to have a companion."

"The cat?"

"What do you think, Dad?"

"The basement is off limits," I said. "I don't want to have to dodge puddles every time I go down for a workout."

"We'll train her right away," Regan said.

"Her? How do you know it's a her?"

"I got some tidying up to do," Oz said.

"I'll help you," Regan said.

"Hold on a second," I said just as my cell phone rang. I checked the incoming number. "I have to take this."

"No problem," Regan said.

As she went inside, I hit the *talk* button.

"Jack, Paul. Something just came to my attention," Lawrence said. "My guys went a little deeper into Fuddy's years as a state cop. Guess who he arrested for arson some seventeen years ago?"

"Dare I say Roper?"

"You knew, didn't you?"

"Hunch."

"Want the particulars?"

"Why not?"

"Some slumlord in the town of Trumbel hired the young Roper to burn an apartment building for the insurance money," Lawrence said. "When it got too hot for him the landlord coughed up Roper to the state police. A young Fuddy made the bust, but three months before Roper's trial was scheduled the landlord up and vanished. Charges were dismissed."

"The landlord ever turn up?"

"No. Any more hunches?"

"High cholesterol and donuts are bad for you."

"Jack, I have a hunch of my own that this could turn ugly on a dime," Lawrence said. "Since this covers three states as far as I know, you might need a friend in the feds here."

"When was the last time you got out of the office?" I said.

"Don't give me that crap," Lawrence said. "I can make this a federal beef and push you out, and put Wally under my wing until his hearing."

"All right, Paul," I said. "If the *if*s and *when*s become the *here* and *now*s, you get the case."

"Side by side or I take it right now."

"Okay, we'll do it like it was twenty years ago," I said.

"Your word on that."

"You got it," I said. "I'll call you back after I break the news to the Sample family that Wally rejected their offer."

"Okay," Lawrence said. "And Jack, be nice."

"Nice is my middle name," I said.

"I thought it was asshole."

Lawrence clicked off. I went back inside and found Regan and Oz in the living room putting some finishing touches on the entertainment center.

"TV, DVD, stereo system with surround-sound, Netflix and all in hi-def," Regan said.

"Never mind that now," I said. "Let's lock up and grab some lunch and talk about this bulldog thing."

"Pug," Oz said.

"Pug, then."

"She's really cute, Dad," Regan said. "Only eight weeks old and Molly will love her, you'll see."

"Grab Molly and let's go," I said.

After lunch I changed into sweats and walked down to the ocean, where I called Sample Iced Tea on my cell phone and asked for Robert Sample.

"Mr. Bekker," he said when he came on the line. "You spoke with Wally?"

"I have."

"And?"

"I'd like to fly in and speak in person."

"When?"

"Tomorrow."

"Tomorrow is Saturday."

"You fabulous five can spare an hour," I said. "I'll be there before noon."

"All right. Noon."

I hung up, tucked the phone into my pocket and went for a six-mile run to burn off lunch. When I returned to the trailer, Oz and Regan were making a list of potential names for the pug.

"We're sort of stuck on a name," Regan said. "A pug is slang for a boxer, right, and all the good names are male. Like Rocky or Dempsey."

I took my chair and glanced at the notepad. "Why not bring her home and see what her personality is first, and then name her after a particular trait of hers you like best," I said.

Regan and Oz glanced at each other.

"Not a bad idea, Dad."

"I know what I name you if I called you by a personality trait," Oz said to me.

I stood up. "I'm going to take a shower. Tomorrow I have to fly to New York for the day."

"That name for my Dad wouldn't happen to be . . . ?" Regan said.

"Never mind my name," I said and stepped into the trailer.

"If they shoe fits, name it," Oz said just as I closed the door.

Chapter Twenty-Six

Fuddy waited for me in the lobby of the Sample Building. He wore a lime-green warm-up suit that fit him like skin. His biceps and chest muscles strained to break free of the thin material.

"Didn't expect you back so soon," he said.

We didn't shake hands.

We didn't speak either, as Fuddy unlocked the sixth floor and we rode up. I stepped off the elevator and he said, "I'll be waiting for you."

"Looking forward to it," I said.

The five were in the conference room. All were dressed in casual clothing. Susan looked to be over her cold. Barbara wore tight-fitting jeans with a black top and black shoes with four-inch heels. Except for Susan, who was drinking tea, all had cups of coffee in front of them.

"Grab a cup if you'd like some," Robert said. "It's fresh."

I helped myself to a cup and sat a few chairs down from Barbara.

"I'll be brief and to the point," I said and took a sip. As with the other day, the brew was excellent. "Wally has rejected your offer and will fight you in court."

"Ha!" Barbara said. "That will be the fucking day."

"Barbara, please," Robert said.

"Bob, kiss my gorgeous ass," Barbara said.

"Excuse my sister, Mr. Bekker. She's always been a bit high-strung," Robert said. "Exactly how does Wally plan to fight us in court and why? He knows nothing of the business world and never seemed interested in learning. Why the change of heart?"

"Wally will pass his psychiatric evaluation and evidence will be presented to the judge," I said. "As for his interest, you would be surprised at how . . ."

"I've heard enough of this crap," Barbara said. "Our lawyers will appeal and stall this in court for years. Wally will be old and gray before he sees a nickel. Tell the little bastard to take the deal or we will take his balls. That is, if he has any."

"For God's sake, Barbara, shut up," Robert said.

"This is getting us nowhere," Susan said. "And as much as I disapprove of my sister's language, she is correct in what will happen. Our lawyers will fight this in court and stall the inheritance for years to come."

I looked at Susan. "Your cold better?"

"Much, thank you."

"As I said before, I'll be brief," I said. "Wally wants his day in court and a seat at your table, and I think he will win. Your father's will is very clear on what he needs to do to gain his inheritance and he understands that fully. And, one more thing. I think he might surprise you on how valuable a resource he can be."

"Sure, if you want gaming tables in the fucking lunch room," Barbara said.

"What if we upped his allowance to a million five?" Robert said.

"You're missing the point," I said. "Wally doesn't want an allowance; he wants to contribute."

"And *you're* missing the point," Barbara said. "Wally isn't welcome here."

"You all feel that way?" I said.

Robert sighed. "It's not that we have any ill will or malice toward our brother, it's just that he's been a . . . what's the word I'm grasping for?"

"Fuckup," Barbara said.

"I'll tell Wally how you feel," I said. "And we'll let the court decide."

I stood up and walked out of the conference room.

Fuddy was standing beside the elevators, key in hand. I stepped into the car and we rode down to the lobby in silence.

Fuddy held the door while I stepped off. "Hey, Bekker?" he said.

I paused to turn around.

"Don't fuck with me. It's unwise."

"I wasn't aware that I was," I said.

"Just don't."

"And if I do?"

Fuddy grinned at me as he released the doors and they closed in my face.

I left the building, claimed my rental car in the visitors' lot, drove around the block and then parked on the street where I could watch the exit for the employee parking lot.

Robert emerged first in a shiny black Lincoln. Susan was next in a Toyota hybrid. Steven drove a Lexus. Amy drove a Volkswagen sedan of some sort.

Barbara didn't show up for another twenty minutes. She was behind the wheel of a Shelby Ford Mustang and when she turned out of the lot I could see her passenger was Mike Fuddy.

I picked up the dark sunglasses and Yankees baseball cap from the seat beside me, put them on and started the engine.

I let Barbara get a block ahead of me and followed her Mustang to a condo complex on the north side of White Plains. Since Barbara owned a home in the town of Rye, the condo had to be Fuddy's.

The complex was gated so there was no way for me to follow the Mustang past the gates, but I didn't need to. I pulled out a small notebook and pen and jotted down the address on the gate. Then I drove back to Central Avenue, found a small restaurant and had lunch at the counter. I asked the waitress for a White Plains phone book and checked for a listed number for Fuddy.

If he had a land line, it wasn't listed.

I called Lawrence from the waiting lounge at the airport.

"Paul, the address for Fuddy checks out; I followed him home," I said. "But he either doesn't have a land line or it's unlisted."

"Looking for anything in particular?" Lawrence said.

"If you mean do I think he'd be stupid enough to call Roper from his home phone, the answer is no," I said. "But I do think he's dumb enough or arrogant enough to be playing gigolo with Barbara Sample."

"The youngest daughter?"

"She's not a nice person," I said.

Lawrence made a noise that sounded like a cross between a chuckle and a snort.

"Call me later," I said.

I hung up and picked up a newspaper in the gift shop for something to read on the flight home. When the plane landed I picked up my car in the lot and drove straight to Hope Springs Eternal.

"When we were kids Barbara used to beat me up and bully me all the time," Wally said. "What she said doesn't surprise me one bit. I actually expected worse."

"Are you sure you want to go forward with this, Wally?" Father Thomas asked.

"I'm sure."

"A million and a half a year for life is a lot of money for no aggravation or responsibility, Wally," I said.

"I don't care," Wally said. "I haven't so much as had a scratch ticket in almost three weeks. I can beat this in court and I will, and then I can help my father's company get out of the bad situation it's in."

"Wait. What?" I said. "What bad situation?"

Wally looked at Father Thomas, who was seated behind his desk in his office. "Do you still have the newspaper, Father?" he asked.

Father Thomas reached under his desk, removed the paper from a trash bin and set it on the desktop. Wally flipped pages to the financial section and ran his finger down the stock market page.

"Here," he said.

I looked.

"Sample Iced Tea closed at 46.73 a share yesterday," Wally said.

"I don't . . . what are you saying?" I said.

"Thirty days ago the stock closed at 67.18," Wally said. "Don't you see? A stock doesn't fall more than twenty dollars a share in a month without something being seriously wrong with the infrastructure of the company."

I looked at Father Thomas.

The priest shrugged. "Wally is a genius when it comes to math," he said.

"What kind of problems?" I said.

"I'm on the outside looking in," Wally said. "It could be any number of individual things or a combination of things that's causing the stock to fall, but one thing is for sure and that is, it isn't good."

"What would cause the stock to fall?" I said. "Wouldn't your family take protective measures against this sort of thing?"

"Traders study financial reports on major companies," Wally

191

said. "Quarterly reports, profits and losses, payroll, production costs, and even lawsuits, and then make their recommendations to their clients based upon what they see as long-term growth of a company. It's always about the math."

"So it's possible to have two billion in sales and still be in trouble?" I said.

"Say you make a hundred dollars a week but your expenses are a hundred and ten," Wally said. "What's going to happen long term?"

"I would imagine a similar situation as with the loan sharks, but without the broken legs," I said.

"Exactly," Wally said.

"Do you think they know that you know, or suspect, the company might be on shaky ground?" I asked.

"Maybe."

"Wally, I want you to keep this to yourself for now. Talk with no one else about this until the court date. Okay?"

Wally nodded.

I looked at Father Thomas.

"I'll keep him in line," he said.

On my way home, I pulled off the road for a moment to call Frank Kagan.

"Frank, do you have a stockbroker?" I said.

"Doesn't everybody?"

"Is he local?"

"Yes. Why?"

"Can you have him at your office on Monday morning?"

"If I had a good reason."

I explained as best I could Wally's theory on the falling Sample Iced Tea stock.

"That's a good reason," Kagan said. "See you Monday."

CHAPTER TWENTY-SEVEN

Oz stirred the coals in the grill to ensure even burning. I unfolded the legs of a long portable table I'd rented in town and tossed on a paper tablecloth. While I set the table with folding chairs and paper plates I kept an eye out for the Hope Springs Eternal van that would be arriving shortly.

Regan had left at nine in the morning to give Father Thomas and Sister Mary Martin a hand with the eight children they would be transporting. Jane had yet to arrive, but I told her noon and it was only a quarter to the hour.

Table arranged, I flopped into my chair with a mug of coffee. Coals graying nicely, Oz took the chair to my left.

"I think I see them," he said.

The white, full-size van turned onto the beach and slowly made its way toward us. It parked beside my car and the side doors slid open. Regan popped out first.

"Hey, Dad!" she called.

Oz and I stood and walked to the van as Sister Mary Martin and Father Thomas got out. The nun wore tan Bermuda shorts with sandals and a gray tee shirt that came almost to her hips. The priest wore basketball shorts with a faded Michael Jordan jersey.

One by one, Regan filed the eight children out of the van. "Dad, give us a hand with the coolers," she said.

"Hi, Father, hi, Sister," I said as I went to the van's open door. "And hi to you, Keri," I said as she hid behind Regan.

"It's okay; say hi back to my dad," Regan said.

Keri peeked around Regan and looked at me.

"Come on, everybody, let's go to the table," Father Thomas said.

Helping Regan carry coolers meant lugging four large ones by myself to the table.

"Mr. Bekker, I think the children shall eat first and play on the beach a bit later," Father Thomas said.

"Oz is grill master; who wants to help?" I said.

"I need to change," Regan said and entered the trailer.

"Come on, everybody, break open the coolers," Sister Mary Martin said. "Mr. Oz needs a hand at the grill."

From behind the grill, Oz said, "Jane's coming."

She drove her cruiser, and the eight children were fascinated to see it arrive and park next to the van. Jane was in full uniform when she got out, and carried a paper bag.

"Are you a police woman?" a girl asked.

"No, honey, I'm a sheriff," Jane said.

"Is somebody in trouble?" the girl said.

"No, sweetheart, nobody is in trouble."

Regan emerged wearing a white tee shirt that came past her knees and holding Molly in her arms. "This is my little girl, Molly," she said.

Jane walked to me. "I need to change. Be right out," she said and entered the trailer.

"Mr. Oz, are those coals ready?" Sister Mary Martin said.

"They is," Oz said.

"Come on, people, let's empty those coolers," Regan said.

"I want a hot dog," Keri said, clinging to Regan's leg.

"Remember what I told you," Regan said.

Keri nodded.

"Okay, then," Regan said. Keri fished a hot dog from a cooler and brought it to Oz at the grill.

Jane emerged wearing a gray tee shirt that went past her knees. "I thought you got a suit," I said.

"I did," Jane said. "Under the shirt. Where's yours?"

"Be right out," I said. I went inside, put on the blue bathing suit I'd picked up in Hawaii and put on a matching tank top.

Oz was busy flipping burgers and dogs when I came out. Regan was talking with Sister Mary Martin. Jane was chatting with Father Thomas. Molly was trying to avoid being strangled by Keri.

By the time we finished eating, the sun was high and hot, and we took the group down to the beach where they played in the sand. A dozen or more surfers in black wetsuits bobbed in the water and rode soft waves.

I carried five folding chairs and spread them out on the sand. Sister Mary Martin and Regan and the kids played at the water's edge. Oz stayed behind to clean up and get things ready for the ice cream party to follow.

While we kept an eye on the kids, I filled Jane in on the latest developments with Wally and Sample Iced Tea.

"Will he pass the evaluation?" Jane asked.

I looked past her to Father Thomas. "Ask him."

"Wally has a very good chance of passing the evaluation and meeting the contingencies of his father's will," Father Thomas said. "Although I'm afraid the battle will only have begun once the will is contested."

"That could take years," Jane said.

"It could, I suppose," the priest said. "But Wally is still very young and believes it's worth fighting for."

Holding Keri's hand, Regan approached us. "Some of the kids want to go in the water," she said.

Sister Mary Martin and a boy were knee deep. She held the boy's hand.

Jane, Father Thomas and I stood up. I removed my tank top

195

and sunglasses and tossed them onto my chair. "Who wants to go in?" I said.

A small boy and a girl came and took my hands. A pair of boys came to Father Thomas. We led them into ankle-deep water.

I looked back at Jane. Two girls about eight years old stood in front of her. Jane sighed and pulled the long tee shirt over her head.

The racing style bathing suit Jane wore was a striking blue. She took the two girls by the hand and led them into the water.

Next to me, Regan nudged me with her elbow and nodded to the surfboarders.

Every one of them stood in waist-deep water, boards floating at their sides, their eyes glued on Jane.

"If they stare any harder their eyes will burn out of their heads," Regan said.

Slowly Jane lowered herself into the water until she was floating and gently guided the girls to float beside her.

I glanced at the surfer dudes. They hadn't moved an inch.

"It's not fair," Regan said. "It's just not fair."

Still holding Regan's hand, Keri said, "What's not fair?"

"That some people are better equipped than others for swimming," Regan said.

Around four in the afternoon we took an ice-cream break. As everybody gathered at the table, Oz and I dished out the various flavors of ice cream. Noticeably absent were Jane and Regan. I spotted them walking along the beach.

I took a dish of chocolate ice cream and a mug of coffee to my chair and sat beside Oz, who had three scoops of a vanilla/chocolate combo.

I spooned some ice cream into my mouth, washed it down with some coffee and nodded at the beach. "What's that about?"

"That be the wise older woman giving the naïve younger woman advice about boys," Oz said. "And if you be smart, which I know you ain't, but if you were, you'd never, ever mention it."

"To which one?" I asked.

Oz ate some ice cream.

"Like I said, if you be smart," he said.

Around five thirty, the gang packed up the van for the return trip to Hope Springs Eternal.

"It was a good day, Mr. Bekker," Sister Mary Martin said.

"Yes, it was."

"I was wondering if we could . . ." Father Thomas said.

"Do it again?" I said. "I don't see why not."

"Dad, I have to ride back and pick up my car," Regan said.

After the van left, Jane said, "I guess I should go change."

Oz and I took chairs and looked down at the rising tide. "A good day," Oz said.

The surfers were gearing up to ride the bigger incoming waves.

Except for one.

He wore a full-body wet suit complete with hood.

He stood out because he didn't have a surfboard.

And he was looking at me.

"Oz," I said. "Go back to your trailer."

"Why?"

"I see something I don't like."

Quietly, Oz stood and walked away.

"Jane!" I said loudly.

"What?" she said through the open trailer door.

"Don't change," I said. "Grab your backup piece and come out here."

A minute or so passed and then Jane emerged wearing the

long tee shirt. She took Oz's vacant chair.

"What's your backup piece?" I said.

"Sig .380, and why do I need it?"

"There's a guy down by the water I don't like the looks of," I said.

Jane focused on the surfers. "Full face mask, no surfboard?"

"Yeah. Let's take a walk."

Jane reached for the beach shoes she'd brought and I said, "Stay barefoot."

We stood up.

"Let's go right toward town and then double back," I said.

We started walking and I held out my right hand. "Give me your hand."

Jane extended her left hand and we came together.

We walked the five hundred or so feet to the water's edge and continued walking on a path as if headed to town.

"He watched us, but didn't budge," Jane said.

"I saw him."

Jane's hand was warm and firm in mine.

"Make like you're picking up a shell," I said.

Jane released my hand and bent over. I turned slightly and stole a glance backward.

Surfer Boy was looking in our direction, but had yet to move.

Jane stood up. I took her hand again and turned us around, and we started walking toward Surfer Boy.

"Grab some shells so we have a reason to stop," I said.

Every twenty feet or so we stopped to pick up a few shells. As we neared Surfer Boy he suddenly came out of the water and started walking away from us.

"He's nervous," Jane said.

"Let's see just how nervous."

We continued walking, stopping every twenty feet to grab a

shell, and as we grew closer Surfer Boy walked faster away from us.

"The beach goes on for two towns," Jane said. "How far are we going to take this?"

"Let him get a big lead," I said.

We continued walking until we reached the spot where Surfer Boy had been in the water. He was now a thousand feet down the beach and quickly widening the gap.

"That's enough," I said.

We walked swiftly back to the trailer.

"Grab your regular piece," I said. "We'll take my car."

"Should I change?"

"No time."

Jane and I sat in my Marquis in the municipal parking lot and waited. I parked in the rear so we could see every car enter and leave and who came and went.

Jane wore her beach shoes, and her gun belt around the tee shirt only made her ample figure appear even more ample. I had tossed on running shoes.

We sat in silence and watched the beach entrance.

After a while, Jane said, "Bekker."

"I see him. Grab the camera from the glove box."

Jane opened the box and removed the small digital camera I kept for just such situations as this one.

"Your cell phone takes photos, you know," she said.

"I never figured out how to do that," I said. "Or send a text."

Surfer Boy stepped off the beach and walked toward the parking lot. He'd removed the mask and I could see his face clearly. He was no more than twenty-five or so, clean-shaven, with broad features.

"Look busy," Jane said.

"What does that . . . ?" I said.

Jane slid over and sat on my lap, and tilted her head toward me while peering through the camera viewer.

"Hold still," she said.

"Like I have a choice."

"Shut up. I'm not that heavy."

Surfer Boy walked to his car. Jane snapped off a half-dozen or more pictures. He got into a tan Ford sedan and she took several shots of the car and license plate.

"New York State tag," she said as the Ford drove off the lot. "There he goes." She tossed the camera onto the seat.

"Can we download those pictures?" I said.

Jane looked at me.

I looked at Jane.

"What?" I said.

She shook her head. "Nothing. Let's go," she said and returned to her seat.

"Is there . . . ?" I said.

"No," Jane said. "Let's go look at those pictures."

CHAPTER TWENTY-EIGHT

"Back there in the car, I thought about kissing you," Jane said.

"I know," I said.

"My marriage ended years ago and I don't even know where the idiot is living," Jane said.

"I know."

"That said, it wasn't the first time I thought about kissing you."

"That I didn't know," I said.

"You don't know a lot," Jane said.

"This is true."

We were in Jane's office, where she had attached my camera to her desktop computer to download the photographs.

After we returned to the trailer, Jane had changed into her uniform. I tossed on a light-blue warm-up suit and followed her in my car to her office.

I could see the photos start to download on the computer screen.

"Question is, will it actually happen?" Jane said.

"Will what actually . . . ?"

There was a knock on the door. It opened and a deputy stuck his head in. "Jane, do . . . ?" he said.

"What the fuck do you want?" Jane said. "I'm busy."

"The manpower reports for next week," the deputy said. "Do you want them or should . . ."

"On my desk," Jane said.

The deputy cautiously entered the office and gently placed the file on the desk.

"Anything else?" Jane asked.

"No."

"Bye," Jane said. The deputy hurried out and closed the door. Jane looked at me. "You didn't answer my question."

"What question?"

"Will it actually happen or was today just a freak occurrence?"

"If it happens at all is always up to the woman," I said. "I don't know much, but I know that. If I have a choice, I choose yes."

"Lucky for you I have no use for sweet talk," Jane said.

"Let me get over being stunned before I start any sweet talk."

"I can just imagine your sweet talk."

I glanced at the computer. "Photos have downloaded."

Jane sat behind her desk and I stood beside her. We looked at the pictures of Surfer Boy's face and the Ford.

"Who the hell is this guy?" Jane said.

"Get a close-up on the tag and let's find out."

Jane entered the New York State tag number into her databank and looked at me. "We have some time to kill if you want to run across the street for some really bad coffee?"

"Sure."

On the way out Jane stopped at the watch commander's desk, where a corporal was on duty. "Be back in twenty minutes," she said. "I locked my office."

The deputy nodded.

"I didn't see you lock your office," I said.

Jane sipped her coffee. "I know, and if I find it locked when we get back I'll know those sissies I employ as deputies were snooping."

I sampled my coffee. It was one step below awful and slightly above terrible.

"This may sound a bit silly, but I'd like to have you come over to my house for dinner," Jane said. "It's been a while since I've really cooked a meal."

"Sure."

Jane nodded. "Tomorrow night okay?"

"Yes."

"Make it seven," Jane said. "So, about this surfer boy?"

"My guess is the Sample family hired him to keep an eye on me hoping I'd lead them to Wally."

"About how I see it. What are you going to do about it?"

"I'm not sure. I'll discuss it with Kagan tomorrow morning."

"Let's find out who Surfer Boy is first so you have something to discuss," Jane said.

"Dale Chase," Jane said. "Age listed as twenty-four. Residence in White Plains. Clean driving and arrest record. That's it."

"That's enough," I said. "Can I get a copy?"

Jane printed a copy for me. I folded it and tucked it into a pocket of the warm-up jacket.

"I gotta go," I said. "Regan doesn't . . ."

"Yeah," Jane said.

I reached for the door.

"Hey, Bekker?"

I turned around. "Yeah?"

"Let's keep the dinner between us for now."

"Sure."

"Where've you been?" Regan said when I entered the trailer. She was watching TV. Some show about bearded guys and duck calls. Molly was on her lap.

I sat next to her. "Working."

"The Wally thing?"

I nodded.

"Jane left her suit in the bathroom."

"I'll get it back to her."

"Thank you for today, Dad," Regan said. "The kids were so excited it's all they talked about on the ride back."

"Good," I said. "We'll do it again. Now about this pug?"

"She won't weigh more than twelve to fifteen pounds."

"I didn't ask what she weighed."

"I really like working at the center, Dad," Regan said. "The kids love Molly, but not all of them. I thought a small dog would . . ."

"Use the pug as a therapy dog?" I said.

"Sort of."

"Good idea," I said and kissed Regan on the nose. I looked at the TV. "I didn't know you liked duck hunting."

Chapter Twenty-Nine

I wore a lightweight, gray suit minus a tie to Kagan's office in the morning. Kagan, as usual, was impeccably dressed in a pin-striped suit with a pale-red tie.

"John Bekker, this is Grant Huber," Kagan said. "Grant is a financial planner and stockbroker with a seat on Wall Street. He's been with me for fifteen years."

Huber couldn't have been more than forty years old. "Mr. Kagan was one of my first clients when I was just starting out," he said, as if reading my thoughts.

"What can you tell me about Sample Iced Tea?" I asked.

"When Frank called me last Friday and asked me to look into it, I did some checking over the weekend," Huber said.

"Let's sit at the table," Kagan suggested.

There was a file on the table, a ceramic coffee pot, three cups and a creamer. Huber took the chair in front of the file. I sat opposite him. Kagan filled three cups with coffee and sat on Huber's left.

I sipped and said, "So what did you find out?"

"It's as Frank said; the stock is falling and shows no signs of an upswing anytime soon," Huber said.

"Why is that?" I asked and sipped some more.

"An analysis of the company," Huber said. "Brokers analyze reports and make recommendations based upon findings. In the case of Sample Iced Tea, it appears on paper that the company lacks leadership and direction since Robert Sample passed away ten years ago."

"Two billion in sales?" I said.

"Means very little if the infrastructure is falling apart. Some of the car companies in Detroit that took bailouts had billions in sales," Huber said. "Sample's logistics are outdated for one thing. Marketing and research have fallen behind as well. The word is the board of directors might vote out Robert Sample Junior as CEO next year if things don't turn around soon."

"Can they vote out an owner?" I said.

"He wouldn't be the first. Remember those ice-cream guys in New England and the men's-clothing-store guy always on TV?"

I nodded.

"Sales remain strong, which is keeping the company afloat and the board silent for the moment, but the falling stock is the tip of the iceberg if there isn't a reasonable improvement," Huber said.

"And you know this from reading reports?" I said.

"It's how it works," Huber said. "Inside information is illegal, but a good analysis can be made from reading public reports and right now the reports aren't good. Hence the falling stock."

"Hence," I said.

"Need anything else?" Huber said.

"Yeah," I said. "Someone to manage my money. Can I come see you in about a month or so?"

Huber gave me his business card. "New clients are always welcome."

After Huber left, I sat with Kagan and had a second cup of coffee while I told him about Dale Chase.

"Do you think the Samples know where Wally is?" Kagan asked.

"If they did they wouldn't be spying on me," I said.

"I suppose," Kagan said. "With court in nine days what difference does it make to them if they know where he is or not?"

"Maybe they think if they talk to him before court they can convince him to take their deal?"

"What about all the other stuff?"

"Working on it," I said. "With or without Wally, somebody will have to answer for murder."

"I'm heading over to talk to Wally, want to tag along?"

"Why not?"

Kagan spoke with Wally and Father Thomas at length in the priest's office. Kagan talked Father Thomas through the process of writing his opinion for the judge and coaxed him on what and what not to say while on the stand.

Wally and I took a walk through the gardens.

"Something I've been meaning to ask you," I said. "Do you really want to become part of an organization that doesn't want you?"

"Are you saying I should take the money and run?" Wally said.

"No. I'm asking how you feel on the matter."

We stopped walking beside the lily pond and Wally looked up at me.

"I know what people think of me," he said. "Loser with a capital *L*, and maybe that's true; I don't know. I do know that it doesn't have to be true given the opportunity, and who are they to tell me no, I shouldn't have that opportunity? Who are they to tell me no. He was my father, too, and they don't have the right."

"Maybe they don't have the right but they have the power," I said.

"I told you, I'm not quitting."

"Even if it drags on for years and years."

"Even then."

"Can you convince a judge that you're worthy of the chance?" I said.

"I'm sure I can if I have my day in court."

"Let's go back and talk to Kagan."

"Bekker, we're just about done," Kagan said when we returned to the office.

"Will Wally be allowed to take the stand in his own behalf?" I said.

"If necessary," Kagan said. "I'm hoping to convince the court it won't be necessary after he takes the psychiatric exam from the court-appointed psychiatrist and they take Father Thomas's reports and testimony into account."

"Maybe you should run through a line of questioning with Wally to prepare him just in case?"

Kagan looked at Wally. "Are you up for that?"

Wally nodded.

"Let's do a run-through of questions tomorrow morning," Kagan said. "Okay with you, Father?"

Father Thomas looked at Wally.

Wally nodded.

"I'll be here at ten," Kagan said.

I was back at the trailer by two. I decided to go for a run and grab a workout afterward. As I ran I let my thoughts free-fall and land where they may.

Dale Chase, a resident of White Plains, turned up in my front yard a few days after I told the Sample clan Wally rejected their offer.

Sample Iced Tea was headquartered in White Plains.

Barbara Sample, VP of Finance, was playing patty-cake with head of security, Mike Fuddy.

Barbara was outspoken and less sensitive than her siblings

when it came to her little brother Wally.

Mike Fuddy was a violent ex-cop.

At Barbara's request, would Fuddy hire Chase to spy on me hoping I would lead him to Wally?

How far were the Samples as a group willing to go to keep Wally from collecting his one-sixth controlling interest in the company?

Murder.

That's how far.

One attempt on Wally's life killed his friend by mistake. Would they try again knowing that the police were now involved and they could wind up on the other end of the stick?

Funny thing about truly wealthy people: they always believe they're smarter than everyone else including the police and will never get caught by an inferior intellect. Very often they're right, and even when they do get caught they have the money to buy the best lawyers to defend them.

Fuddy was strong-arm all the way. I doubted that as chief of security he was of much use to the company on a corporate level. Why employ a man like him at all? His strength was in intimidation and muscle, and while that could be useful working at the docks I didn't exactly see the necessity of it at a company that made thirty flavors of iced tea.

My guess was that Barbara persuaded Fuddy to get rid of Wally before the court date. Fuddy recruited Roper who, believing Wally was occupying his home, blew up the wrong man.

I suddenly realized that I'd meant to run three miles out before I turned around and I'd run four. I made a U-turn and headed back.

My thoughts turned to Jane.

I like to think of myself as an honest man. Truth be told, Janet and I were not a good fit. I don't want to and can't change as much as she wanted me to and she wants somebody I am not.

The marriage could have worked for a while. Then the strain would have stretched it until it broke at the seams.

I've always found women confusing and difficult to figure out. Even my wife, Carol. You'd think that being married to someone for eleven years, you'd get to know their thought patterns on certain things, but you'd be wrong. I was much better at figuring out a crime than what Carol really wanted for her birthday or Christmas or even dinner on a night out.

I've known Jane twenty years or more. She is the least pretentious person I know. What you see in Jane is exactly what you get. But, as a friend and colleague. Relationships on a personal level tend to change things.

I was five hundred yards from the trailer and could see Walt's sedan parked beside the Marquis. He was seated in a chair beside Oz.

I broke out of a jog and into a run, and arrived at the trailer drenched in sweat.

"You want a towel or you just gonna shake off like a wet dog?" Oz said.

I flopped into my chair.

"I spoke with Jackman a little while ago," Walt said. "He said to tell you the arson squad found what they believe to be an igniter from a high-end barbeque grill in the rubble."

I nodded and wiped sweat from my eyes.

"I couldn't make one of those," Walt said. "Could you?"

"No, but I'm not a professional arsonist."

"Where do they learn this shit?"

"Have you tried searching Google?" I asked. "You can Google blueprints for a nuclear bomb."

Walt looked at me and I knew that later he would try it.

"Where's Regan?" I asked.

"At the school," Oz said.

I nodded again and glanced at my cell phone on the table. There was a message from Paul Lawrence. "Give me a second," I said.

I punched in the number. For once, Lawrence answered his own line.

"Jack, we found your arsonist Adam Roper," he said.

I swallowed hard. "Where?"

"Some kids playing at the landfill in Newark found him buried in a mountain of sand," Lawrence said. "They saw what they thought was a finger poking out and started digging."

"Shit," I said. "Cause of death?"

"M.E. is working on it, but preliminary reports look like he was beaten to death."

"That's two," I said. "Both connected to Sample and Fuddy. They say things come in threes."

"What aren't you telling me, Jack?"

"We had a beach outing for some of the kids from Regan's old hospital," I said. "There was a man spying on us from the water. Jane and I tailed him and he fled. We traced his tags to White Plains. Name is Dale Chase. He's a kid of twenty-four."

"I'll see what I can find out," Lawrence said. "Jack, you watch your ass."

"Yeah."

"What's the tag?" Lawrence asked.

I told him and he hung up.

I set the phone aside and looked at Walt.

"Were you saving that one for my birthday gift?" Walt said.

"It happened late yesterday," I said. "I was going to tell you as soon as I ran it down and had something to tell."

"What's going on?" Oz asked.

"Is the house ready to move in?" I said.

211

"Power on, phones in, cable working, all except the alarm installed."

"I'd like you and Regan to go there tonight and stay there," I said. "It's home, you might as well live there."

Oz glared at me. "Hide out there is what you mean," he said.

"Oz, I . . ."

"Six months ago she got beat up by the psycho hit man and now this new asshole," he said. "How many times you gonna put her in danger before you quit trying to be Dick friggin' Tracy?"

"You can yell at me later when this is finished," I said. "Right now I need you to do this for me."

"I was twenty years younger, thirty pounds heavier and I knew how to fight, I'd kick your ass," Oz said.

"Kick it later," I said. "Go pack and take my shotgun, but don't let her see it."

"And what are you gonna do?" Oz said.

"What time will Regan be home?"

Oz looked at his watch. "Half hour."

"I'll talk to her," I said.

Oz stood up. "Get me the shotgun."

I retrieved the shotgun and a box of shells from my safe and gave them to Oz. He carried them to his trailer.

"He's right, you know," Walt said.

"No, he isn't because he's never been a cop," I said. "You've been a cop almost thirty years and raised a family. Did you once quit because some bad guy put you in danger? If that were the case, there would be no cops and nothing but bad guys. Why is it different for you and not me?"

"Fuck you," Walt said.

"Fuck you, too," I said.

"Asshole."

"Dick."

"Fuck you."

"You said that already. Are you going to help me or not."

"You need to ask?"

"No. Follow Regan and Oz to the new place and check it before you let them go inside," I said.

Walt nodded. "It's county so I can't have a car swing by overnight."

"I know. I'll ask Jane."

Walt looked down the beach toward town. "Car's coming," he said.

"That's Regan."

"Take everything you need because you're not coming back here until I say it's safe," I said.

"For crying out loud, Dad," Regan said.

"The court hearing is in nine days," I said. "This is just a precaution, that's all."

"You said that last time, and I got the snot beat out of me and Aunt Janet wound up in the hospital," Regan said.

I looked at Walt.

"She has a point," Walt said.

"You're no help," I said.

"And while Oz and I are in hiding, what are you doing?" Regan said.

"What I signed on to do," I said. "Get Wally to court in one piece and then the job is over. Okay?"

Regan nodded. "I'll go pack."

Regan gave me a hug and kiss and then stepped back and looked up at me.

"I need a dad, you know," she said.

"I'll be fine," I said. "Walt will follow you and Oz and check the house. I'll call you later, okay?"

Regan nodded. She opened her car door where Molly was asleep in back and got behind the wheel. Oz was already in his car and took the lead. Regan followed.

I looked at Walt.

"I got your back, asshole," he said. "You watch your front."

Walt got into his car and followed Oz. I sat in my chair and called Jane.

"Change of plans," I said. "Can you come here?"

"The beach?"

"Yes."

"On duty or off?"

"A little bit of both," I said.

"Should I bring food?"

"That might not be a bad idea."

CHAPTER THIRTY

Jane is Irish and as fair-skinned as they come. In summer months there's just a hint of freckles on her face. Her usual complexion is just short of milk. When she laughs her cheeks turn a light pink. When she's angry her nostrils flare and her cheeks and neck glow red. I've picked up on those little traits over the years so I can read her mood most of the time.

We sat at the table and as I gave her the update, her cheeks glowed a deep red and her blue eyes seemed to turn a light shade of green.

When I was done, she pulled out a soft pack of cigarettes and lit one. "Fuck this guy," she said as she exhaled smoke through her nose.

She pulled out her cell phone and punched in a number. "How many cars on patrol tonight?" After a moment, she said, "I want one car to swing by for a security check at the Hope Springs Eternal complex and another at this address."

She looked at me. I gave her the address to the new home.

She repeated it and then said, "Anything unusual at all gets looked at. Call me immediately on my cell number if something breaks." She hung up and looked at me. "Okay?"

I nodded.

"What do you think the life expectancy of that asshole on the beach is right now?"

"Chase? Depends on his connections, but things come in threes, right?"

215

The sun was down and a cool breeze was blowing in off the ocean. "Let's talk inside," Jane said.

She had a suitcase of emergency clothing in the trunk of her cruiser as all experienced cops do. I grabbed it while Jane carried a bag of groceries and we went inside.

We sat at the tiny kitchen table. I filled two mugs with coffee. Jane lit another cigarette.

"I'm not a pour-my-heart-out kind of woman, Bekker, but I am an honest woman," she said. "My tolerance for bullshit is very low, but you know that already. We've known each other a long time and I've always suspected there was a spark between us there in the background. It stayed in the background all this time because the time was just never right for us. Is it now?"

"Are you asking if it's really over between me and Janet?"

"Yes."

"It's over."

"I won't put up with lies and bullshit, not even from you."

"It's over."

Jane sipped coffee and inhaled on her cigarette.

"So who do you suspect is the bad guy in this Sample thing?" she said. "Is what's-his-face Fuddy capable of murder? Are the five Sample siblings capable of asking him to commit it, or is there an outside source that we don't know about controlling things?"

"Fuddy is the genuine article," I said. "A toughie with a bad attitude and I suspect he's murdered before, if not for money then out of anger or even pleasure."

"As tough as you?"

"No, but close."

"So, with billions on the line and no desire to add a sixth Sample into the controlling mix, it's possible they put their little heads together with Fuddy and offered him some incentive to remove Wally from the scene?"

"More than possible," I said. "As Fuddy is already shacking up with Barbara Sample, sex isn't a motivator for him. It has to be a payoff and a big one."

"It always comes down to money, doesn't it," Jane said. "In one form or another."

"It heads the list," I said. "Followed by sex, revenge and power."

Jane stood up and put her cigarette out in the sink. She tossed the butt into the trash can, turned and looked at me.

"I'm not ready yet for . . ." she said.

I looked at her. "Doing it?"

"You sweet talker, you," she said.

"It comes natural," I said.

"Is what you call a shower in there safe?"

"If by *safe* you mean is someone going to stab you through the curtain while you're washing your hair, yes, it's safe," I said. "Just don't lift the drain while you're in it or you might let the rats in."

"Cute," Jane said and left the kitchen.

I drank some more coffee and thought about Wally while Jane took a shower. After a while, she came into the tiny kitchen wearing a knee-length gray tee shirt and white socks.

"I guess there's no need to tell you I weigh a bit more than the one-thirty-five I've been claiming for years," she said and took a chair at the table.

"Does it matter?" I said.

"No. Do you want to check on the house?"

"It couldn't hurt."

Jane picked up her cell phone and dialed a number. When her deputy answered, she said, "It's Jane; anything to report?"

She listened for a moment, and then hung up. "All is quiet on the western front," she said.

"Want to turn in?" I asked. "You get Regan's bed."

Just after two in the morning, I awoke when Jane crept into my bedroom and crawled into bed next to me.

"Bekker, are you awake?" she whispered.

"I am now," I said.

"This isn't a sex thing," Jane said. "I can't sleep in Regan's tiny bed. I keep falling out."

"Sure."

"Are you okay with that?"

"Fine."

"Just so you know, I toss a lot," Jane said.

"So you could punch me in the eye in your sleep?"

"Possible," Jane said. "More likely is you may wake up with me hugging you."

"Also fine," I said. "However, I won't wake up at all unless you let me go back to sleep."

"Is there anything weird you do in your sleep, like snore?"

"No, I don't snore, but I have been known to wet the bed from time to time."

"Oh, shut up."

CHAPTER THIRTY-ONE

We watched the sun come up from the table in front of the trailer. Jane smoked a cigarette to go with her coffee. I fought the urge to beg one from her pack and drank my coffee solo.

I wore my blue warm-up suit. Jane tossed on a robe I forgot I had.

"I have to go to work," she said.

I nodded and sipped.

"That wasn't so bad just sleeping, was it?"

"Just sleeping is good," I said. "I try to do it at least once a night."

"You know what I mean."

"If by *you know what I mean,* you mean do I believe in the caveman adage that a man should take a test drive before entering into a relationship first, no, I don't," I said. "And if I did believe that and something did happen, only an idiot would think it was the man's choice in the matter."

Jane glanced at me. "Sometimes you're smarter than you look," she said.

"I'll take that as a compliment," I said. "Want some breakfast before you go?"

I worked the heavy bag and tried to keep my mind free, but my mind had a mind of its own.

As I pounded the bag with stiff jabs and right hooks, images of Jane kept running through my thoughts like a winding river.

She was like a coiled snake that could unleash tremendous power at a moment's notice. I've witnessed her take down three bad guys in the blink of an eye because they underestimated her, a mistake I would never make.

I attacked the bag with combinations, right and left hooks and jabs until my shoulders ached and I couldn't throw one more punch.

I removed the bag gloves and dropped to the elevated push-up station. Somewhere around the twenty-fifth push-up I lost count as Jane crept back into my thoughts.

The budding relationship between us had roots going back a very long time, even if I'd never admitted it, even to myself. I chose to bury it for various reasons. Those reasons no longer existed. However, my limited track record with women was not very good, to say the least.

Horrible at best.

The last push-up, around one hundred and fifty, had me glued to the ground.

I stood up and toweled off and then did some pull-ups, and finished off with ten minutes with the weighted jump rope. Then I went inside for a mug of coffee and a towel and took my seat outside. I checked my cell phone. There was a message from Kagan's office. He must have wanted to give me an update on how it went with Wally's coaching.

I punched in the number.

"John Bekker for Mr. Kagan," I said.

"Mr. Bekker, Mr. Kagan is in the hospital," the receptionist said, flustered.

"Why? What happened?"

"He was beaten."

"What hospital?"

"County. It's the closest to the office."

"Did he say what happened?"

"He can't say anything. He's unconscious."

"I'm on my way."

I set the phone down and then picked it up again and punched in the number for Jane's cell phone.

She answered on the third ring. "Bekker, what's . . . ?"

"Frank Kagan was beat up last night," I said. "Who took the report?"

"Hold on."

I held for five minutes.

"Deputy Spears," Jane said. "We had thirty calls last night. None at your house or the hospital complex, so my people didn't notify me."

"I'm going to the hospital," I said.

"I'll get Spears out of bed and meet you there."

The attending physician in the ICU met with me in the waiting room down the hall from Kagan's room. "I'm afraid he's still unconscious," the doctor said.

"Do you know what happened?"

"He was brought here by ambulance at ten thirty last night," the doctor said. "A sheriff's deputy was called to the rear parking lot of Mr. Kagan's office building when a teenage couple was looking for a dark spot to make out in and they saw him on the ground."

"Mugged?"

"There are a thousand dollars and seven credit cards in his wallet."

"Can I see him?"

I followed the doctor to Kagan's room, where he was wired to machines and an IV bottle. Every few seconds one of the machines would register something and blip.

I looked at the doctor. "There's not a mark on his face," I said.

"I didn't say there was," the doctor said. "He was severely beaten in the stomach, kidneys, back and ribs. He's suffered internal damage and bleeding, and he'll probably be out for at least another twelve to twenty-four hours."

"I'm waiting for the sheriff and a deputy," I said. "Okay if I wait here?"

"Don't disturb him and when they arrive, please talk in the waiting room."

The doctor left and I moved a bit closer to the bed. Kagan's face was partially blocked by the oxygen mask, but even close up I couldn't find so much as a scratch on it.

I turned and looked out the window at the view seven floors below. I spotted a cruiser turn into the visitors' parking lot and disappear underground.

I went out to the hallway to wait for Jane.

Janet came off the elevator. She turned down the hall and walked directly to me. "One of the girls spotted you in the lobby," she said. "You're not here for you or Regan, I hope?"

"Frank Kagan," I said.

"That mob lawyer."

"Civil, not criminal."

"Why is he here?"

"He was beaten unconscious."

"Is he going to be all right? What did the doctor say?"

"Internal damage and bleeding," I said. "He expects him to wake up sometime tonight or tomorrow."

"So, you don't know what happened?"

"No."

Janet nodded. "So, how are you?"

"Fine. The house is ours. Regan has a part-time job working for Sister Mary Martin three days a week."

"That's wonderful," Janet said. "Mark misses her a lot. Maybe he can stay over sometime?"

"As much as he wants."

She was silent for a moment. She looked down at the floor for a split second and then looked at me.

"Jack, about everything that's happened," she said.

The elevator binged and Jane and Deputy Spears got out.

"Calamity Jane is here," Janet said.

Jane and Spears walked to us.

"Hello, Jane," Janet said.

Jane nodded. "Janet."

"Well, I hope Mr. Kagan recovers soon," Janet said. "I have to return to my floor."

She walked to the exit door before the elevator, opened it and left the floor.

"Kagan's room?" Jane said.

I opened the door and we entered.

"There's not a mark on him," Jane said.

"From the neck up," I said.

"A pro worked him over."

"Looks like," I said. "Let's talk in the waiting room."

We went down the hall. There were chairs for twelve in the waiting room, but we were the only occupants.

Jane looked at Spears. "Go over it again."

"Nine thirty last night a call came through that there was an unconscious man in the parking lot of an office building," Spears said. "I thought it might be just another drunk who fell, but I could see right off by the suit he wore it wasn't. I called for an ambulance to take him to the hospital."

"Did you check the lot for evidence?" I said.

"As best I could in the dark, but there was nothing to see," Spears said. "I didn't even find any traces of blood on the ground."

"Okay, take the cruiser back to the office," Jane said. "I'll get a ride from Bekker."

Spears left the waiting room.

"Let's grab some coffee in the cafeteria," I said. "I need to make some calls."

While Jane grabbed two cups of coffee from the serving line, I called Walt at the station and told him about Kagan.

"You were right to have Regan and Oz go to the new place," Walt said. "This is getting messy."

"It's going to get messier the closer we come to the court date," I said.

Jane arrived with the coffee and took a seat.

"Only now it looks like we don't have a lawyer," I said.

"What happens when all Kagan's mob buddies find out he was attacked?" Walt said. "They consider him one of their own. They won't let this pass without payback."

"I thought of that," I said. "We won't let it be known for now. The last thing we need is a bunch of wise guys in the mix, especially since all we have for evidence is a paper-thin paper trail that's circumstantial at best."

"When's the hearing?"

"Seven days."

"Not much time to find a pinch hitter."

"No."

"Keep me posted."

"Yeah."

I set the phone down and took a sip from my cup.

"How much expense money do you have?" Jane said.

"As much as I need."

"I can have off-duty people do a special detail at the complex and your house," Jane said.

"Do it." I grabbed my phone and called Paul Lawrence.

"It took some rule bending, but guess where this Dale Chase works and goes to school?" Lawrence said.

"I'll guess if you guess who got beat up and is in the hospital unconscious," I said.

"Who?"

"Frank Kagan."

"Shit," Lawrence said. "Is it related? With these mob lawyers you never know."

"A week before the hearing where Kagan was planning an all-out frontal assault, what do you think?"

"I think you're right," Lawrence said. "Chase is enrolled in Pace University in White Plains and works part time as a security guard at Sample Iced Tea."

"That makes his boss Mike Fuddy," I said.

"I think it's time me and some of the boys took charge of this," Lawrence said. "We need to find evidence that links Sample Iced Tea to two murders and a beat-down that isn't circumstantial."

"Can it wait until after Wally's hearing?"

"When?"

"One week."

"I do what I can from here until after the hearing," Lawrence said. "Then this little shop of horrors goes to Justice and I run with it, and that includes an independent internal audit of the Sample books."

"Agreed," I said.

Jane looked at me as I hung up and reached for my coffee. "I got the gist of it," she said.

I sipped and set the cup aside. "It could work," I said.

"What?"

I grabbed the phone and searched the memory log, then hit redial.

A stuffy male voice answered. "Crist residence."

"John Bekker for Campbell Crist," I said.

"The ladies are out at the moment."

225

"Tell either to call John Bekker right away," I said.

"They aren't expected back before dinner."

"That's fine. Take down my number."

I set the phone down and looked at Jane.

"Carly Simms filling in for Frank Kagan," Jane said. "Think she'll do it?"

"She'll do it," I said. "Simms never met a challenge she backed down from."

Jane nodded. "So what did Janet have to say?"

"Nothing. Let's check on Kagan."

We returned to Kagan's room and spoke briefly with the doctor. I left him my cell and asked to be called when Kagan awoke.

I drove Jane to her office. "What do you think if we took your cruiser to see Wally and then to my house?" I said. "We could have the off-duty deputies follow in their cars."

"I'll set it up," Jane said. She used her cell phone to call her office and spoke with the watch commander.

"Done," she said after she hung up. "Twenty-eight an hour for each special detail for an eight-hour shift."

"Make it a ten-hour shift," I said.

"Who first?"

"My house is closer."

We arrived at the municipal building and I parked beside Jane's cruiser. "As soon as they arrive we'll head out," she said. "In the meantime, sit tight."

While Jane went inside, I called Father Thomas and explained what happened and what my plan was for a deputy.

"Will he recover?" he said.

"They didn't want him dead. Just out of commission for a while," I said. "That's why no head shots. He'll recover but not in time for the hearing."

"What will we do? Wally needs a lawyer to represent him in court."

"I know. I have an idea. I'll see you in a little while."

I spotted Jane and two male deputies in full uniform walking to my car. I got out and met them at Jane's cruiser.

"Deputy Price and Deputy Robertson," Jane said.

Price looked like a kid of around twenty-three. Robertson seemed like a veteran.

"Price takes your house, Robertson, the hospital," Jane said. "They'll follow in my cruiser."

The drive to my house took about forty minutes. "He's kind of young," I said.

"Price?"

I nodded.

"He's twenty-four and has three years in. He's been in the National Guard for six years and drives a tank. I think he can do the job."

"He looks like a twelve-year-old Brad Pitt," I said.

"He does, doesn't he?" Jane said.

I looked at Jane and she grinned at me.

"Again with this," Regan said. "Dad, we're trying to build a home here for us. How can we do that if every time I turn around you turn the place into a shooting gallery?"

"It's not a . . . this is just a precaution," I said. "It's better to have and not need than to need and not have. Oz, explain it to her."

"Your daddy not as stupid as he looks," Oz said.

"Not helping, Oz," I said.

"So we have to have some stranger sleeping on the sofa every night?" Regan said.

"He better not be sleeping," Jane said.

"Can he stay out of the way?" Regan asked.

"As much as possible," Jane said.

"Do we have to feed him?"

"Just a little water and face him toward the sun," I said.

"All right, where is he?" Regan said.

Jane opened the front door. "Deputy Price."

And in walked young Brad Pitt. Behind me I heard Regan produce a sound very much like a soft gasp.

"Deputy Price, this is Regan, Bekker's daughter, and their friend Oz," Jane said.

"Hello," Price said.

I looked at my daughter. Her mouth was open. Her eyes were locked on Price.

"I'll take you on a tour of the house and show you all the doors, locks and windows," I said.

"I'll do that," Regan said.

She took Price by the arm and guided him to the kitchen.

"How come we never get a hot female deputy around fifty years old?" Oz said.

"You did this on purpose," I said to Jane.

"You asked for a special detail and that's what I delivered," Jane said.

"Seem reasonable to me," Oz said.

After about five minutes Regan and Price returned. Regan still had her arm linked with his. "That took long enough," I said.

"Be quiet, Bekker," Jane said.

"It's a simple enough setup," Price said. "Don't worry, Mr. Bekker. We'll be fine. I'll take good care of your daughter."

"That's not . . ." I said.

Jane grabbed my arm. "Let's go, Bekker."

I nodded. On the way out I heard Regan say to Price, "So what would you like for dinner?"

I was about to turn around when Jane yanked me out the door.

★ ★ ★ ★ ★

"Would you relax?" Jane said as she drove us to see Father Thomas. "Nineteen-year-old girls go through crushes every five minutes."

"Emotionally Regan is still thirteen," I said.

"So are you and look how well you've done," Jane said.

I was about to reply with a snappy comeback when my cell phone rang. I checked the incoming number and then said, "Campbell, John Bekker."

"Our house manager called and said you're trying to get in touch with us," Campbell said. "We're in the car."

"I need Carly, actually," I said. "I need a lawyer to fill in for Frank Kagan. He was beaten and is hospitalized and . . ."

"Frank Kagan," Campbell said. "How badly?"

"Bad enough, but I think he'll recover," I said. "Can I talk to Simms?"

"Let me put the call on speaker and you can fill us in."

There was a second or so of silence and then Carly Simms said, "Hi, Bekker, it's been a while."

"I need your help," I said. "Let me fill you in and then tell me what you think."

I took about ten minutes to explain the situation and did my best to ignore the cigarette Jane had lit up.

"All I've done is a few accident cases and assist in criminal research since moving to Florida," Simms said. "I don't think I can . . ."

"She'll do it. We'll be there tomorrow," Campbell said.

"Who's the lawyer here?" Simms said.

"I'll pick you up at the airport," I said. "Call me later with the flight number."

"I didn't say I would . . ." Simms said.

"Tootles," Campbell said and hung up.

I stuck the phone back into my pocket and looked at Jane.

"She'll do it," I said.

"I'm very sorry to hear about Mr. Kagan," Father Thomas said. "We will pray for him at evening mass tonight."

"How badly is he hurt?" Wally asked.

"Pretty banged up," I said. "He'll recover, I'm sure, but not in time for court."

"So, what do we do now?" Father Thomas said.

"Maybe I should take the deal and just go away," Wally said.

"This has gone way beyond that now, Wally," I said. "Two men murdered, another beat up and a federal investigation is about to begin. Your best bet to help your father's company is to stay the course and win in court."

"Without Mr. Kagan?" Wally said.

"With another lawyer," I said. "Someone I trust."

"Who?"

"You'll meet them tomorrow," I said. "In the meantime go over all the preparation notes Kagan gave you and be ready."

Wally nodded.

"And try not to worry," I said. "Both of you. A deputy will be on duty right outside all night."

I left the office and went outside where Jane stood against her cruiser with a cigarette dangling between her lips.

"Where's Robertson?" I said.

"Taking a swing around the complex."

"Maybe we should check on . . ."

"She's in good hands, Bekker," Jane said.

"That's what worries me."

CHAPTER THIRTY-TWO

I added a few logs to the trash-can bonfire and then took my chair next to Jane. The fire crackled loudly as tiny sparks rose up and flew away on a soft breeze. We sipped our coffee and watched the fire. Jane reached over and took my hand.

A moment or so later, her cell phone rang. She checked the number and answered the call. "Price, it's Jane," she said.

She listened for a moment and then said, "I don't have a problem with it if her father doesn't. Call him on his cell phone."

Jane hung up and looked at me.

"What don't you have a . . ." I said as my phone rang.

"John Bekker," I said.

"Mr. Bekker, Deputy Price. Regan . . . I mean, your daughter and Mr. Oz would like to know if they can go shopping for a puppy tomorrow. I get off at eight and start my regular shift, but I can drive them there and drive them home if you'd like."

"Very thoughtful of you, Deputy Price," I said. "My daughter is a very good cook, isn't she?"

"Why, yes, she is, sir," Price said.

"Goodnight, deputy," I said.

"Good night, sir."

I hung up and tossed the phone onto the card table at my side. "He's very polite, your deputy," I said.

Jane grinned at me and the glow of the fire reflected off her face. "I already told him if he even thought of getting out of line I'd remove his boys with garden shears and feed them to your

231

new puppy."

I looked at her.

"And that goes for you, too," she said.

"What does that . . . ?"

"She isn't through with you yet."

"What are . . . you mean Janet?"

"Yes, Janet. Of course Janet."

"She's marrying Clayton," I said.

"Why are all men so damn stupid?" Jane said.

"We're born that way," I said. "It only gets worse as we age."

"Joke if you want, but a woman can always tell when another woman isn't over a man," Jane said. "And she isn't over you. Yet."

"What exactly are you talking about?" I said.

Jane rolled her eyes. "Stupid," she said. "Look, before I wind up playing the role of home-wrecking, other woman, I need to know that you're over her. Otherwise, whatever the hell might be happening between us won't happen."

"I knew it was over in Hawaii when she wouldn't return my calls and then went to Chicago for a month of training and Clayton happened to spend the weekend with her," I said.

"It doesn't mean you're done with her."

"In this case it does."

"You're sure?"

"Yes."

"Good." Jane took my hand again.

The fire crackled. We were silent for a few minutes.

"Worried about Regan?" Jane asked, breaking the quiet.

"A little."

"And Wally?"

"A lot."

"Regan will be fine and you can't control the courts," Jane said.

"I just want to make sure he stays alive long enough to make it to court," I said.

"You like the little dweeb, don't you?"

"He's a real pain in the ass, but yes, I do."

"I can say the same thing about you."

"Yeah, but I'm taller."

"Speaking of dweebs, what do you think Walt would do if he saw us sitting here holding hands?"

"Probably laugh himself to death," I said.

"I'm going home before I do something I'm not ready to do yet," Jane said. "Is that okay with you?"

"I may be stupid in a lot of ways, but I'm smart enough to know, as I said before, the choice is never the man's," I said. "Even if we're dumb enough to think it is."

"There's hope for you yet, Bekker," Jane said.

I walked her to her cruiser, where our bonfire date ended with a sweet, very soft kiss before she opened her door and got behind the wheel.

"That's the preview." Jane started the engine. "The main event is yet to follow," she said, and drove away.

CHAPTER THIRTY-THREE

Campbell Crist told me their flight would arrive at ten thirty-five. It landed ten minutes early. I waited behind the gate for passengers to emerge. There was no missing these two. When a pair of tall and strikingly beautiful women, one blond, the other brunette, are holding hands and pulling carry-on luggage through an airport terminal, they get noticed.

Both wore slacks, sleeveless blouses, four-inch heels, yellow, straw sunhats and dark glasses. They had wonderful tans to complete the picture. As they passed through the gate and walked over to me, Campbell said, "Shall we make every man with a boner in this airport jealous?"

"Let's do," Simms said.

And they hugged me and kissed me on the cheek.

"Still driving that jalopy?" Campbell said.

"It gets me where I'm going," I said.

"Bekker, all you need is an old raincoat and a cigar," Simms said.

"Have any luggage?" I said.

"Everything we need is at the estate," Campbell said.

"Let's go," I said. "I'll fill you in on the way."

"This good deed doesn't go unpunished," Campbell said.

"You want a favor in return," I said. "Ask."

"We will," Simms said. "After the court date."

★ ★ ★ ★ ★

During the hour-long ride I filled the ladies in on the events from day one to this morning. They kept silent until I had finished.

Seated next to me, Simms said, "So, you finally quit smoking."

"For Regan's sake, I'm trying. What about Wally? Can you help him?"

"I didn't fly here to do him any harm," Simms said.

"Relax, Bekker," Campbell said from behind me. "So, tell us what you've been up to? How are Janet and Regan?"

"Both are fine, but Janet is back with her ex-husband," I said.

"The shoe didn't fit, huh?" Simms said.

"No."

I turned into the driveway for Hope Springs Eternal and parked in front of the office building.

"Are you coming in?" Simms said to Campbell.

"Whatever for?"

"Suit yourself," Simms said.

I escorted Simms to Father Thomas's office and made the introductions. Wally stared at her with mouth agape. "You're a lawyer?" Wally asked.

"Close your mouth, sonny boy, and have a seat," Simms said. "And to answer your question, no, I am not *a* lawyer. I am *your* lawyer. Bekker, go take Campbell to lunch or something."

I went outside and found Campbell standing beside the Marquis.

"So, this is where my father paid all those years to ease his guilt," she said.

After Regan witnessed her mother being murdered she was traumatized to the point she refused to speak and was sent to Hope Springs Eternal for the decade I jumped inside a scotch bottle. Eddie Crist, mob boss of the East Coast, believing his

235

son was responsible for the hit put out on me that led to my wife's death, paid the bill for Regan's treatment and left her a nice trust fund.

"Want to take a tour?" I said.

Campbell took my arm and we walked around the complex. We took in the gardens, the athletic field, farming fields, the school, the library, entertainment hall, dining hall and small church.

"It's quite the setup," Campbell said.

"Want some coffee?" I said.

"I could do with some."

We entered the dining hall, where lunch had just concluded but coffee was still available. I filled two cups and we took a table by the window.

"Do you know I just turned forty-three?" Campbell said.

"I didn't know. Happy birthday."

"Once a woman hits forty she hates birthdays."

"You're as striking looking as ever," I said. "Both of you ladies are."

Campbell took a small sip of coffee. "I can make one phone call to my father's friends and your problem will simply disappear," she said.

"And two murders might go unsolved in the process," I said. "Besides, the real problem is getting Wally to pass his court exam. If he's deemed unfit he won't collect his inheritance and a sixth of the company."

Campbell nodded. "So, we let Carly do her thing?"

"Yes."

"She's damn good, you know."

"I know."

"I suppose you do."

Simms was county prosecutor for ten years before she was arrested for murder a year ago. She was framed, and I helped find those responsible. Frank Kagan arranged a safe hiding place at the Crist mansion where Campbell lived after Eddie died from cancer.

"So, what happened between you and Janet?" she said.

"We weren't a good fit," I said.

"Why do women always want to change the man they want?" Campbell said. "That's what it was all about, right?"

I sipped some coffee.

"You know who I always thought was more your type is that crazy sheriff; what's her name?"

"Jane Morgan."

"That one, yes. She's nuts, you know. Just like you."

My cell phone rang. I dug it out and checked the number. "It's the hospital," I said and hit *talk*. "John Bekker."

"Mr. Bekker, this is Doctor Balfour. You asked me to call you when Mr. Kagan was awake. He's awake and is asking for you."

"Can I see him?"

"Yes."

"Tell him I'll be there shortly."

I hung up and looked at Campbell. "Frank's awake. I'm going to see him. You girls want to tag along?"

"If you're going to chauffeur us around you really must get a better car," Campbell said. "We're pretty spoiled at this point."

"He's determined to pass the psychiatric evaluation come hell or high water," Simms said. "He'll need some coaching, but there's still time for that. He'll need to show the examining psychiatrist and the judge that he is responsible and has kicked his gambling habit."

"I owe you one," I said.

"You do," Simms said.

"And we'll collect," Campbell added from behind me.

I turned off the highway and headed to the hospital. "But

you won't tell me what it is?"

"We will," Simms said. "After this is over."

Sitting up in bed, Kagan looked at Simms and Campbell at my side and said, "My good God, is that Campbell Crist and Carly Simms?"

"I was going to bring flowers," I said. "I decided on them instead."

Campbell kissed Kagan on the cheek. "How do you feel, Frank?"

"Like a truck ran me over."

"Do you remember what happened?" I said.

"Help me sit up."

I was about to lift Kagan when the ladies beat me to it. Each took an arm and gently lifted him until he was sitting up in bed.

"I worked late on touching up the Q&A for the judge," Kagan said. "I left the office around nine fifteen or so and went down to the parking lot. It was dark. I've been meaning to have lamps put in, but we rarely work after dark."

He reached for the glass of water on the table beside the bed and took a sip. "I was about to unlock my car . . ."

"Were there any other cars in the lot?" I said.

"No. I had the keys in my hand and then I felt this sharp, overpowering pain in my right kidney. Nothing like I'd ever felt before. At first I thought I'd been shot. But when I fell to my knees and looked up I saw a man standing over me. He . . ."

"Did you see his face?" I said.

"He wore a ski mask," Kagan said. "And the pain was from his fingers. He had a grip on me like a vise. I would have passed out except he let me go. So he could beat me up. The next thing I remember is waking up here a little while ago."

"Did he say anything?" I said.

"Not a word," Kagan said. "Although, from what little I saw,

I had the sense he was grinning behind that mask the entire time."

"Frank, I'm going to take over for you and assist Wally Sample for his court date," Simms said. "Are you up for a little chat?"

"I am," Kagan said.

"I'll be outside," I said. I took Campbell's arm and we went to the hallway.

"He's awake and talking with Carly Simms, who is taking over for him," I said to Lawrence when he answered his phone. "I think Wally has a legitimate shot at passing his evaluation. How are you doing?"

"So far all Justice sees is mismanagement of a company that had been successful for a very long time," Lawrence said. "What's really a puzzle is how a strong-arm character wound up employed there in the first place."

"I have no doubt it was Fuddy who worked Kagan over," I said.

"Two murders and a beat-down," Lawrence said.

"So far."

"And no real evidence except for circumstantial."

"So far."

"I'm flying up with a team the day of the court date," Lawrence said. "Hopefully I'll have some inside dirt on the books by then. In the meantime you watch your ass."

I hung up, and then called Walt and told him about Kagan. He said, "Simms will get Wally through this. How about your end?"

"Regan and Oz are protected," I said. "So is Wally. If Fuddy tries anything he'll have to come after me."

There was a short pause on the line.

"That's what you're setting up, isn't it?" Walt finally said.

"I don't like my family being spied on and having to hide

them out because some asshole with an anger management problem enjoys his work too much."

"I don't suppose it will do any good to tell you to watch your back," Walt said. "So let me say I'm here if you need me."

"I know," I said.

I hung up and called Jane. "Can you pick me up at the trailer later? I want to stop by and check on Regan."

"Six o'clock okay?"

"Perfect," I said. "Just in time for dinner."

"Should I wear my regular gun belt or the formal one for special occasions?"

"Formal one?"

"It's pink with cute little hearts."

"Sorry I asked."

I told her about Kagan.

"Simms will get it done," she said. "I've seen her act in court before. She's damn good."

"I know. See you at six."

I returned to Kagan's room, where Simms was wrapping things up. Campbell was in the chair, reading a fashion magazine.

"We're done for now, Bekker," Simms said.

"I'll give you a ride home," I said. I shook Kagan's hand. "By the way, I could use some additional expense money."

"Stop by the office. My girl will write you a check."

"I'll begin coaching Wally on taking the stand tomorrow," Simms said.

"Is six days enough time?" I said.

"In my opinion the little idiot is a mad genius," Simms said. "I can only take him so far, though. The rest is up to him."

"Are you driving us through the gates?" Campbell said.

"It's a tenth of a mile from the gates to the house," I said.

"You really must get a better car," Campbell said. "I can't have the help seeing us in this heap."

CHAPTER THIRTY-FOUR

I had time for a run and a workout, and after six miles at a steady pace along the ocean I cranked out push-ups, pull-ups and a thirty-minute session on the heavy bag. Dripping sweat, I went inside my trailer for a shower and a change of clothes. I grabbed a tan suit, white shirt, loafers and made a pot of coffee and waited outside for Jane to arrive.

Around a quarter to six I spotted her cruiser turning onto the beach and stood up. As she slowed the cruiser to a stop, I locked the trailer door and when I turned around Jane had opened the passenger door for me.

"All is still quiet on the western front," she said as I got in. "Price and Robertson report no suspicious activity, although the puppy did pee on the new carpet."

I looked at Jane.

She grinned and punched the gas, and the cruiser burned sand.

Seating arrangements were as follows: Oz at the head of the table. Jane and I to his left. Regan and Deputy Price to his right.

The puppy, all four pounds of her, was asleep in a cushy doggie bed on the floor, wrapped in a blanket.

Molly sat beside the bed and watched her new friend sleep. Molly seemed curious about the puppy, as if unsure if it was a good or bad thing to have around the house. She touched the puppy with her paw and made a soft squeak.

Conversation centered around the luscious steak tips Oz had prepared on the new grill and the training of the still nameless puppy. "First she needs to be housebroken," Regan said. "Then I want to take her to companion-dog training school."

"Where?" I said.

"If I may, Mr. Bekker, the training academy has a guard-, guide- and companion-dog training program," Price said.

I looked at him.

"We have two K-9 units," Jane said.

I looked at Jane.

"Companion training takes about four to six weeks," Price said.

"I'm well aware of what the academy has to offer, Deputy Price," I said.

"I meant no disrespect, sir," Price said. "It's just that there are many new developments in place since you went through the academy twenty-five years ago. A lot of the old training is obsolete."

Next to me I could feel Oz's grin.

I felt a vein in my neck bulge. Just before I let this snot-nosed kid have it, Jane squeezed my right knee under the table until I settled down.

I looked at the puppy. Molly was halfway in the bed and sniffing her.

"I don't know much about dog training," I said. "But I do know they respond better if they have a name."

"We're working on that, Dad," Regan said. "I would like to name her by a character trait as you suggested, but so far the only trait she displays is, she has to pee a lot. I can't exactly call her 'pee a lot,' can I?"

I looked at the dog bed. Molly had wormed her way in—she and the puppy were cuddled tightly together and sound asleep.

"Cuddles," I said. "Name her Cuddles."

After dinner and dessert—Regan had baked a chocolate cake—I stacked dishes in the dishwasher while Oz rinsed and handed them to me. Jane was on her phone to Robertson, and Regan and Price were in the backyard with Cuddles and Molly.

"How close did that boy come to getting his ass kicked?" Oz asked.

"You'll never know," I said.

Jane ended her call and said, "Bekker, I want to take a ride over and see Robertson."

I closed the door to the dishwasher. "Oz, you watch them," I said. "And by watch them I mean six feet separates them at all times."

"Want I should carry the shotgun around the house?" Oz asked.

"Yes," I said.

"No," Jane said. She looked at me. "You coming?"

"I'm going to wring his freaking neck," I said.

"Good deputies don't grow on trees," Jane said, grinning at me.

"Neither do daughters."

"Would you relax?" Jane said. "All he's done that I see is take your place at the dinner table and call you old."

I looked at her.

"It's not what he said, but that's what you heard, isn't it?" she said.

I stared out the window.

"Here's your choice for the evening's entertainment," Jane said. "You can brood and sulk all alone like the idiot you are, or you can enjoy the company of something curvy, blond and scrumptious. Pick one."

I looked at Jane.

"Good boy," she said.

"I don't know what it is, Jane, but I can't shake the feeling I'm being watched," Deputy Robertson said.

"How often are you making perimeter checks?" Jane said.

"Every fifteen minutes since I came on at six."

We were standing beside Robertson's cruiser just outside the front gates of Hope Springs Eternal. "But you haven't seen anybody?" Jane asked.

"No. It's just a feeling."

"Bekker, let's take a look around," Jane said. She removed her flashlight from her belt and we walked through the open gates.

"They lock them at eight thirty," I said.

"In ten minutes," Jane said.

We walked the entire complex, interior, gardens, fields and buildings, and didn't see one thing we could label as suspicious.

"What do you think?" Jane asked.

"I think we should walk it again counter-clockwise," I said.

The dorm rooms were dark, the small church and offices dark, the grounds still and quiet.

We returned to the front gates just before ten. Robertson's cruiser was missing. The gates were locked.

"I can't put my finger on it, but I agree with Robertson," Jane said. "I have the creepy feeling I'm being watched."

"We could stay the night as backup," I said.

"We could. We won't," Jane said. She called her dispatcher on her cell phone. "It's Jane. Pull a car from the rotation and send them to Hope Springs Eternal as backup for Robertson until eight in the morning."

Robertson's cruiser arrived at the gates. He got out and looked at us. "Anything?" he asked.

"No, but quiet doesn't mean safe," Jane said. "I'm getting

you a backup for the night. Open the gates."

Robertson had the key for the gates and opened them. We walked out to Jane's cruiser.

"We'll wait until the second car arrives," she said.

The second cruiser didn't show up for thirty minutes. Robertson made two additional perimeter checks. Jane smoked two cigarettes. I leaned on her cruiser and let my thoughts flow.

"Do you always take up a post at the gates after making a perimeter check?" I said to Robertson.

"It's the only place that allows me a view of the grounds and access if need be," Robertson said.

I looked behind us at the dark road that led to the complex. It was at least a half mile to the closest home and without street lamps. Anybody or anything could hide in the darkness even fifty feet away and you'd never see them.

Lights suddenly appeared on the road.

"Jane," I said.

"That should be Wilkes," she said.

He arrived less than a minute later, got out of the cruiser and reported to Jane.

She took a few minutes to explain the detail and added, "One car stays at the gates while the other is on patrol. I don't want so much as a mouse getting in there without you seeing it."

Around two in the morning I opened my eyes, untangled myself from Jane's legs and went to the kitchen for a glass of milk. I sat at the small table and sipped. I heard Jane move around in the bed and a moment later she joined me.

"One good thing about this trailer is you never have far to go to get from one end to the other," she said as she tied the belt of my robe that hung off her.

"Want to sit outside for a bit?" I asked.

★ ★ ★ ★ ★

I was tossing wood onto the bonfire when Jane came out of the trailer with two glasses of milk.

"I warmed it up," she said and gave me one glass. "It will help you get back to sleep."

Jane sat in a chair and took a sip. I sat next to her and watched the fire.

"We didn't miss anything, if that's what's bothering you," she said.

"How do we know that?" I asked.

"You're the best damn cop I know," she said. "But you can only take things so far with what you have. This court date is in what, five days?"

I nodded.

"After that, let the FBI solve the murders and whatever internal problems they have at Sample Iced Tea."

"Fuddy is behind them and the attack on Kagan," I said. "What I can't figure is motive."

Jane sipped her milk.

"Unless it's as simple as Barbara Sample is pulling his strings using sex to get him to do her bidding?" I said.

"If he's got a screw loose, as you say, it wouldn't be too difficult to get him to do just that," Jane said. "It's a matter of pushing his buttons."

"I think I need to find out," I said.

"How?"

"We have a secret weapon."

"What's that?"

"Carly Simms," I said.

Jane looked at me. "That could work."

"I'll call her in the morning."

Jane took my hand.

"What you said earlier in the car about I heard what I wanted to hear," I said. "Do you remember saying that?"

"I also remember saying you're an idiot," Jane said. "What's your point?"

"What if Fuddy is so far gone he's acting on his own, thinking it's what Barbara Sample wants from him?" I said.

"Voices in his head?" Jane said.

"He wouldn't be the first to hear a talking dog giving him orders."

"And to follow those orders to please the master."

"It's plausible," I said.

"I'm tired, Bekker," Jane said. "The milk is kicking in. Mind if I go back to sleep?"

"Sure," I said.

"You?"

"I'm going to sit here and think a while," I said.

"Want me to stay?"

"No, go ahead," I said. "I won't be long."

An hour or so later, I found Jane curled up in a ball in my bed, sound asleep. So far the only thing we've done together was sleep, so I did the only thing that made sense and curled up beside her.

CHAPTER THIRTY-FIVE

I sat in a corner of the library and watched as Simms coached Wally through his testimony in preparation for his court appearance. From her long history as a prosecutor, Simms knew how to squeeze every last drop from a witness, no matter how inept they might be.

And what was nagging at me was anybody's guess.

I had no doubt Fuddy was guilty of murder and assault, but proving it wasn't as easy as it sounded. That might require Paul Lawrence and all the resources Justice could muster.

"A mouse," I said aloud.

Simms turned around and looked at me. "What?"

"Nothing," I said. "I'll be right back."

I left the library and walked over to the office building.

Jane said last night she didn't want so much as a mouse getting past her deputies at the gates.

But what if the mouse was invited in?

Father Thomas was in his office with Sister Mary Martin. They were working on budget reports when I knocked on the door.

"Sorry to bother you, but I have an important question," I said.

"No bother at all," Father Thomas said.

"How many outside contractors have been on the premises in the past few weeks?" I said.

"I'm not sure."

"Can you check?"

"I keep the files," Sister Mary Martin said.

"Can we see them for the past three weeks or so?" I asked.

"I'll get them."

Sister Mary Martin left the office.

"What are we looking for?" Father Thomas said.

"I'm not sure," I said. "Just a hunch."

Holding several files, Sister Mary Martin returned. "Food deliveries, laundry supplies, cable service for the entertainment room, flowers for the chapel, the plumber for the clogged shower in the gym and that's about all," she said.

"Food, laundry and flowers are regular vendors?" I said.

"Like clockwork."

"What was wrong with the cable?"

"I'm not sure," Sister Mary Martin said. She scanned the work order.

"Poor reception," she said. "It's been fine since."

"Let me see that," I said.

She gave me the paper. It appeared legitimate, with a clear, legible signature.

"Who called the cable company?"

"I did," Sister Mary Martin said. "After the children called me to the entertainment room and the cable was out."

"Did you make an appointment on the phone?"

"Yes, for the next day."

"And no problems since?"

"None."

"What exactly are you searching for?" Father Thomas asked.

"Somebody who was here that shouldn't have been," I said.

"Do you still need these?" Sister Mary Martin asked.

"No, thank you."

She walked to the door and then paused to turn around. "That reminds me," she said. "I need to call the alarm company to repair the gates."

"What's wrong with them?" I said.

"The buzzer sticks."

"Show me."

"The gates are kept locked at all times these days, I'm afraid," Father Thomas said.

In sunlight I had a better view of the locking mechanism and the white box mounted midpoint on the interior gate wall.

"Our number one priority is the protection of the children, of course," Father Thomas said. "But in case of emergency the gates can be opened without the key by pressing a release button."

"It's tested once a week," Sister Mary Martin said.

She opened the box and pressed the emergency release button. It buzzed and the lock on the gates snapped open. I pulled the heavy gate inward a few feet and then pushed it closed.

It didn't lock, though, and I was able to yank the gate open.

I checked the lock and pushed it in a few times. "Hit the button," I said.

Sister Mary Martin pushed the button. There was a buzz and I pushed the lock in again with my finger.

I closed the gate and jiggled it hard. The lock took and snapped into place.

"Call the locksmith today," I said. "Don't use the buzzer until the lock is replaced."

"He'll make the thirty days without gambling, that's no problem," Simms said as I drove her to the Crist mansion. "It's the evaluation I'm concerned about."

"The coaching not going well?" I said.

"It's going fine. In a classroom without any real pressure," Simms said. "Under the microscope of a hostile psychiatrist and then in court where a hostile lawyer will use every dirty trick in the book to fuck him over is another story."

"So, do your thing tomorrow and maybe soften them up a bit," I said.

"That's my plan," Simms said. "Take me through the rundown one more time."

"It could work," Jane said. "It could work better if you had some backup."

"You have a sheriff's department to run," I said. "And Wally, like it or not, is under your protection. I need you to keep him alive for his court date or all this is for nothing."

"And then turn it over to the FBI," Jane said.

"Yes."

"And maybe take a little vacation together and we can come out of the closet."

"What do you mean 'come out of the closet'?" I said.

"First dinner in public at a really nice restaurant where I can dress up and feel like a woman, and we bring Regan and her date if she has one," Jane said. "I'm not a sneak-around kind of girl."

"And then?"

"The last time I took a real vacation Clinton was doing parlor tricks with a cigar," Jane said.

"What do you call a real vacation?"

"We'll work that out later."

"If we go somewhere is it with or without?" I said.

"She has Oz, a dog and a cat and a job," Jane said. "And from the looks of things a possible boyfriend who happens to be well trained and well armed."

"Without?"

"Most definitely without."

"I have no problem with any of that, but I have a request of my own," I said. "Before we go anywhere I'd like to have a man-to-man with the possible boyfriend."

Jane looked at me from behind her desk.

"If he wants to date my daughter he needs to know her history," I said. "That's only fair to both."

"I think I agree with you," Jane said.

"Don't sound so shocked. It happens."

"Just don't make a habit of being right."

"I'll fill you in later."

"I can hardly wait," Jane said as she broke every ordinance on no smoking by reaching for her cigarettes and lighting one up.

CHAPTER THIRTY-SIX

"I'm not entirely sure this is legal," Simms said as we walked from the rental car to the squat bank of apartments where Dale Chase lived.

"It's illegal now to knock on someone's door and ask to speak to them?" I said.

The vestibule door was unlocked. There was a bank of mailboxes on the left with intercom buzzers beside each box. The door that led to the interior lobby could be opened with a key or after being buzzed in by a resident.

Chase lived in 3B. I pushed the intercom button. Several seconds later he said, "Who is it?"

"John Bekker," I said into the intercom.

"Who?"

"The man you spied on at the beach," I said. "You remember me. I followed you and you took off."

"I don't . . . who . . . I think you have the wrong apartment," Chase said.

I pressed the intercom button again.

"I'm calling the police," Chase said.

"Go ahead. Who do you think told me where you live?"

"What . . . what do you want?"

"Just to talk to you, that's all."

"About what?"

"I think you know," I said. "Of course, I could call the PD myself and we can talk at the police station?"

The buzzer sounded and I pushed the door inward. There was one elevator and we rode it to the third floor.

I didn't have to knock on 3B. The door was open and Dale Chase was waiting for us in the hallway. He looked at Simms. "Who's this?" he said.

Dressed in her best miniskirt power suit with four-inch heels, Simms was a force to be reckoned with as she said, "I'm the lawyer who could put you away for seven to ten years, that's who."

Chase looked at me. "You said just to talk."

"I didn't say about what," I said. "Inside."

We followed Chase into his studio apartment. He closed the door and said, "I have class in one hour."

"Not today," Simms said.

"You got any coffee?" I said.

"I can make some."

"Make it and we'll sit and have a nice conversation about life."

Up close, Dale Chase was a scared-looking kid. His eyes were filled with fear and he bit his lower lip as he went about brewing a pot on the small countertop.

Simms and I sat at his tiny table as he poured coffee into three cups that didn't match and probably came from a yard sale.

"You have one chance at not being dragged down to the police station and charged with a half-dozen counts of accessory charges," Simms said. "And that means one lie and Bekker drags you to the police, and one thing he's good at is dragging."

"Accessory charges . . . all I did was what Mr. Fuddy asked me to," Chase said.

"What exactly did he ask you to do and did he tell you why?" I said.

"He said the company was involved in some big lawsuit that

could ruin its reputation, something like that," Chase said. "He said you were causing all sorts of problems and asked if I could do some surveillance work for him. That's all he asked and that's all I did. He paid me a thousand dollars and I really needed it for tuition."

"What kind of surveillance work?" Simms said.

"Tail him, see where he goes, what he does," Chase said. "Like that."

"Pictures?" I said.

"Some. I gave them to Mr. Fuddy."

"Developed?"

"What? No. The card from the digital camera."

"It's a new world, Bekker," Simms said.

"How many times did you tail me?" I said.

"Three times."

"Where and when?"

"Police station to your home on the beach. Your home to that lawyer's office. That hospital in the middle of nowhere to your home on the beach. And that cookout on the beach. After that I told Mr. Fuddy you made me and I gave him the card from my camera."

"Did you keep a log?" I said.

Chase nodded. "I gave him that, too."

"We're on our way to see the Sample family," I said. "You're coming with us."

"Why?"

"Because confession is good for the soul," I said.

"And because it beats rotting in prison," Simms said.

Fuddy was in the lobby of the Sample Iced Tea building when the three of us arrived. At the sight of Chase, Fuddy's jaw all but dropped.

"What is . . . what are you doing with them, Dale?" he said.

"Don't answer that," Simms said.

"We have an appointment with the Samples," I said.

Fuddy glared at Chase. "You, too?"

"Don't answer that," Simms said.

Fuddy looked at Simms. "Who the fuck are you?"

"Take us up to six," I said. "And this time you're invited."

We entered the elevator and Fuddy unlocked six. As we rode up he glared at me. "I warned you, Bekker. You don't know what you're fucking with here."

"I know exactly what and who I'm fucking with," I said. "Do you?"

The door opened. "I guess we'll find out," Fuddy said.

"I guess so," I said. "And leave it unlocked. We're expecting company."

We stepped out and walked to the conference room.

The Samples were seated at the table. Two men in power suits were with them.

"Mr. Bekker, these are our attorneys representing us in court," Robert Sample said. "Mr. Ferrer and Mr. Jacob."

"This is Carly Simms," I said. "Representing Wally at the hearing."

"What happened to Mr. Kagan?" Robert said.

"Your thug beat him up," Simms said.

"What . . . who are you . . . I don't understand," Robert said.

"You asked for this meeting," Jacob said. "I assume it has to do with Wally's court appearance in three days. We want to express our . . ."

"Shut up," Simms said.

"What? Excuse me," Jacob said.

"Go right ahead and excuse yourself," Simms said. "It doesn't matter to me."

"Mr. Bekker, what is going on here?" Robert said.

"I'll make it simple," Simms said. "Your man Fuddy will be

257

investigated by the FBI for murder, extortion, assault, harassment and arson."

The room was silent for a moment. I didn't look at him, but
I could feel Fuddy's seething glare on my face.

"My question to you is why would you ever hire such a
violent, unstable man as your security director?" Simms said.

There was a knock on the door. Captain Willard stepped in
and said, "Sorry I'm late. Traffic."

"We just started," Simms said. "We were just explaining how
the FBI is investigating Mr. Fuddy for murder, arson and a host
of other goodies."

Willard looked at Fuddy.

Fuddy glared at Simms. "Prove it," he said.

"I was led to believe this meeting was about Wally Sample,
not Mr. Fuddy," Ferrer said.

"One and the same," Simms said. "So please tell us how you
came to hire a dirt bag like Fuddy in the first place."

"I don't have to listen to this," Fuddy said.

"Take one step and I'll slap you in cuffs," Willard said.

"Mr. Sample?" Simms said.

Robert looked at his attorneys. Ferrer nodded.

"I don't know where to begin," Robert said.

"Begin by keeping your fucking mouth shut," Fuddy said.

Willard opened the door and nodded. Two uniformed officers entered the room. Willard nodded toward Fuddy. "If he
opens his mouth, taze and cuff him and take him away."

"Go on, Mr. Sample," Simms said.

"Out of nowhere, Fuddy shows up and demands a meeting,"
Robert said. "He has . . . he claimed he was working as a
bouncer at a major casino in Atlantic City and had dozens of
photographs of Wally gambling and losing heavily. He claimed
he had photos of Wally meeting with loan sharks and such."

"Did he?" Simms said.

"Yes."

"And he blackmailed you?"

"Yes."

"What were his demands?" Simms said.

"One million dollars up front, plus a job and salary of one hundred and twenty-five thousand dollars per year or he gives the photos to the gossip magazines and Sample Iced Tea gets dragged through the mud," Robert said. "We're a family-owned company with a longstanding reputation to consider. One million and a job against losing our reputation was not an option."

"Prove it," Fuddy said. "Any of it. You can't."

"Shut up," Willard said.

"So now that Wally is back in the spotlight you paid Fuddy to kill him," Simms said. "I don't see the benefit in that. Besides photos of Wally you're now an accessory to murder one, and . . ."

"What are you talking about?" Robert said. "We had nothing to do with anything other than paying extortion to Fuddy for his silence."

"Are you saying he acted on his own?" Simms said. "Wouldn't he be killing his meal ticket by removing Wally? Why would you continue to pay extortion if the reason for paying it is removed?"

"If some compromising photos are worth one million and a job, how much is accessory to murder worth?" I said. "Kill off Wally and the photos are worthless, but the threat of implicating the Sample Iced Tea family in murdering their brother right before he inherits his fair share and a one-sixth ownership is worth how much for Fuddy's silence? Five million? Ten?"

"That is just sick enough to work on a bunch of corporate cowards like you five," Simms said.

"Fuck you, Bekker," Fuddy said. "Prove it. Prove any of it."

"I don't have to," I said. "My friends at the FBI will. All you have to do is wait for them to knock on your door."

Fuddy glared at me. "Fuck you," he said and charged across the room.

The two uniformed officers grabbed his arms. Fuddy flung them off as if they were children and raised his right fist at me. Before he made contact, Willard hit him in the back with his taser. Fuddy went down to the rug.

"Cuff him, take him to the station, book him and stick him in a cell," Willard said.

"What charge?" one of the officers said.

"Aggravated assault and resisting arrest," Willard said. "We'll let the FBI deal with all that other stuff later."

The officers cuffed Fuddy's hands behind his back and yanked him to his feet. Still reeling from the taser, Fuddy was like human Silly Putty as they dragged him out of the room.

"There is another matter," Simms said. "A rather embarrassing one, I'm afraid."

"And that would be?" Jacob said.

Simms looked at Barbara Sample. "It won't look good that you're shacking up with Fuddy, considering his present set of circumstances."

Barbara stared at Simms for several seconds. Then her mouth drew back into a thin, hard line. "You fucking bitch," she said.

"Name calling," Simms said. "Yikes."

"Barbara, is this true?" Robert asked.

"I followed you and Fuddy to his condo," I said to Barbara.

"For God's sake, Barbara, what were you thinking?" Robert asked.

"Below the waist like she always thinks," Amy said.

"It wouldn't do you any harm to get laid once in a while, big sister," Barbara said. "It might even clear up your skin."

"Did you know about Fuddy's plan for killing your brother?" Simms said.

"No, of course not," Barbara said. "I knew about the photos

and extortion, but there was nothing I could do about that."

"Except sleep with the guy blackmailing us," Amy said. "Honestly, Barbara."

"This is not going to look good for us or the corporation, is it?" Robert asked.

"No," Simms said. "But, then again, none of it will once this story breaks and the media gets ahold of it."

"Oh, good God," Robert said.

"The board will have us all removed," Steven said. "Our company will fall into the hands of a board-appointed CEO. We're ruined as a company and a family."

"It gets worse," Simms said.

"How?" Robert asked. "Could it possibly get worse?"

"I plan to beat the pants off you in court and have Wally fully instated as a full partner. I strongly suggest you retain the best criminal defense attorney money can buy, because you'll be spending a lot of it."

"But, we're the victims here," Robert said.

Simms looked at me. "They can't be this dumb, can they?"

"I think we're done here," I said.

"Wait, just wait," Robert said. "You can't drop an atom bomb like this in our lap and run off like you're late for a lunch appointment."

"Sure we can," I said.

I turned to Willard. "This silent young man is Dale Chase," I said. "He works here as a part-time security guard. Fuddy convinced him to follow me around and take pictures. He's a victim in Fuddy's plot and if you take him to the station he'll write you a statement as such. He'll testify in court against Fuddy in exchange for no charges. Right, Dale?"

"Yes, sir," Chase said.

"From the looks of things, Robert, you need some damn expensive lawyers," Willard said.

"We can recommend the best in the state," Ferrer said.

"You're pretty much fucked," Simms said. "All of you."

"Unless," I said.

"What? Unless what?" Robert asked.

"Wally's psych evaluation isn't contested at his hearing and he's allowed to take his rightful place as sixth controlling member of the company," Simms said. "In exchange for your cooperation, Bekker will ask his friends at the FBI to do all they can to make sure it is known that Sample Iced Tea is the victim in a major blackmail scam, and in no way guilty of any crimes."

Robert looked at his lawyers.

Ferrer and Jacob both nodded.

"Give Wally a chance," I said. "He's really smart and he has a lot of good ideas."

Simms looked at Willard.

"We'll follow you to the station," she said. "I'm sure you'd like statements from both of us."

"You sure know how to show a girl a good time, Bekker," Simms said. "I'll give you that."

I took her to an Italian restaurant on Central Avenue in White Plains. She had a glass of red wine with dinner. I went with Sample Iced Tea, lemon flavored. The stuff wasn't half bad.

"What did your friend at the FBI have to say?" Simms said.

"Paul and a team are flying here the day after Wally's hearing," I said. "Unless they can directly link Fuddy to murder they'll go with extortion and blackmail and some lesser charges of harassment with Chase's testimony. Without being able to prove murder and arson, Paul said he can swing it so publicity paints Sample Iced Tea as the innocent victim. He figures on fifteen years, out in ten for Fuddy unless they can make a case on the murder and arson charges."

"Unless he confesses," Simms said.

"He won't."

"It's still not a bad haul."

"No. About your fee," I said. "Kagan won't blink at whatever bill you submit."

"My fee is that you keep your word and do us the favor you promised."

"Which is?"

"I'll let Campbell have that honor."

"Want dessert?" I said. "I saw chocolate cheesecake on the menu."

"Yes, damn you."

"To Wally," I said and lifted my glass of iced tea.

Simms clinked my glass with her glass of wine.

"To Wally," she said.

I called Jane from my room at the motel in White Plains.

"I miss you, Bekker," Jane said. "Damn you."

"That's the second time I've been damned tonight," I said.

"You asked Simms if she wanted dessert."

"Chocolate cheesecake," I said.

"You have to learn us women over forty are prone to mood swings," Jane said. "Especially about our weight."

"I'm figuring that out."

"What time will you be back?"

"Plane lands at noon."

"Let's celebrate your victory with a home-cooked meal."

"Whose home and who cooks?"

"Don't be a wise ass."

"Can I be just a regular ass?"

"Seven thirty at your place," Jane said. "And bring back cheesecake. We can pig out and watch the sunset."

"But you said . . ."

"So I did," Jane said and hung up.

Chapter Thirty-Seven

Somehow Frank Kagan managed to leave the hospital and make the trip to Manhattan for Wally's hearing.

The hearing was held in a courtroom in superior court in lower Manhattan. Simms acted as primary defense, Kagan as secondary. Father Thomas gave testimony to Wally's mental fitness and readiness to assume his rightful place in Sample Iced Tea.

The entire Sample family and Ferrer and Jacob sat on the opposing side.

Ferrer asked the judge if Robert Sample could make a statement.

Carefully reading his prepared statement, Robert told the judge that he and the entire Sample family rejoiced in their brother's recovery and welcomed him into the fold as a full member of the Sample Iced Tea Corporation.

The judge called for a short recess to confer with counsel in his chambers.

Father Thomas sat in the front row beside me. "Wally has asked if he could stay two extra weeks to finish our sessions before he starts work in his new position," the priest said.

"In case he falls off the wagon," I said.

"He's scared."

"He's just gone from bum owing thousands to loan sharks, to millionaire corporate executive," I said. "Wouldn't you be scared in his shoes?"

"Terrified."

After about an hour, measured as three cigarettes before my promise to Regan, the judge and attorneys returned to the courtroom.

There was no need to hear the judge's decision. The smile on Simms's face told me all I needed to know.

CHAPTER THIRTY-EIGHT

The late afternoon sun lit up the grass in my new backyard and it glowed a deep emerald green.

Oz sat with me at the patio table and we watched Molly and Cuddles roll around and snip at each other. Molly kept her needle-like claws retracted and Cuddles did more licking with her tongue than nipping with her tiny, sharp teeth.

"I think she make a fine therapy dog once she trained," Oz said.

"Speaking of training, whose turn is it to walk the little puddle bucket?"

"I went last time," Oz said.

"Okay, but you and Regan have to share duty for the night," I said. "I have some loose ends to tend to."

"That loose end wouldn't happen to be honey blond about five foot seven, looking like Marilyn Monroe singing 'Happy birthday, Mr. President' wearing a sheriff's uniform?" Oz said. "Would it?"

"Never mind and what time does Regan get home from work?"

"Around five thirty."

I glanced at my watch. "Just in time for her next walk."

I went inside for the leash and buckled Cuddles in. We went around the side of the house and through the gate to the street.

Just as a sheriff's cruiser pulled into the driveway.

Deputy Price emerged wearing dark sunglasses. He removed

them as he walked over to me. "Hello, Mr. Bekker," he said.

"I thought the detail ended three days ago," I said.

"Yes, sir, it did."

"So, why are you here?"

"I wanted to talk to you about Regan."

Cuddles was yanking on the leash.

"She's going to pee on my shoes," I said. "Walk and talk."

We walked to the curb and turned right. Our steps were small as Cuddles had a very short stride.

"Now, what about Regan?" I said.

"We discussed it and . . ."

"Who is we and what is it?" I said.

"Us. Regan and I, and we talked it over, and with your permission we would like to date," Price said.

"Each other?"

"What? Yes, sir, each other."

Cuddles found a nice spot in the gutter and let go her tiny bladder.

"Deputy Price, there are . . . what is your first name?"

"Phil."

"There are some things you need to know about my daughter, Phil," I said.

"Yes, sir. Regan has told me about what happened to her mother and the years she spent at the hospital," Price said. "She's even told me that emotionally she's not quite where she needs to be and still sees a psychiatrist once a week."

"She told you all that."

"We had a lot of quiet time to kill while I was on special detail."

"Understand this," I said. "My daughter's mental state is very fragile."

"I know that," Price said. "And I give you my word I will be a gentleman and do nothing to hurt her."

"If my daughter cries even once you will think a building fell on you," I said. "Is that understood?"

"I understand."

"Good."

"Mr. Bekker?"

"Yes."

"She cries at movies with animals when they get hurt," Price said. "Especially dogs and cats. Does that count?"

"I think you're on safe ground with that one," I said. "She'll be home in a while. Oz is in the backyard if you want to wait."

Price smiled and put his sunglasses back on. "Yes, sir," he said.

I continued walking Cuddles and as we reached the end of the block my cell phone rang. I checked the number and said, "Paul, how's it going?"

"Jack, you won't believe this," Lawrence said. "Bail was set at four hundred thousand dollars and the son of a bitch posted."

"Fuddy is loose?" I said.

"They took his passport and froze his bank accounts, but he's loose until trial or until I can prove otherwise and they lock him up again."

"Did you ask for higher bail?"

"Without murder and arson charges, that's the highest the judge would go."

"Will you be able to build a case?"

"On the blackmail and extortion," Lawrence said. "And if we put him away fifteen to twenty that gives me lots of time to build a murder case."

"Even without murder one that's not chump change," I said.

"Jack, I don't like the looks of this guy," Lawrence said. "He's unstable to say the least. Downright insane to say the most. I've assigned a team to stake out his condo for the time being."

"He's a slick bastard, Paul," I said.

"The team I assigned are fifteen-year vets," Lawrence said. "Want some help?"

"The AG would never allow outside contractors on something like this."

"Just watch that son of a bitch," I said.

"I'd love to make murder one stick on this asshole," Lawrence said. "In the meantime, I'll let you know if he pulls something."

I hung up and walked Cuddles back to the house.

Price and Oz were in the backyard. Regan hadn't come home from work yet.

"Are you off duty?" I said.

"Yes, sir."

"Stick around for a bit until you're on duty," I said. "I'll clear it with Jane for you to stay the night."

CHAPTER THIRTY-NINE

"The judicial system is for shit," Jane said when I told her about Fuddy.

"The law is the law," I said. "The judge set bail at max and the bastard spent some of his extortion money to post."

We were in the kitchen at the trailer. She was at the stove, making a stir-fry. She had switched out her uniform for a pair of jeans, a sweatshirt and walking shoes.

"Wally is still with Father Thomas," I said.

"Want me to reinstate the protection detail for them?"

I nodded.

"Your house?"

"I already did that."

"Price?"

I nodded again.

"Regan?"

"Don't ask."

"You can't keep a glass bubble around her forever," Jane said.

I sat at the table. "I feel old," I said.

Jane set aside the wooden spoon she was using, reached over and goosed me on the rear end.

"You're only as old as the woman who feels you," she said, and sat on my lap.

"Are you wearing a gun?" I asked.

"Of course."

"Where?"

"Maybe, just maybe, if you eat all your dinner, including your peas, I will finally let you find out," Jane said. "If that cheesecake you brought back is as good as you say."

When the moon is full the sand at the beach looks almost like snow. It's so bright there's no need to turn on the outside floodlights.

I filled mugs with coffee and sliced off two pieces of cheesecake. We sat at the small patio table and watched the moon glisten off the ocean.

"I've decided to get serious about a diet," Jane said as she forked a hunk of cheesecake into her mouth. "Tomorrow."

I looked at her. Even in the pale moonlight her eyes were Paul Newman blue.

"How is the cheesecake?" I asked.

"Scrumptious. I think my diet will be to avoid all fruits and vegetables."

I sliced into my piece and washed it down with a sip of coffee. "I ate all my peas," I said.

Jane looked at me. "So you did."

"And I was wondering if you'd care to show me where you hide your weapon," I said.

Jane set her fork on her plate, stood up and took a seat on my lap. "I suppose it's time, don't you think?"

"I do."

"You're not feeling too old?"

"The cheesecake revitalized me."

"How can a woman resist such a sweet talker as you?"

"It's a gift," I said. Out of the corner of my eye I spotted twin white dots on the beach.

I focused on them.

"Jack, now is the part where we do a *From Here to Eternity* kiss on the sand," Jane said.

"Turn around," I said.

Jane shifted her position and spotted the oncoming lights. "Walt?" she said.

I shook my head. "Let's go inside."

We got up, went in, closed the door and turned off all the lights.

I opened the kitchen drawer where I'd placed my .45 earlier and held it as we peered through the curtains.

After several minutes, the car arrived. It parked next to my Marquis and kept the lights on as the door opened.

Mike Fuddy got out. A massive .44 Magnum revolver was in his right hand. He opened the rear door, reached in and yanked Keri out by the hair. Duct tape covered her mouth.

"Bekker, I know you're in there," Fuddy shouted. "I brought you a little parting gift from me to you."

He yanked Keri's hair and the little girl started to cry.

"How the . . . ?" Jane gasped.

"The surveillance photos Chase took that day on the beach," I said. "The hospital name is on the van."

"Bekker, come out, come out, wherever you are," Fuddy said in a creepy singsong voice.

"Let me call my SWAT team," Jane said.

"No time for that," I said. "And he's just sick enough to kill that child if they set foot on the beach."

"I'll huff, and I'll puff," Fuddy said, gleefully.

"I'm going to have to eat this one." I looked at Jane. "Can you take him?" I asked and handed her the .45.

Jane nodded.

"Come on, Bekker, don't be a sore loser," Fuddy said. "Come on out and play with us."

"Wait for him to release the little girl before you take the shot," I said. "If she isn't clear, don't do it. I'll let him beat on me until she's clear."

I walked to the door.

"Jack," Jane said.

"I'll be all right," I said. "Just wait until she's clear to take the shot."

I opened the door and stepped outside, and looked at Fuddy.

"Your problem is with me, Fuddy. Let the little girl go," I said.

Fuddy yanked her hair again. Keri made a muffled sobbing noise behind the duct tape.

"Fuck you, Bekker," Fuddy said. "The FBI, the cops, they all want a piece of my ass and all because you can't leave things alone. Well, first I'm going to kill you and make her watch and then . . ."

"Just get it over with," I said. "If your balls are as big as your mouth."

Fuddy lurched forward and cracked me in the jaw with the eight-inch-long barrel of the .44. The heavy steel was like getting cracked with a baseball bat and I fell backward against the wall of the trailer.

Still holding Keri by the hair, Fuddy took a step forward and cracked me in the face with the .44 a second time. I saw stars and slumped to my knees.

"Not so tough now, are you?" Fuddy said.

I looked up into Fuddy's eyes. He was gone and he wasn't coming back. It might be possible to make a case for insanity for him, but his insanity was fueled by hate and anger and not mental illness.

The third crack with the .44 knocked me over to the sand. My nose and mouth were filled with blood and I had to spit so I could breathe.

"Get up, Bekker," Fuddy said. "I thought you were a tough guy. I thought you were a real man."

I rolled over and looked at the black, steel-toe boots Fuddy wore.

I started to get up and he kicked me in the stomach with the right boot. "I thought you said you wanted to work out, Bekker," Fuddy said.

I went down again.

"Not so tough-talking now, are you?" Fuddy snarled.

He kicked me in the ribs, the stomach and back and face. With each kick he made a gleeful kind of grunt.

"I told you not to fuck with me, Bekker," he said. "I told you."

I rolled onto my back and looked at him through blurry eyes.

"Is that all you got?" I said. "I didn't take you for a sissy, but what do you expect from a guy with a name like Fuddy."

And that put Fuddy over the edge.

He flung Keri aside. She fell to the sand and he tucked the .44 into his belt. Then he reached down and took hold of my tee shirt, and yanked me to my feet.

I looked at Keri. She was inching away from us on all fours, but was still too close for Jane to take a shot.

"How do you like working out with me, Bekker, huh?" Fuddy said.

"Fuck you," I said and spit blood in Fuddy's face.

He screamed and punched me in the nose. I hit the wall of the trailer. As I bounced off, he punched me in the stomach, and then kneed me in the chin. He grabbed my hair and slammed my face into the trailer and then took my right arm and threw me onto the patio table. It cracked under my weight and I went down hard.

I looked for Keri. She was finally clear.

Fuddy followed me. As he was about to bend over, Jane said, "That's enough."

I rolled over and looked at her.

You haven't seen anything until you've seen a blue-eyed, beautiful honey blond aiming a Glock .45 pistol at the bad guy.

Fuddy looked at her. His right hand inched toward the .44 tucked into his belt.

"Do it so I have a reason," Jane said.

Fuddy locked eyes with her in a silent dare.

Then he smiled and reached for the .44.

Jane shot him in the chest. He staggered backward and looked at her with amazement. She shot him a second time in the chest and he dropped to his knees.

"Third time's a fucking charm, asshole," Jane said and shot him in the forehead.

She lowered the Glock and rushed to me. I said, "The little girl."

She went to Keri, lifted her into her arms and carefully removed the duct tape. Bursting into tears, Keri buried her face in Jane's chest.

I fought to my feet, staggered over to my chair and flopped down. Blood ran down my face and I wiped it away with my tee shirt.

Holding Keri, Jane sat in the chair next to me. "Jesus Christ, Bekker," she said.

"Do you think you could give me a cigarette and not tell Regan?" I said.

"Yes."

"And then take me to the county hospital?"

"Yes."

"And stop at Pat's for some donuts on the way?"

"You're pushing it," Jane said.

I looked at the Atlantic Ocean, at the moonlight shimmering on the water.

"Nice night," I said.

Jane shifted Keri to her lap, reached over and took my hand.

275

"Dear God, I hate to see what you think is a bad night," she said.

CHAPTER FORTY

I passed out or fell asleep in Jane's cruiser on the way to the county hospital. I wasn't sure which, but it didn't really matter. The result was the same. I was gone.

I woke up for a bit in the emergency room and looked at a doctor who appeared young enough to still be in high school as he took my blood pressure.

"His vital signs are good, let's get him to X-ray," I heard the doctor say.

When I opened my eyes next, a different doctor was talking to Jane.

"He has three broken ribs on the right side and four bruised ribs on the left," the doctor said. "His nose is broken, but from the looks of things it's been broken several times before. His right cheekbone and sinus cavity are fractured as well as the eye socket. However, it's the internal injuries that concern me. There is a great deal of blood in his urine."

"The man had steel-toe boots and kicked him in the back and ribs," I heard Jane say.

"That explains the blood in his urine," the doctor said. "I'm going to give him something to sleep as I'm afraid those broken ribs are going to be quite painful."

When I woke up next the sun was shining through the window. Wires and tubes were in my arms and a few other places. The white curtain was drawn around the bed.

I heard Regan say from the other side of the curtain, "My

dad allowed that guy to do this to him?"

"He had to, honey, in order to save Keri's life," I heard Jane say. "It was the only way to get him to release her so I could take a shot."

Then I heard Regan start to cry and I couldn't see it happening, but I knew Jane was holding her tight.

A sharp pain went through my side and a few moments later I grew sleepy again.

Much later in the afternoon, I awoke again and from behind the curtain I heard Walt say, "How long will he be in here?"

"Doc says at least a week," I heard Oz say.

"In that case let's go to the cafeteria for some coffee," Walt said.

My ribs were suddenly on fire and before I knew it I drifted off again. I must have been on an automatic painkiller dispenser of some kind.

Three days later I was sitting up in bed. Jane, Walt, Oz and Regan were in the room with me. I had just finished eating what passed for lunch.

Oz was eyeing the tray on the serving trolley. "You gonna eat that Jell-O?" he asked.

"Probably not," I said. "I'll let you have it if you take Regan for a walk so Walt, Jane and I can talk a little business."

"Forget the Jell-O, Oz," Regan said. "I'll spring for lunch in the cafeteria."

"Got you first paycheck, huh?" Oz said.

Regan kissed me softly on the forehead. On the way out of the room, she said, "No, but I do have my dad's wallet."

Jane pulled up a chair next to the bed. Walt stood at the window.

"Well, the little girl is safe, the bad guy is dead, and Wally is on his way to take his place as an executive at Sample Iced

Tea," Walt said. "Except for a few minor bruises, I'd say you . . ."

"Minor bruises?" I said. "My face is . . ."

"Slight details," Walt said.

"Kagan told me to tell you he'll write you a check, plus a bonus as soon as you get out of here," Jane said.

From the hallway, I heard Campbell Crist say, "If you doctors stare any harder, you'll stroke out."

"Give them a break, Campbell," I heard Carly Simms say. "They're men."

"Men," Campbell said as if she'd just stepped in something really disgusting. Then they were in the room and Campbell said, "Well, you never really were that good-looking to begin with."

"That's a terrible thing to say to a man in his condition," Simms said.

"What . . . ?" I said.

"We've come for our payback," Campbell said.

"If you could give us a minute alone with Johnny Handsome here," Simms said. "We have a private matter to discuss."

Jane glared at the ladies.

"It won't take long and we'll return him to you exactly as we found him, beat up and broken," Campbell said.

"We'll be in the cafeteria with Regan and Oz," Jane said and kissed me lightly on the lips.

Walt and Jane headed for the door.

"I see you and the Barbie Doll finally hooked up," Campbell said.

"Who is she . . . ?" I heard Jane say from the hallway.

"Let it go, Jane," I heard Walt say. "Let it go."

Campbell and Simms giggled.

"So what is your pound of flesh?" I asked.

"Well, Bekker," Campbell said as a nurse entered the room.

"Excuse me, ladies," the nurse said as she drew the curtain around the bed. "I need to remove Mr. Bekker's catheter."

"Should we leave?" Simms asked.

"No, it will only take a moment," the nurse said. "Just stay on the other side of the curtain."

"So, Bekker, since the Supreme Court decision made it legal, Carly and I wish to be married," Campbell said.

"Congratulations," I said.

The nurse lifted my hospital gown.

"As my father is dead and so is Carly's, we would like you to give us away at the service," Campbell said. "Once your face is normal again, or as close to normal as it's going to get without looking like the gnome who lives in the bell tower."

"You said you would be nice," Simms said.

"That was nice," Campbell said.

"So, how about it, Bekker?" Simms said.

"I'll do it if you two would get the hell out of my hospital room," I said.

"Excellent," Simms said. "We'll be in touch."

I watched the nurse slip on rubber gloves and reach for the catheter.

"Oh, one more thing," Campbell said. "We would like you to father our children."

"What?" I yelled as the nurse yanked the catheter free.

ABOUT THE AUTHOR

Al Lamanda is a native of New York City. He is the author of the novels *Dunston Falls, Walking Homeless, Running Homeless, Sunset, Sunrise, First Light* and *This Side of Midnight.*